THE CHRONICLES OF
Vladimir Tod

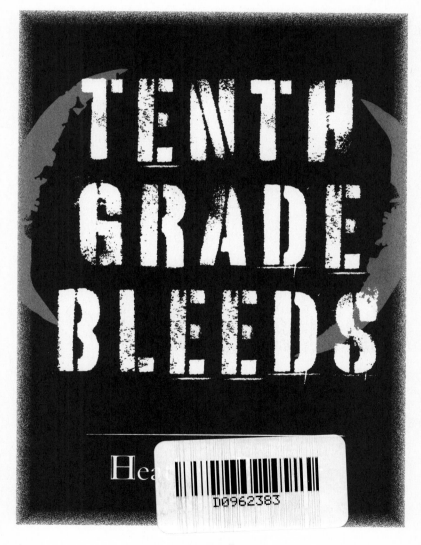

TENTH GRADE BLEEDS

Hea

D0962383

speak

An Imprint of Penguin Group (USA) Inc.

SPEAK
Published by the Penguin Group
Penguin Group (USA) Inc., 345 Hudson Street, New York, New York 10014, U.S.A.
Penguin Group (Canada), 90 Eglinton Avenue East, Suite 700, Toronto, Ontario, Canada M4P 2Y3
(a division of Pearson Penguin Canada Inc.)
Penguin Books Ltd, 80 Strand, London WC2R 0RL, England
Penguin Ireland, 25 St Stephen's Green, Dublin 2, Ireland (a division of Penguin Books Ltd)
Penguin Group (Australia), 250 Camberwell Road, Camberwell, Victoria 3124, Australia
(a division of Pearson Australia Group Pty Ltd)
Penguin Books India Pvt Ltd, 11 Community Centre, Panchsheel Park, New Delhi - 110 017, India
Penguin Group (NZ), 67 Apollo Drive, Rosedale, North Shore 0632, New Zealand
(a division of Pearson New Zealand Ltd.)
Penguin Books (South Africa) (Pty) Ltd, 24 Sturdee Avenue, Rosebank, Johannesburg 2196, South Africa

Registered Offices: Penguin Books Ltd, 80 Strand, London WC2R 0RL, England

First published in the United States of America by Dutton Children's Books,
a division of Penguin Young Readers Group, 2009
Published by Speak, an imprint of Penguin Group (USA) Inc., 2010

This book is a work of fiction. Names, characters, places, and incidents are either the product
of the author's imagination or are used fictitiously, and any resemblance to actual persons,
living or dead, business establishments, events, or locales is entirely coincidental.

5 7 9 10 8 6

CIP Data is available.
ISBN: 978-0-525-42135-1 (hc)

Speak ISBN 978-0-14-241560-3

Designed by Jason Henry

Printed in the United States of America

▼ ▼ ▼

To you,

for being who you are

───────── ACKNOWLEDGMENTS ─────────

It would be easier to thank all of the people who have contrib-
uted to my success by writing "thanks, everyone," because
there have been so many people that have blessed my life that
I am positive I'll leave out at least one or two. To those I do
forget—my deepest apologies.

I'd like to thank Maureen Sullivan, who is quite possibly
the smartest woman on the planet, and whom I am blessed to
be edited by. Also, Michael Bourret, who isn't just brilliant, but
funny and insightful too—qualities that make him the best lit-
erary agent that any author could ever have. To everyone at
Dutton—you are amazing people and the magic that you perform stuns me every time I am witness to it.

Jackie Kessler—you are the best friend a gal could have,
and I'd happily face hellfire with you (besides . . . you have the
map). Dawn Vanniman—I love you, sis! Kylie McAuliffe—a
most loyal Minion and fangtastic contest winner. And, once
again, thanks to Paul, Jacob, and Alexandria—you are my everything. I am absolutely amazed by your support, your dedica-
tion, and your unfailing belief in me. Without you, none of this
would be possible.

Most importantly, thanks must go to my Minion Horde, of
which you have just become a part by picking up this book.
Without you, my Minion, I am nothing, and Vlad is but a piece
of fiction. In your hands, he becomes real. Thank you, from
both of us.

CONTENTS

The Chronicles of Vladimir Tod

TENTH GRADE BLEEDS

1
ENTER IGNATIUS

IGNATIUS DREW THE CURVED BLADE along the whetstone slowly, the gritty sound filling his ears. It had to be sharp, sharp enough to slice into bone if necessary. He didn't expect to kill the halfling boy, only to damage him, break him, before dragging his nearly lifeless body before the council, as he'd been hired to do. But if the boy gave him any trouble at all, Ignatius would take his bloody pleasures slowly, so that the boy felt every bruise, every cut.

He almost hoped the boy would fight back, give him an excuse to torture him. After all, he had it coming. His very existence was an abomination.

Small sparks flew from the blade, and at last, Ignatius pulled metal from stone. He ran his thumb along the steel, splitting his pale skin open. Blood—rich, red—dripped from the cut before it healed closed again.

He was hungry. It was always better to hunt when he was hungry. He hadn't eaten in months, in eager anticipation of that insatiable need pushing him through the capture and, perhaps, the kill.

The council had been clear: "Bring us Vladimir Tod and your reward will be immeasurable." They never mentioned in what condition to bring him, had only barely stressed that he should be living. Little did they know, Ignatius didn't require payment. Causing the boy's suffering—and perhaps even his death, he thought with a pleasant shiver—would be reward enough.

The boy who would be the Pravus. The thought enraged Ignatius further, and he returned his blade to the whetstone, working it slowly, smoothing the edge into a razor.

Soon. Once the final paperwork was signed, his hunt would begin.

And Vladimir Tod would be made to suffer.

2
At Summer's End

VLAD SQUEEZED HIS EYES TIGHT and listened to the thumping of his heartbeat and the whoosh of his blood as it pumped through his vampire veins. Well, half-vampire veins, anyway. His stomach had been rumbling loudly for the last half hour, and the hunger eased the task of locating his uncle with nothing more than his vampire intuition. Otis hadn't thought that it would. Actually, he'd presumed quite the opposite—the same way Vikas had been surprised during their training sessions in Siberia last year when Vlad confessed he found it easier to push into people's minds when he was hungry. It turned out Vlad was a freak in that regard as well. But maybe that wasn't such a bad thing. After all, the hunger seemed to sharpen his vampire skills.

He tightened his stomach muscles and refrained from pushing into Otis's mind. As his uncle had said, sensing a vampire's location wasn't about tapping into his thoughts. It was about reaching out with your blood, your very vampire cells, and feeling the presence of one of your kind, gauging the distance they stood from you.

With a deep breath, Vlad reached out and sensed his uncle's presence northwest of where he stood on the front porch of his Aunt Nelly's house, the house he'd called home for five years. The corners of his lips rose in a half smile as he spoke to Otis with his thoughts. *"Oh come on! That's too easy. Go farther away! You're only a half mile out. Even Henry could detect you at this distance."*

"Your drudge couldn't detect the Stop & Shop with the aid of a GPS."

Vlad laughed aloud, brushing his black hair out of his eyes and dropping his gaze to his shoes, the smile still firmly fixed to his lips. *"How am I doing, anyway?"*

"Exceptionally well, Vladimir, but I'd wager you don't need me to tell you that. In fact, better than any vampire I've ever encountered. Most can detect our kind up to roughly six hundred yards. But you . . . you're clearly gifted in this regard—your father would be proud. Now, clear your mind and try again in five minutes."

He sat on the steps and stared up at the star-speckled

sky. A cool breeze brushed his cheek. As of tomorrow, summer would be at its end, and Nelly would no longer have an open mind about his late-night activities—even those with Otis. He had hoped this evening could last forever, but the first day of school was looming, and with it, something disturbing that he'd been pushing out of his mind all summer.

There was no stopping it. Not anymore, anyway. He'd whined, pleaded with, and appealed to his uncle until he was blue in the face. But there would be no further delay. It was inevitable. It was time.

Uncle Otis was leaving.

Worse yet, there was absolutely nothing that Vlad could possibly do to prevent it.

It wasn't just that Otis was going away again that jangled Vlad's nerves; it was the fact that he'd gotten used to Otis's comforting protection in the past few months. What was Vlad supposed to do if his former friend Joss decided to return to Bathory and unleash his Slayer skills all over again? He didn't think it was mathematically possible to survive another stake through the heart. Surviving it once was bad enough. And it had raised the possibility that he just might possibly be, maybe actually *really* be, the Pravus. The half-vampire, half-human, ruling-over-vampirekind, enslaving-the-human-race subject of prophecy that Elysia had been watching out for for centuries. Just thinking about it gave Vlad the chills.

And even if he really were the Pravus, he seriously doubted that D'Ablo would back off for another entire year, especially since the last time Vlad saw the fanged jerk he had all but mimicked Arnold Schwarzenegger's catch-phrase of "I'll be back."

Man, sometimes it really sucked being a vampire.

Especially a teen vampire.

Whose vampire uncle was about to pull outta town and leave him to his own defenses.

Vlad stood back up and listened to his heartbeat: slow, strong, amazingly healthy after his encounter with Joss last year. After a moment, he reached out to Otis and felt his presence. Only this time he didn't just feel him standing three blocks away; he could almost *see* him there, leaning casually with his back against the streetlight across from Mr. Craig's old house. It was as if he were watching the scene through the lens of a large, omniscient camera.

He furrowed his brow. *"Otis, are you standing across from Mr. Craig's house, leaning against a pole?"*

Otis's voice, hesitant in Vlad's mind. *"Vladimir, you're supposed to be judging my distance from you. Are you tapping into my thoughts? I can't feel you in there."*

"No. I'm watching you. At least, I think I am. From the outside."

Otis grew very quiet and walked quickly out of view from the camera in Vlad's mind. Then the camera clicked off, and Vlad chewed his bottom lip in contemplation. In moments, thanks to his vampire speed, Otis was making his way up the street to where Vlad stood. His face seemed paler than usual, his eyes large and wide, almost suspicious. When he opened the gate, he frowned, his eyebrows drawn together as if he were distressed. "How did you see me, Vladimir? Exactly what were you doing?"

Vlad shrugged, his nerves fraying some—he'd seen that look in Otis's eyes several times over the summer, and each time had ended up reminding him what a freak he was, even in the vampire world. "I didn't do anything different, just reached out with my blood, the way you taught me. Why?"

Otis shook his head. "Vampires can't tell who it is we sense or precisely where they are, only how far away from us they're located and how many there are."

Vlad sighed. "Great. I can't do the simplest thing without screwing it up with my weirdness."

"It's not a curse, Vladimir. It's a blessing." But in Otis's softly spoken words lurked a lie.

Vlad's jaw tensed, but he kept his tone light. "Then you be the Pravus. I'm too tired to reign over vampirekind, let alone enslave the human race."

Otis smiled, but it was forced. Behind his casual pose Vlad sensed fear. "Is that what you want, to do as prophecy deems you will—if, in fact, you are the so-called Pravus?"

"I don't know. Being godlike might have its perks." The corner of Vlad's mouth rose in a smirk, but then he shrugged with one shoulder and dropped his gaze to the ground between his feet. "But even if I am—and . . . well, I think we both know that's a very real possibility."

Otis shifted his feet, and Vlad braced himself. Vlad wasn't stupid. He hadn't failed to notice Otis's changed behavior—the discomfort and awkward, nervous glances ever since Joss had put him in the hospital with a stake through the heart. Only the Pravus could have survived something like that. Worse than the idea that he could be a danger to humans everywhere, and a tyrant to his fellow creatures of the night, was that his uncle, his last living relative, was living in fear of him . . . or rather, of what he might be, and probably was.

"Even if I am the Pravus, it's like you told me, Otis. A man is the choices that he makes. And I fully intend to make good choices, to be a good man. Like my dad was." He met Otis's eyes then and smiled, hoping his words would be enough to calm Otis's fears, if only for the evening.

But Otis still looked troubled.

Vlad looked up into the night sky. "It sucks that summer is almost over. No more late nights outside with you, learning new skills. Not that there could possibly be much more to learn."

"Oh, there's one or two that I haven't taught you yet." Otis winked. "Are you hungry?"

"Famished." Vlad's fangs slipped down from his gums in

acknowledgment. He ran his tongue across their tips and met Otis's eyes. "By the way, I wanted to thank you. You know, for not feeding on humans while you're here. I know it hasn't been easy, living on bagged blood when you're used to feeding straight from the source. But I really appreciate the effort... even though you'll probably gorge on whole families after you've left Bathory."

Otis chuckled but, Vlad noticed, he didn't negate Vlad's jibe. "And I want to thank *you*," he said.

"For what?"

Otis turned and led the way up the steps of the porch. He opened the front door, holding it for Vlad, then followed his nephew inside. "Many things. For putting up with an old fool's superstitions. For outshining our brethren in wisdom and skill. For allowing me to share your home. And mostly, for helping me to see your father, Tomas, again, through you."

Vlad felt his cheeks flush a little. "It's not like I even had a say about you staying here—there was no way Nelly would let you stay anywhere else. And neither would I. You belong here with us, Otis."

Otis grew quiet for a moment, and then nodded, as if making a momentous decision. "Come, Vladimir. I want to show you something."

Otis led him into the kitchen, where he rummaged through several drawers before finally withdrawing a paring knife. "There is power in blood. I'm certain you know this. But something I have not yet taught you is how that power may be utilized for your protection, and the protection of those you care for. And with me leaving … well, I'd feel better if you knew more about how to protect yourself."

Otis placed the knife on the counter between them and kept his voice low, as if afraid that they would wake Nelly, or maybe, Vlad thought, afraid that Nelly would overhear. "Reach back, Vlad. Do you recall me carving my name in Elysian code into that small box in your dresser two years ago?"

Vlad nodded. How could he forget it? He'd thought Otis was some psychotic vampire, marking him for death. It was funny how wrong he'd turned out to be.

Otis pushed up his left sleeve, revealing the thick black tattooed symbol on his wrist. When he placed it near Vlad's own tattooed wrist, both symbols glowed brightly. "I was marking you, vowing with my life to protect you by inscribing my vampire name into one of your possessions. It was a warning to any vampire who wanted to cause you grief that they would have me to deal with. You remember my explanation of that?"

Vlad smiled at their tattoos and offered a nod. "Of course I do. But what's with the knife?"

"Marking someone is taken very seriously in the vampire world. But it is more of an oath, a vow, than an element of power. The real power of our Elysian names is when they are used in the creation of glyphs." Otis plucked the knife from the counter and pressed the tip against the soft pad of his pointer finger. The shiny metal broke the skin, allowing a crimson bubble to form. Vlad's stomach rumbled. He and Otis exchanged somber looks—one hungry vampire to another. Otis nodded apologetically. "Normally I'd just bite my finger, but I fear the taste of blood—even my own—would be too much to bear at this point. And I made a promise to you that I intend to keep. No feeding from the source while I am here in Bathory."

Otis placed his bloodied finger against the wood of the nearest cupboard door and, with his blood, drew his name in Elysian code, the tattooed symbol on his wrist. As he did so, the blood soaked into the wood. Seconds later, the wood began to burn where his blood had touched. Otis looked at Vlad. "Open it."

Vlad furrowed his brow and reached for the knob, but it was stuck fast. "I can't."

"I know. I empowered that as a locking glyph. As I drew my name, my mark, I fed my intent into the blood with my thoughts." Otis smiled, but beneath his smile there was something else—concern, maybe. Or fear. Again, fear. "In blood, there is power. But your name is powerful as well. Combined, you can protect loved ones and precious objects, keep secrets, even harm unwanted trespassers. Glyphs are crucial to vampire society, to our way of life.

But they are also dangerous, Vladimir, when used incorrectly or not respected. Use your glyphs wisely, and keep your distance from those that glow red."

Vlad ran his finger along the glyph, wondering briefly what Nelly would say about the unusable cupboard and its damaged surface. "Why?"

But Otis either didn't hear his question or didn't acknowledge it, because he washed off the knife in the sink and turned back to Vlad, almost anxious. "Now, your turn. Nip the end of your finger just a bit. We don't want the blood to flow too well. It'll smear your glyph, and a flawed glyph won't work."

As Vlad bit into his finger, Otis turned his head, shivering. Suddenly Vlad felt enormously bad for restricting his uncle's diet. As the blood blossomed out of the small cut, Vlad squeezed, encouraging the wound to remain open.

Otis closed his eyes. Vlad could feel his uncle inside his mind. His presence was comforting. *"Now visualize, for example, that none but you can open the knife drawer."* A pause, then *"Excellent. And now you simply write your name on it, with your blood, in Elysian code."*

Vlad breathed deeply, dragging his bloody finger along the drawer, drawing the symbol that was his vampiric name, the image that was forever burned into his left wrist. When he'd finished, he met Otis's now open eyes. "How do we know it worked?"

Otis pulled the knob, but the drawer was locked tight. He smiled proudly. "It seems to have worked just fine."

Vlad examined his handiwork, a smile finding its way onto his lips, but his smile faltered when he realized what an enormous mess would be awaiting Nelly in the morning. "How do you remove a glyph, anyway?"

"Only the glyph's master can remove it, and it must be washed away with spring water." Otis moved to the refrigerator and rummaged around inside for something. Successful, he withdrew a small plastic bottle. He tossed it to Vlad, along with a rag. "Fortunately for you, it comes in bottles now. Your father and I used to walk for miles to locate a spring."

Vlad poured some water on the cloth until it was soaked, then wiped at the marked drawer front. His glyph sizzled a bit and then evaporated completely, leaving the drawer just as it had been, with no sign of the apparent damage his blood had caused to its surface. He tossed the rag to Otis, who scrubbed the cupboard door clean. "Let me guess. Uphill? Both ways? Through four feet of snow?"

Otis chuckled. "At times, yes. We faced many obstacles seeking out springs in our younger days, when we were still learning how to use glyphs. I'll never forget the time we had to cross straight through a grouping of roughly a hundred members of the Slayer Society, who were all regaling one another with boastful tales about how many vampires each had killed. The only spring for miles was at the center of their encampment."

Vlad's eyes grew wide. "They didn't see you?"

"Of course they did. But for all of their apparent skills, not one attacked. We were approached by a small group, stakes at the ready. They asked to see our Society Coin. All slayers carry a coin as proof of their membership in the Slayer Society. Tomas withdrew just such a coin from his pocket and told them of the three vampires that we had just slain, not a mile from their encampment. 'Three at once,' he bragged. When in all actuality it had been three Slayers that he and I had just feasted on, which is how he'd come by the coin. And they believed his ridiculous tale." Otis grinned at Vlad's disbelieving stare. "Have I mentioned that your father was a master of mind control?"

3

RETURN to BATHORY HIGH

VLAD ZIPPED UP HIS BACKPACK and glanced at the clock. He was running late for his first day as a sophomore at Bathory High, and was exhausted from his late-night rendezvous with Otis. He stretched his thin arms over his head and yawned, his fangs pressing easily through his gums as a reminder that he'd yet to consume his morning meal. A second later, his stomach growled, as if agreeing that it was time to eat. Vlad pulled three blood bags from the freezer, stacked them in a pile, and bit into the plastic, breaking through the layers until cool, sweet, delicious blood seeped into his awaiting mouth. He sucked quickly and drained the bags. It wasn't enough to satiate his gnawing hunger. Lately it seemed like nothing was.

"A word, Vladimir." Otis placed his old leather doctor bag on the table beside Vlad's backpack and yawned. It was funny how easily a vampire could get used to sleeping during the day and roaming around at night. Switching back was another story.

Vlad tossed the bags in the biohazard container beneath the sink and ignored his rumbling stomach. His fangs had already shrunk back, but slowly, as if forewarning him that his hunger couldn't be ignored for long. He turned to Otis, half knowing what was coming and unwilling to hear it.

Otis paused, pressed his lips together, as if taking a moment to gather his thoughts. Then he took a deep breath and began his now familiar lecture. "Your hunger . . ."

Vlad couldn't help but snap, "What about it?"

"It's been growing considerably over the summer, don't you think?"

Vlad shrugged and dropped his gaze to the plank floor. He'd been hoping nobody would notice. But Henry had remarked on it several times, Nelly complained about it constantly, and Otis kept flashing him these overly concerned glances. It seemed a guy just couldn't keep a secret in this town.

Well, apart from that whole being a vampire thing.

"I assure you, it has. I've seen it, and you've struggled with it, Vlad." Otis paused again, this time leaning closer, his eyes very serious, his tone no-nonsense. It wasn't like Otis to get all parental. "It's time we seriously discuss a change in your diet. Before you lose control of your appetite and harm someone close to you."

Vlad's jaw tightened, and he shook his head adamantly. "No way. I'm not killing anyone just because I need a snack."

Otis's tone remained insistent, but gently so. "It is not necessary to kill. And there are alternatives to taking blood against a human's will. Donors, for instance."

Vlad mulled this over for several moments, wondering exactly why Otis hadn't brought up using a donor before— not that he was interested in feeding from a human, of course. He certainly didn't lie awake thinking about it late at night, daydreaming about the taste of it. No way. No sir. He was completely in control of his enormous thirst. "What do you mean, donors?" he asked.

"There is a group of humans—drudges, actually—who donate their services in order to help a small, unusual sect of vampires—those against the idea of killing humans or forcing them to act as sustenance. The humans donate of their own free will, with no direction from their masters. So you see, you *can* feed on humans, Vladimir, without taking their lives."

Vlad's stomach rumbled its eagerness. He made sure to take a breath before saying, "I guess that would be okay."

Relief flooded Otis's eyes. "Good. Thank you for keeping an open mind. However, there is a minor problem with this option. This sect... it's located in Paris. So you would have to attend school there in order to partake every day, the way that your body seems to require."

"Paris?" Vlad shook his head once again. Clearly, his uncle had lost his mind. "I can't move to Paris, Otis."

"It would be different if you were a monthly feeder, Vladimir. But as your appetite seems more demanding, we have to make adjustments. I have good friends there who will care for you, watch out for you."

Vlad picked up his backpack, which was heavy with school supplies, and swung it over his shoulder. "What about Nelly? She won't be safe without me here."

Otis swallowed hard. When he spoke, it came out in hesitant, worried gasps. "Vladimir... with your growing hunger and your refusal to drink from unwilling humans... soon she may not be safe *with* you here."

Vlad furrowed his brow. He'd never hurt Nelly, no matter how hungry he got. Otis should know better. He headed for the front door. "I'm not going."

Otis followed him all the way to the porch, his voice pleading. "Then let me teach you how to hunt. Just in case."

"No." Vlad moved down the steps and out the gate, leaving Otis and his bizarre ideas behind.

Henry was waiting for him across the street. "Dude, where's your girlfriend?"

Vlad tried to hide his smile at the mention of Meredith—*the* Meredith Brookstone—being his girlfriend, but he couldn't. "She's not walking with us. Her dad kinda thinks I might be a serial killer."

"On account of what, exactly?"

"On account of I'm dating his daughter, I think."

Henry nodded toward Otis, who was still standing on the porch, watching them as they finally disappeared between houses. "What was that all about anyway?"

"Nothing." Vlad's grip on his backpack tightened as he relived the conversation. He still couldn't believe Otis had suggested that he might someday be a threat to Nelly. And he was leaving tonight! Talk about picking a crappy time to get someone mad at you. And as if that weren't bad enough, bringing it up on his first day of school was exactly what Vlad didn't need.

"Oh man, I forgot to tell you." They stepped out from between the houses and rounded the corner to face the front steps of Bathory High. "Snelgrove got a new job."

"Oh yeah? As what? I'd kill to see the middle school principal shoveling dog turds for a living." Vlad chuckled, but his amusement wasn't long-lived. Standing on the top step was a familiar face, twitching his little mouse nose distrustfully and watching passing students like he was some kind of prison warden.

"Actually . . ." Henry winced. "He took over being principal of the high school."

Vlad sighed, defeated. First Otis's lecture, now Snelgrove. The only thing that remained was for Eddie Poe to tell everyone he was a monster, and Bill and Tom to shove him into a locker, and his day would be complete. "Great. Today officially sucks."

Henry pulled him by his sleeve and whispered with a chuckle, "Dude, you're a vampire. Every day sucks for you."

"Vlad!" Across the sidewalk stood a pretty girl with chocolate brown hair and a penchant for wearing pink. Vlad grinned. Meredith.

She crossed the street and kind of skipped over to him, smiling, her pink backpack bouncing against her back. "I was hoping I'd see you before class."

"Ditto." Vlad's heart thumped solidly against his chest, nice and strong. A few popular kids walked by, wrinkling their noses at him, but nothing they could do would bring his mood back down. He had a girlfriend. A real live actual girlfriend. And nothing could take that away. Not Snelgrove, not Eddie, and not even a million snotty looks from the popular kids.

And there had been a million snotty looks from the popular kids. They'd started during last year's Freedom Fest, when Vlad had hung out with Meredith all night. And with each look, Vlad's stomach had shrunk a little in fear. It seemed everyone but Meredith knew he didn't belong at her side. Even Vlad knew it. Meredith deserved better.

Meredith smiled at Henry, then crooked her pointer finger, gesturing for Vlad to come closer. When he did, she whispered in his ear, her breath all warm and sugary-sweet. It sent chills up his spine. "I missed you. Maybe we could get together after school, just the two of us?"

He reached up, brushing her soft hair from her ear, and whispered, "Can't tonight. My uncle is leaving and I need to see him off. But let me ditch Henry after school tomorrow and we can meet up at Eat around three-thirty, okay?"

She turned her head, lightly brushing her lips against his cheek in response.

Vlad's heart nearly exploded from joy overload.

The food at Eat, the town's diner, wasn't exactly fantastic, but it was a place where they could be alone, without fear of Henry feeling left out or of Meredith's father swooping down and stealing her away from the clutches of a homicidal maniac—i.e., her boyfriend. Suddenly, Eat seemed like paradise. And while it wasn't technically called Eat, that's what its single neon sign screamed into the streets. More of a command than a sign, really.

Meredith joined Melissa Hart at the bottom of the steps, and they walked up them with a bouncy gate. Vlad gazed after Meredith, still feeling floaty on the inside. Henry cleared his throat, his mood suddenly sullen. "We'd better find our lockers. Bell rings in five minutes."

He led the way and Vlad followed, struggling to keep his happiness undercover. He knew it bothered Henry that he was seeing Meredith and that Henry wasn't seeing

Melissa, but it wasn't like Vlad had planned it that way, or that he was going to spend much time feeling guilty over it. For once, Henry was struggling with girl issues, and Vlad wasn't.

Truth be told, it was kind of nice.

"Don't think I'm not watching you, Mr. Tod," Principal Snelgrove snarled as Vlad walked by. Vlad waited until the coast was clear before rolling his eyes.

But just inside the doors stood someone whom Vlad was worried about, someone who'd also been watching him, and strapped to his neck was a brand-spanking-new digital SLR camera.

Eddie Poe.

The boy who'd seen Vlad's eyes flash that weird irides-cent purple last year, the boy who'd photographed him floating up to the belfry. The bane of Vlad's existence had just upgraded his equipment. And he was watching Vlad closely, as if waiting for him to latch onto the nearest cheerleader's neck right here in the middle of school.

As if Vlad would bite a cheerleader. The thought left a bad taste in his mouth.

Vlad nodded curtly to Eddie, who did the same, gestur-ing to his new camera. Then Vlad pursed his lips and headed to locker number 313.

Ever since Eddie had seen Vlad's eyes flash purple, he'd been following Vlad around, snapping pictures, staring. Your basic stalkeresque activities. But Vlad could handle that. What really made him crazy was the sudden surge of hungry confidence that Eddie's budding obsession had brought on. At every turn, Eddie seemed to delight in taunting Vlad, as if waiting for the day he would snap and reveal his darkest secrets. It was as if Eddie had found a way out of his pit of nobody-ness, and Vlad was the one holding the ladder.

Vlad pulled his padlock from his backpack and slipped it into the hole in the locker's door, then stuffed his notebooks, pens, and other school supplies inside. His locker already looked messy. Vlad closed the door.

Eddie was waiting for him. And he wasn't smiling.

Neither was Vlad. "What do you want, Eddie?"

"Just to show you my new camera. You like it? I saved up all summer for it. Must have mowed every lawn in Bathory to afford this baby." He patted the camera gently, his eyes never leaving Vlad's.

Vlad shrugged. "It's nice, I guess. I don't know much about cameras."

"I do. I know about lots of things." Eddie's normally quivering jaw set, a determined look in his eyes. Determined to expose Vlad's secret. "Anyway ... see ya around, I guess."

"Yeah ... and you can bet I'll be seeing you." Vlad watched Eddie walk away, his mood plummeting. He'd never be normal. He'd never fit in. And this kid was out to tell the world why.

Henry walked past Eddie, glaring at him the entire time. Eddie shrank away, and Vlad felt just a little bit better about their encounter. Henry opened his locker. "So what did the *National Enquirer* want anyway?"

Vlad shrugged. "The usual, I guess."

He glanced over at Eddie, who had stopped at the drinking fountain for a sip, and bit his bottom lip. "He's not going to stop until he exposes me, Henry. He's different this year. Last year he was just annoying. But now . . . it's like he's got something to prove, and that something is me."

Henry grabbed his English and science books and closed his locker. His forehead was creased, as if he was troubled. "Don't worry about it, Vlad. We'll figure something out. After all, it's just Eddie Poe. He's nothing. He's empty space."

Vlad nodded, unsure if he agreed with Henry's assessment of the situation. Eddie might be a nobody, but a determined nobody could find his way into being a somebody if the right opportunity presented itself. Trying to push those troubling thoughts from his mind, he frowned down at his schedule. He didn't share any classes with Henry or Meredith this year, which didn't exactly give him a lot to look forward to. After receiving a friendly slug in the shoulder from Henry, he grabbed the teal book with a picture of what looked like a brain holding hands with a piece of broccoli on the cover and headed down the hall to first period.

Health class. Whoever had decided that forcing kids to sit in a room together while a teacher blushes and stumbles over the ins and outs of sex and drugs and puberty was a good idea should have realized that kids already know most of the stuff by the time they hit high school, and the stuff they don't know, they really, *really* don't want to hear from an old windbag like Mr. Cartel.

Mr. Cartel was born before the beginning of time, and he seemed to look fondly on those pre-dinosaur years, as he couldn't help but comment on how things had been when he was a kid. Vlad had heard the horror stories about health class with Mr. Cartel. He'd been warned about the weird wheezing noise he made when he breathed, and about the fact that every time he was forced to say the word *gonads* he would stutter. But Vlad hadn't been prepared for the life-size posters of two naked people and all their naked bits. Nor had he been prepared for the desktop models of the human reproductive systems.

Oh. My. God.

Vlad's face flushed as he did a quick head count on the way to his desk. Twelve girls, eight guys, one very old teacher, and way too many naked parts at the front of the class. It was like a scene out of his worst nightmare.

Suddenly he was relieved that Meredith didn't share first hour with him.

He took a desk in the back, as far away from all the nakedness as he could possibly get. No one, of course, was sitting in the front row. Mr. Cartel waited quietly until the bell rang, then leaned back in his chair and regarded the class with a somber expression. "Welcome to health. In this class, we will discuss physiological changes in a body as it ages, the reproductive process, the dangers of sexually transmitted diseases, the dangers of drugs and alcohol, and we will spend an entire month discussing how smoking cigarettes damages the human body."

Vlad sank further down in his seat with each item the teacher had listed until he got to drugs, alcohol, and tobacco—he already knew those were things to be avoided if he planned on living past twenty. And not just because of the way they harmed his body—if he touched any of them, Nelly would kill him for sure.

Mr. Cartel cleared his throat and shifted in his seat a little before standing up. He picked up a long, wooden pointer and, much to Vlad's horror, smacked the pointer against the nether regions of the man on the poster. "The human reproductive system is a complicated and fascinating subject. We will study each part thoroughly, from glands to g-g-g-gonads . . ."

Vlad felt his face grow so hot that he was fairly certain he was glowing. He sank even further down in his seat and waited for the nightmare to be over.

After napping through geometry and accidentally freezing Mrs. Patterson's beaker to the lab table in chemistry, Vlad stumbled into a lunchtime oasis. Meredith had saved a seat for him and Henry sat across from her, making moon eyes at Melissa Hart as she made her way through the lunch line. Vlad slid in beside Meredith and managed a smile. "Is it graduation time yet?"

Meredith laughed, sweet and giggly, making Vlad's insides all gooey. "Is it that bad so far?"

Henry snorted. "Not all of us lucked out with challenging courses like art and Sucking Up to the Teacher 101, Meredith."

Meredith wrinkled her nose in that cute way she did whenever she was irritated, and brushed a stray hair from her eyes. "It's called teacher's assistant, and maybe if you worked harder at your grades, you'd get to do it for a semester, too. Besides, art isn't exactly easy."

Henry shrugged and Vlad changed the subject—he wasn't in the mood for another tiff between those two. "Cartel's going to make this the longest year yet."

A grin spread across Henry's face. "Only if he keeps talking about gonads. Man, that guy can stutter. In second period we kept asking him questions, knowing the answer involved gonads, just to hear him rattle through the word a couple dozen times. It was funny."

Vlad chuckled, but Meredith didn't. In fact, she looked a little repulsed. Apparently, a girl's idea of funny was very different from a guy's.

Melissa sat down on the other side of Meredith, much to Henry's dismay. The two girls were deep in conversation when Henry leaned across the table and raised his eyebrows with a smirk. "So . . . did you get a look at the woman on that poster?"

Vlad laughed aloud, shaking his head. "Dude, did you see the date on that poster? She's way too old for you."

4

A LONG GOODBYE

THAT AFTERNOON, AS VLAD MADE HIS WAY from the school to his house sans Henry, he had the unsettling, unshakable feeling that he was being followed. He turned around several times, but found no one. Finally, as he was crossing the street, he whipped around fast enough to spot a head ducking behind a tree. With a sigh, he approached the tree and ducked around it to find Eddie and his new camera. "What are you doing, Eddie?"

Eddie forced a smile. "Just walking. What about you?"

Vlad knew he was lying—they both knew it. He shook his head, weary of Eddie's antics already. "Nothing. That's all I'm doing, Eddie. And that's all you'll ever catch me doing by following me. So why don't you get another hobby?"

He turned and crossed the street. As his foot touched pavement, he heard the click of a camera behind him. The sound made the corner of his mouth twitch in irritation.

By the time Vlad got back to the house, he was completely annoyed with Eddie, but overshadowing his annoyance was the fact that he dreaded the conversation that he knew was waiting for him there. He slipped through the front gate as quietly as he could, moved up the path to the front steps, made his way across the porch, and opened the door an inch. Then he paused, tilting his head to see if he could hear his uncle Otis moving around in the house.

Nothing. Not so much as a footstep. Maybe Otis had given up the argument in light of his coming departure.

With a relieved exhale, Vlad counted his blessings, stepped inside, and headed for the stairs.

"I believe an apology is in order, Vladimir."

Vlad cursed himself for not using his vampire honing skills. What good were talents like these if he couldn't remember to use them? He stopped in his tracks and turned to face Otis, who'd been leaning against the wall to the left of the front door, waiting.

Apparently, he wasn't about to skip town without finishing his rant on Vlad's growing hunger.

Vlad's stomach grumbled its agreement, and he couldn't

help but wonder whose side it was on. "I'm not apologizing, Otis. Not for disagreeing with you. I mean, okay, maybe I shouldn't have walked out like that, but I—"

Otis held up his hand, silencing Vlad. "I'm not asking you to apologize. I'm apologizing to you. No one knows better than you how in control of your hunger you are, and if you say that you can resist harming those around you, I have no choice but to trust you."

Then Otis met his gaze and softened. "I'm just trying to give you as much good advice as I can before leaving tonight."

The corners of Vlad's mouth rose in a knowing half smile. "I'll miss you too."

A sadness overwhelmed Otis's eyes, and he reached out and gave Vlad's shoulder a squeeze. He didn't speak, and Vlad understood why. Because the argument over Vlad's growing appetite was much more about how hard it was for Otis to leave him once again than it was about the fear of Vlad snacking on his friends and family. Of course, Otis *was* still concerned about that, but not, Vlad surmised, as much as he was worried about leaving Vlad behind, with only an hour's drive between him and the Stokerton council.

Vlad dropped his backpack at the foot of the stairs and glanced at the suitcases that sat there. The sight of them sent a hairline fracture through his heart. "Did you pack already?"

Otis sighed and ran a hand through his hair, ruffling it. "Not yet. Truth be told, I've been avoiding it all day."

Vlad turned over one of the luggage tags and smiled to see that his and Nelly's address had been scribbled on it in Otis's horrific handwriting—an unspoken acknowledgment that no matter where he traveled this was his home. "Y'know, Otis . . . maybe you should stay."

"Vladimir, I—"

"No. Hear me out a second." Vlad's heart thumped harder. He had to fight to retain a calm tone. Even so, his voice rose with insistent need. "You like it here, right? And so far, having you around has been a lot safer than having you anywhere else."

Otis seemed on guard, which only made Vlad's words come out faster, spilling over his tongue in a desperate ramble. "You've been here for almost four months, and the Stokerton council hasn't bugged you once, even though this would be a pretty obvious place for you to hide out. I've never seen Nelly so happy . . ."

Vlad's voice caught in his throat. ". . . and I'm learning so much from you."

Otis averted his eyes, but it was too late. Vlad had already seen the "no" lurking within them. Vlad bit down on the inside of his cheek to keep the tears at bay. "Tell me why you can't stay. Because it's not making much sense to me that you should take off to Siberia when you've got it so good here."

Otis sighed. "Vladimir . . ."

"Is it the Elysia thing? Needing to be among your own kind? Because you have that with me, Otis. I'm a vampire too. And I really feel better when you're around."

"You are completely right on all counts."

But something dark flickered in his eyes, crushing Vlad's hopes before they could even bloom. Vlad opened his mouth and closed it again, not daring to ask what that flicker meant.

Otis wet his lips, his expression troubled, sorrowful, but certain. "Even so, I cannot stay. Please, Vladimir, I need you to trust me on this. My staying here may endanger you and Nelly."

A panicky feeling had wormed its way into Vlad's chest. He couldn't explain it, but the idea of Otis leaving him again—especially after all that he'd been through with Joss staking him last year and D'Ablo hinting that he wasn't fin-ished with Vlad—made his stomach twist and turn. Frus-trated, Vlad threw his hands in the air. "Can't someone else look for that ritual?"

Otis raised his voice suddenly. "Who? There is no one but me! And Vikas, of course. But his time is stretched."

Vlad knew he was pushing his uncle, but it was all he had left to cling to. In but a few hours, Otis would be gone again. Vlad wasn't sure just how much more of this he could take. "Isn't there a glyph or something we can place to pro-tect all of us, or to keep the council from finding you?"

Otis shook his head, his tone calm once again. "It's not as simple as that. I can hide from one, maybe two vampires utilizing glyphs, but hiding from all of Elysia is a fool's errand."

Vlad's jaw tensed. He fell silent, and stood very still for a moment before speaking. "My dad managed well enough."

Otis closed his eyes in defeat. "Well, we can't all be as crafty as your father, can we?"

Vlad winced. "I just wish—"

"I know. Believe me, I know." Otis turned away from him and gazed out the window near the front door, his shoulders slumped. In Vlad's mind, he heard Otis say, *More than anything, I wish I could stay, too.*"

Vlad's face dropped. He had expected defeat when he'd entered this battle, but the taste of it was still bitter. "Do you need help packing?"

"Why don't we save that for after dinner?" Otis smiled weakly over his shoulder at Vlad. "I want to try my hand at cooking. I believe Nelly would like that. I have no taste for human food anymore, but in my previous life, I was quite the chef."

Vlad shook his head. "I'll just nuke some O positive, if you don't mind."

"Actually I'd prefer it if you'd dine with us." Otis turned to face him with a curious grin. "I'm making blood sausage."

A half hour later, the kitchen was an enormous mess. Otis had several pans and a variety of bowls out on the counter, only a few of them in use. The smell of blood filled Vlad's nostrils, dizzying him with hunger pangs. It took every ounce of his willpower to keep from lifting the big bowl of blood from the counter and slurping down every last drop.

Vlad picked up the wooden spoon and stirred the spiced crimson before turning to his uncle. "Y'know, I might as well have a bag or two of blood. As good as this might smell, animal blood doesn't do much for me in the way of vitamins and minerals."

"Not surprising. Most vampires find animal blood less than enjoyable to the palate and not helpful in the least when it comes to nutrients. But you needn't worry. I'm making our blood sausages from human blood."

Vlad shifted uncomfortably.

Otis hurried to add, "And with the argument we had this morning in mind, I'm using blood from the freezer. And with as much as I'm using, Nelly will need to stock up again."

They exchanged smiles before Otis scooped up bits of diced onion and dropped them in the bowl. He rinsed his hands in the sink, and as he reached for the towel, he quipped, "Unless, of course, you're interested in trying fresh blood."

Vlad knew his uncle was joking, but still he flinched. "Doesn't it bother you that you're hurting people when you feed from the source?"

Otis smiled. "About as much as it bothers you that you're hurting plastic bags, Vladimir," he said, his tone teasing. "Don't think of them as people. Think of them as sustenance."

"Is Nelly sustenance?" It was a low blow, but Vlad was still hurting from his uncle's plans to leave him ... again.

Otis stiffened. He met Vlad's gaze, his eyes haunted. Seeing them gave Vlad a grim surge of satisfaction. "That's not fair," Otis said.

Vlad set the spoon on the counter and folded his arms in front of him. "It's perfectly fair. You're so concerned about my appetite and the safety of the people I'm around. What about you? Do you ever think you might forget that Nelly is anything more than food?"

Otis's jaw hung open. His throat emitted several stunned sounds before he shook his head sharply and said, "Vladimir, I would never harm anyone I care about."

Vlad picked up the spoon again and stirred the onions into the herb-blood mixture, but he kept an eye on Otis. "I know. But it doesn't feel good to be accused, does it?"

The front door opened and Nelly called out, "Otis? Vlad? Are you home?"

Vlad rolled his eyes a little. After all, all of the downstairs lights were on and Otis's car was in the driveway.

Unless they'd gone for a long walk and needed a beacon to find their way back, it was pretty obvious they were home. "We're in the kitchen."

As Nelly stepped into the kitchen, the grocery sack she was holding slipped from her fingers. Otis caught it moments before it hit the floor. She stared wide-eyed at Vlad and then at Otis.

Otis placed the bag on the plank table and returned his attention to her, his brow furrowed. "Is something wrong, Nelly?"

Vlad's brow furrowed too. Nelly's face had gone completely white, and her eyes kept flitting from Vlad to Otis to the room around them.

Vlad turned to survey their surroundings for the first time since Otis had started preparing the meal. His uncle, as it turned out, was not a tidy cook, to say the least. Strewn about the kitchen were large, sharp knives, bits of ground meat and chopped vegetables, skins that the sausage would eventually find its way into, and blood. Lots and lots of blood.

Nelly's eyes finally stopped to focus on the large bowl of blood on the counter in front of Otis, then on his blood-soaked apron, moving up to meet the bewildered expression on his face. "What happened in here?"

Suddenly the realization fell on Otis that to a human, the scene around them made it look as though he and Vlad had been making a nice stew out of the neighborhood children.

Laughter escaped his lips. "Nelly, this isn't what it looks like, I swear. I'm sure it seems we were gorging ourselves on the Johnsons down the street, but we are innocent."

Nelly looked relieved. "I'm sorry. I just wasn't expecting to come home to a scene straight out of *Psycho Slasher Chainsaw Guy from Hell.*"

Vlad coughed. He was almost certain Nelly had never seen that movie, though the previews had been enough to give her an idea of the plot. He wondered for a moment if she had any idea that he and Henry had seen it last year under the pretense of watching a nice, severely-lacking-blood-and-gore spy movie instead.

Vlad looked down at the front of his shirt, which was spattered with small red dots. Several had dried into a rusty brown color. He chewed his bottom lip for a moment, troubled somewhat by Nelly's reaction. Even after all this time, Nelly still worried she'd come home to find him acting like some sort of animal. She'd never voiced it, but Vlad knew that was how she must feel. After all, it had to be hard for her to live with a vampire all these years. It would be like being a pizza living with Henry for an extended period of time. Say, ten minutes or so.

The thought made Vlad a little sick to his stomach.

Otis took Nelly's hands in his and said, "I would never bring the fruits of my hunts into your home, Nelly. You never have to worry about that. And your ward is rather like a vegetarian, so there's no cause for alarm there either. We were simply making blood sausage for dinner."

Nelly's eyes lit up. "You're cooking?"

Otis's voice became softer, sweeter. "It's the least I could do."

Vlad almost retched at their flirting. It was the only obnoxious thing about Otis staying with them. He slipped his soiled shirt over his head and headed for the stairs, muttering that he needed to change ... not that he thought they'd hear him. He still wasn't sure how he felt about the obvious attraction between Nelly and Otis. On one hand, if they ended up married, he'd have the coolest family on the block. But on the other ... the idea of them dating was kind of weird.

Plus, the thought of walking in on them making out was positively repulsive.

After slipping upstairs to his room and changing his shirt, Vlad took his time rejoining them for dinner. Otis cooked Nelly's blood sausages and served them with a side of spiced potatoes and buttered asparagus. Vlad's and Otis's—much to Vlad's delight—were served raw. Vlad lifted one up to his mouth and bit into it, his fangs popping through the fleshy casing. The feeling gave him an excited chill, but he said nothing to Otis about it. Even so, his uncle smiled at him as if to say, "See how pleasant it would be to suck the life out of people?"

After Vlad had drained three sausages, he sat back in his seat, surprisingly satisfied. Nelly smiled at him. "I'll take care of the dishes. Why don't you help Otis get ready?"

Vlad nodded and slowly turned his eyes to Otis, who had finished his meal some time before and was watching Nelly with a sad expression. Without hesitation, Vlad spoke to his uncle telepathically. *"You're going to miss her so much. I can see it in your eyes. Stay, Otis. Please."*

But Otis wouldn't hear it. Vlad felt a definite crunch in his head, a signal that Otis had cut him off. Vlad pursed his lips. Otis stood and pulled a watch from his pocket, noting the time. "Thank you, Nelly. It would be nice to spend a moment alone with Vladimir before I leave."

Vlad and Otis wordlessly carried Otis's suitcases upstairs. Otis unzipped the largest suitcase, opened the large bottom drawer of the antique bureau Nelly kept in the corner of the library, and began moving neat stacks of his clothing from the drawer to his luggage. Vlad turned away, unable to watch his uncle choose to leave him and Nelly behind.

Otis's voice sounded raspy. "Would you mind gathering my toiletries together? They go in the smallest bag."

Vlad grabbed the bag and walked into the bathroom. He took his time filling it—not that he was concerned with neatness or that Otis might fret over leaving his toothbrush behind. He just knew what was coming. It was goodbye. And he really, really didn't want to face it again. Every time

Otis had left him behind, Vlad found it harder to be without him.

Not to mention the fact that whenever Otis wasn't around, people tried to kill him.

As he slipped Otis's shampoo into the bag and zipped it closed—slowly—his uncle appeared in the doorway, a meek smile affixed to his lips. "All set out here."

Vlad handed him the toiletries bag, and Otis led him back out into the library. Once they were there, his uncle stopped, looking very much like he wanted to tell Vlad something, but he couldn't seem to find the words. After a long silence, he said, "Trust only yourself in this world, Vladimir."

Vlad blinked, uncertain what Otis was talking about. Did he mean not to trust even him? Was it his way of saying he wasn't coming back? Vlad pushed the thought away and picked up one of Otis's suitcases. As he helped carry the bags down the stairs and out to Otis's car, he felt like someone had placed a cinder block on his chest. And the cinder block got heavier with every step he took.

Otis placed the bags inside his car and closed the trunk before joining Nelly on the porch. Vlad knew they were whispering, but didn't care to hear just what. Time seemed to move very slowly. It was like falling. Vlad knew it was happening, that pain was coming, but he just couldn't stop it. And then suddenly, Otis brushed his lips against Nelly's cheek and time picked up again. The hurt of his uncle leaving swelled up inside of Vlad and poured forth out his eyes in hot tears. Otis moved down the stairs and without missing a beat or uttering a sound, he swept Vlad into a tight embrace and spoke with his thoughts. *"I love you, Vladimir. I don't believe I've ever told you that, but I do. And I want you to know that no matter what the future holds, I will return to you. Nothing can keep me from you. You and Nelly are my family, more so than even Elysia itself."*

The tears poured down Vlad's cheeks. "Then why? Why can't you stay?"

Otis's breath was warm on Vlad's hair. It reminded Vlad too much of his father and those long ago moments when his dad would rock him back to sleep after a nightmare. "Vladimir, we've been through this. I can't endanger you anymore than I already have. This goes further than the crimes I am charged with, Vladimir. D'Ablo and I have a tense history, and he would gladly draw out my pain by harming everyone that I have come to hold dear."

Vlad sniffled. The panicky feeling in his chest had started to subside, but only a little. "Why hasn't he found you yet? He has to know you'd come here."

In Otis's eyes lurked dark secrets, and Vlad yearned to know what his uncle was keeping from him. But Vlad wasn't sure he was brave enough to ask. Otis said, "Vikas and other friends have been leading my enemies down false trails by placing drops of my blood around the world. And of course, I've placed glyphs all over Bathory to hide my presence here from D'Ablo himself, glyphs that I washed away earlier this afternoon. When I come back, I'll place more."

Vlad dried his face on his sleeve. When he spoke, his voice cracked. "When will that be?"

Otis sighed, and with a glance back at Nelly, he withdrew the keys from his pocket. "I don't know. Soon, I hope. But I must leave now. Before D'Ablo realizes I am here."

Vlad blurted, "Will you at least come back for my birthday?"

"I will absolutely try. But no promises." Otis opened the driver's-side door and slid into his seat. He gunned the engine to life and shut the door, then rolled his window down and smiled.

"Practice your glyphs. If you run into any problems, you know how to reach me." He tapped his temple twice before backing out the driveway and heading down the road that would lead him out of town.

Vlad could only watch helplessly.

Time passed, but Otis's car still kept shrinking.

Just like Vlad's insides.

He turned and made his way into the house, headed straight upstairs, and lay on his bed.

He couldn't recall having fallen asleep, but suddenly his chest tightened in panic and he sat bolt upright, his eyes searching the now pitch-dark room for his alarm clock. It was 2:00 A.M.

Vlad wondered where Otis was by now—if he'd already boarded his plane in Stokerton and was on his way to Siberia or if he'd changed his mind and had headed back to Bathory to stay. He reached out, just like Otis taught him, and tried to detect Otis's presence. To his delight, he sensed that a vampire was near. Maybe two doors down.

Vlad sighed in relief. He pushed, just as he had this morning, but couldn't see his uncle. In fact . . . it didn't even really feel like Otis at all. He wasn't sure how he knew it, but he was growing fairly certain that the vampire that was now as close as his front porch wasn't his uncle. Vlad held his breath for a moment and reached out with his mind. *"Otis?"*

But Otis didn't answer.

The vampire was inside his house now, maybe on the stairs. Closer, closer. Vlad jumped from his bed and spun around, certain the vampire he sensed was in his very room, but all he could see was dark. His heart rammed against his ribs, in a flying panic, but Vlad didn't dare scream—he couldn't endanger Nelly by drawing her into his room with a strange vampire. His breaths came out in rapid puffs, as if the air had suddenly chilled.

And that's when gloved hands clamped slowly onto his shoulders.

Vlad froze, speechless. The vampire, whoever it might be, was right behind him.

"Vladimir Tod. How I have been looking forward to seeing you again."

Vlad knew that voice. It was cold, cruel, and in every nightmare he'd had since the end of his eighth-grade year.

D'Ablo.

5

An Unexpected Visitor

VLAD TURNED TO FACE THE INTRUDER, the vampire respon-sible for so much of his pain and terror over the past two years, and set his jaw as best he could. His heart slammed against his ribs in solid, terrified beats. He was screaming on the inside, but his lips remained totally silent as he defiantly stared D'Ablo down, his left eyebrow starkly raised as if the vampire's intrusion had only been a minor surprise. Vlad didn't speak, didn't even try, because he knew if he opened his mouth, his screams would find their way up and out and into the world. Instead, he pretended that he wasn't scared out of his mind and scanned the room with his peripheral vision for anything that could be used as a weapon.

The corners of D'Ablo's thin lips curled up in a smile. He held his hands outward, as if to show that he was unarmed. But he was always armed with his fangs and vampiric strength—something Vlad's ribs refused to forget after their encounter in his eighth-grade year. Of course, if D'Ablo was always armed, so was Vlad. But Vlad wasn't exactly comforted by that knowledge.

D'Ablo's smile eased. "I'll dispense with the pleasantries. After all, it's ridiculously apparent that we share . . . distaste for each other."

Vlad snorted. Distaste. That was a good one. Nice and understated.

"You have something that I want." D'Ablo regarded him for a moment, as if waiting for him to ask what. Then, seeing that Vlad had no intention of speaking, he continued. "Tomas's journal."

At this Vlad's other eyebrow rose in surprise. "My dad's journal?"

Then a crease formed on his forehead as his eyebrows fell. "Why? What do you want it for?"

"Sentimental reasons. A small memento, is all." D'Ablo tightened his gloves on his hands.

The air between them grew thick with tension.

Vlad shook his head slowly. "No way. You can't have it."

D'Ablo didn't look surprised at all. In fact, he looked like that was the reply he'd been expecting. "You may not be aware of this fact, but Tomas and I were extremely close before he abandoned all of Elysia for the likes of you. I respected him, revered him, even. And now that he has died—an act that is so rare for a vampire to undergo—I find myself missing my old friend more than I had anticipated."

D'Ablo's expression changed then, but only slightly. A brief blip of honest pain crossed his eyes. Seeing it made Vlad take a step back.

D'Ablo took a step closer. "You have hundreds of items to remember Tomas by. Give me this. Give me his journal."

Vlad chewed his bottom lip thoughtfully. On one hand, he had the feeling that D'Ablo might be giving him a chunk of heartfelt truth—something that freaked him out completely. On the other, if he handed the journal over, something in his gut said that it was a trick and that he'd be paying for it in one horrible way or another. After all, D'Ablo was probably the biggest jerk Vlad knew, vampire or otherwise. So why trust him?

"I know you and Tomas were close, actually," Vlad said. "He was even your vice president, as I heard it. Your right-hand man on the Stokerton council. I'm sure you two must have been close."

"We were."

"Of course that makes it even more twisted that you've tried to kill me. Twice now, isn't it?" He looked at D'Ablo, whose expression changed dramatically at the jibe. It was almost as if this fact had never occurred to him. He looked somewhat pained. For a moment, Vlad pitied him. He shook his head again. "Not the journal. You can take something to remember him by, but not that."

D'Ablo grew quiet, and Vlad really didn't think he was mulling over what else of Tomas's belongings he might be interested in taking back with him to his office in Stokerton. It was more likely that D'Ablo was debating exactly how to manipulate Vlad into giving him what he wanted. Or maybe how to kill him. Attempted murder would definitely be the more familiar path.

D'Ablo's features tensed. His hands, gloved in their usual shiny black leather, tightened into fists and then loosened again. When he spoke, his words were hushed and crisp. "Is there no way that I can persuade you?"

Vlad felt himself relaxing a bit. It couldn't be mind control that was easing his muscular tension—Otis had taught him well not only how to detect such attempts, but also how to block them. And it certainly couldn't be confidence, as he was freaking out on the inside and it was all he could do not to run screaming into the night. Whatever it was, Vlad didn't trust it. He met D'Ablo's eyes with a cold gaze. "Why are you trying to *persuade* me at all? Why don't you just attack me and torture me until I tell you where it is? What's with this bizarre attempt at decency?"

And there it was, in D'Ablo's cold, steel gray eyes. Vlad

didn't need telepathy to see it or understand it—not that D'Ablo would allow him even a glimpse of his twisted mind, Vlad was certain. But he could see it, the reason that D'Ablo was talking to him instead of attacking him on sight.

He really believed that Vlad was the Pravus.

And part of him, small as it might be, was afraid of that. And it looked like D'Ablo hadn't yet figured out a way to take Vlad's life because of that fact. After all, his attempts at both ripping Vlad to shreds and trying to turn him into a walking shish kebab via wooden stake had failed miserably.

Vlad straightened his shoulders, releasing the lungful of breath he'd been holding. "Tell me why you want it, exactly."

An impatient light flashed across D'Ablo's eyes. Poised on his tongue was a blatant lie. "Simply to remember him by."

Vlad knew better. If D'Ablo wanted the journal, there was a solid reason for it—one that wasn't merely sentimental. "And if I offered you some pictures or a few of his favorite books?"

D'Ablo shook his head, a wave of low laughter escaping him. He'd grown tired of this game. In a blink he was inches in front of Vlad, squeezing his leather-covered hand tightly around Vlad's throat, until Vlad could feel his lungs tighten in panic. Vlad tore at D'Ablo's hands, but his attacker held fast, whispering bluntly into his ear. "The journal or your life, boy. I'll give you some time to think it over."

Then, just as suddenly as he'd attacked, D'Ablo released

his grip and turned toward the door. Vlad coughed and gasped as air entered his lungs once again. D'Ablo's hand was on the knob when he managed to choke out, "That's not gonna be easy if the Pravus can't be killed."

D'Ablo smirked and opened the door. He met Vlad's eyes and shook his head. "That's not what I meant. But you'll see soon enough."

Vlad blinked, utterly confused. He reached out with his mind, calling to Otis for help . . . but Otis was silent.

As D'Ablo stepped outside, he spoke again, this time without looking back. "Sweet dreams."

His words were followed by chilling laughter.

6

In Anticipation of Blood

IGNATIUS SLIPPED THE CURVED BLADE into the leather holster on his leg. It wasn't the only tool he would need in torturing the Tod boy, but it was by far his favorite. The blade was an extension of himself, and had shed nearly as much blood. They were one. Symbiotic, in a way. The blade hungered for blood, but needed Ignatius's actions and strength to acquire it. And Ignatius . . . he hungered for justice, something only the blade could provide for him. Soon they would taste both.

Lying on the table was a stack of papers, all stamped with the official seal of the Stokerton council. The top paper held the signatures of every council member. They had granted him official permission to hunt the boy at last. It was about time.

Now Ignatius's only concern was how to find the boy alone . . . and in total darkness.

His allergy to the sun—so severe that he would burn even from the light that reflected off the moon at night, so terrible that it could not be overcome by mere sunblock— was an embarrassment that he had dealt with since the moment he'd been reborn into vampiric society. He had never let it hold him back from completing a task. Never. And it wouldn't stop him this time.

He would capture Vladimir Tod . . . and make him bleed until his screams were silenced.

7
HALLOWEEN

VLAD SUCKED THE SWEET CRIMSON LIQUID through a straw, careful not to smudge his now green face. Dressing as Frankenstein (or, technically, Frankenstein's monster) for Matthew's annual Halloween party turned out to be a bit more challenging than he'd thought, and he hadn't even left the house yet. The makeup was a pain to put on, let alone *keep* on. And the bolts he'd attached to his neck with FX putty kept drooping. Still, it wasn't as if the costume or the party or even D'Ablo's visit over two months ago was stressing him out—even though, admittedly, Vlad had been watching around every corner for D'Ablo's return. It was Henry.

"I just don't understand what made you change your mind about going, that's all. We always go to Matthew's Halloween party together." Vlad frowned at Henry, who was leaning up against the kitchen counter sans costume, his arms crossed in front of him. "Is it because Meredith is coming with me? Because it's not like you'd be a third wheel or anything."

"It's not that." Henry shook his head. "I'm just getting too old for this kinda stuff."

Vlad gaped openly at his best friend. "Dude, we're the same age! And anyway, who cares? It's the funnest night of the year. Why shouldn't we dress up and goof off?"

Henry shrugged. "I just don't feel like going, okay?"

But Vlad knew exactly what Henry's reasons were for not going to Matthew's party this year. For one, Melissa Hart had already accepted a date with Mike Brennan—and these days, Henry only seemed to have eyes for Melissa. And for two, Melissa and Meredith were practically inseparable, which likely meant that the four of them were going to spend quite a bit of time together at the party ... and Henry would feel left out. Vlad got it. He really did. But he also knew that he would do everything in his power not to make Henry feel like a tagalong, and he needed Henry to believe that.

Vlad sighed, dropping the empty blood bag and straw into the biohazard box under the sink. It wasn't just that Vlad wanted Henry to come. Henry's presence made it a whole lot easier to share the same air as the popular kids, and to ward off any nasty comments about Vlad. His best friend was an ever-present safety catch.

When he looked at Henry, it pained him. His friend seemed so stressed out lately, and there was little Vlad could do to alleviate it. "Look, I know how much you like Melissa, Henry—"

"Then help me."

Vlad blinked. "How?"

Henry uncrossed his arms and placed his hands back on the counter, hunching his shoulders. He held Vlad's gaze for a moment before answering. "Find out if Melissa likes me."

Vlad shrugged, hoping Henry wasn't asking him to do what he thought he was asking him to do. "I guess I could ask Meredith—"

"You know that's not what I mean." Henry's mouth was a thin, determined line. "Read her mind. Tell me whether or not I even have a remote chance with her."

Vlad couldn't believe what he was hearing. Reading the minds of hot girls at the mall was one thing. But sneaking around in Melissa's private thoughts just to give Henry an edge—an edge Henry didn't need at all with any other girl at Bathory High—just seemed wrong. He knew Henry only asked out of desperation, but that still didn't make it right. He shook his head. "I can't do that, man. Sorry."

Henry's face flushed. His voice shook slightly. "What

good are all these vampiric powers if you can't even help out a friend?"

"I'm not saying no to be a jerk. I just don't feel right about traipsing around inside Melissa's head." He looked at Henry and sighed. "I'm sorry. I just can't."

"So you're a hypocrite."

"No, I just know right from wrong."

Henry dropped his gaze, defeated. Several moments of awkward, tense silence passed, until finally he spoke, giving way to a drastic subject change. "Have you had any luck reaching Otis?"

Vlad watched him for a moment. Resisting the temptation to peek into his friend's thoughts, Vlad toyed absently with the bolt on the left side of his neck. "Not yet. It's weird, I haven't been able to reach him since he left town."

Henry shrugged, not looking completely invested in the conversation. "Maybe it's a distance thing?"

"Might be. I mean, I had no problem with distance in the training room in Siberia, but outside that room ... well, it's harder to reach people sometimes." Vlad furrowed his brow. "I hope he's not keeping me out of his head for some reason."

"I'm sure he's not. Don't worry about it."

But Vlad was worried about it. The quiet in his mind was terribly unsettling. But he trusted Otis. And if Otis said he'd be back soon, he'd be back soon.

The doorbell rang, and Vlad gave Henry one last

pleading glance before bolting for the door. Before he reached it, Henry already had his jacket on and was saying his goodbyes to Nelly.

When Vlad opened the door, Meredith smiled at him, looking even cuter this year as the bride of Frankenstein. Sure, the idea of matching costumes had given him indigestion at first, but Vlad was quickly catching on to this having a girlfriend thing. Stay your own person, have your own opinions, but if the girl you hope to kiss after the party suggests you wear dorky matching outfits, then you'd better act like Dorkapalooza is on your top-ten list of fave things to do. Vlad smiled back and said, "Nice hair."

Her tresses were heaped in a black-and-white-streaked mound atop her head, standing a foot high at least. She giggled. "Thanks. It took my mom three hours and two cans of hairspray, but I think it'll hold."

He was about to make a witty comment about how she looked really beautiful, bride of a fictional monster or not, but then Henry brushed by on his way out the door. Vlad frowned. "Come on, Henry. You don't even have to dress up, okay?"

Henry's eyes flicked to Meredith and then to Vlad. He gave a halfhearted shrug. "I told you, man. I just don't feel like going."

Then Henry trudged down the front steps and across the yard. Vlad watched him with troubled eyes. Meredith tugged his sleeve. "It'll be okay. We'll still have fun. Don't worry."

Vlad dropped his gaze for a moment. Not even the promise of a happy night semi-alone with Meredith could wash away his concerns. His best friend was clearly troubled by something. Vlad just hoped that something wasn't him.

While Nelly and Meredith exchanged pleasantries, Vlad thought about Henry and what might be on his mind. He knew Melissa was in there somewhere—after all, Henry had never had a problem getting girls to like him, and Melissa had shown absolutely zero interest in his charms so far. It had to be a bruise to his ego. But Vlad suspected that wasn't the only thing troubling him.

Lately, whenever Vlad would hover in front of his best friend or open the *Encyclopedia Vampyrica* in front of him, inciting his eyes to flash iridescent purple, Henry's mood would shift, and then he'd sulk for days. Vlad had a sneaking suspicion that maybe being Vlad's drudge—Vlad's human slave, all because of a single bite—was getting to Henry in the worst way. The kind of way that meant that Henry was so bothered by it that he couldn't even bring himself to tell Vlad.

Of course, this was all speculation on Vlad's part. And he might be completely wrong about why Henry had been acting so sullen lately. Maybe it was nothing. Maybe he really just didn't feel like dressing up and going to Matthew's party. It was possible. Vlad highly doubted it ... but it was possible.

"Vladimir?" Nelly's voice broke into his thoughts, and he blinked at her. "Did you hear me?"

He shook his head. "Sorry. I was just thinking about something. What did you say?"

A brief flash of concern crossed her eyes. "No later than eleven tonight, okay?"

Vlad let out a sigh. "It's been eleven for the past two years. Y'know, I am older now."

Nelly nodded thoughtfully. "You're absolutely right. Older and able to get into more trouble. Better make it ten."

Vlad groaned and rolled his eyes as he headed for the door. "Fine. See you at eleven."

Meredith chattered all the way to Matthew's house. For the most part, Vlad listened and laughed at all the right spots. But tainting their precious time together was the matter of Henry, and the gnawing feeling that Vlad was somehow responsible for his cloudy mood. Not to mention his dire stress at the idea of attending a party without his best friend to protect him.

As they stepped up onto the front porch, Vlad saw the flash of a camera from the corner of his eye. Eddie.

Vlad tensed and forced himself to ignore the little twit, difficult as it was.

Meredith turned to Vlad, a small crease in her forehead. "Are you okay, Vlad? You seem ... distracted."

He hadn't realized it was that obvious. He said, "It's Henry. He's been acting really weird lately."

Meredith nodded with understanding. "I bet it's because of what happened with Melissa."

Vlad's eyes probably couldn't have gone any wider if he tried. "Something happened?"

She nodded, sighing loudly. "Henry asked her out in the middle of the student council meeting last week, right in front of everyone. She said no, of course—she's always thought Henry was kind of a jerk, y'know? On account of how he dates all sorts of girls, but never really has a girlfriend."

On Henry's behalf, Vlad winced. Once a girl had listed your name in the jerk category, there was little hope of recovery.

"So anyway, Melissa told him no. But... well, she also told him that it didn't matter if he got down on his knees and begged her, she'd never go out with him. Not in a million years." She shrugged. "But it's not like it matters, right? I mean, Henry can get any girl."

"Any girl but Melissa, you mean." Vlad chewed his bottom lip thoughtfully for a moment before meeting her eyes. "The problem is that it really does matter to Henry."

Meredith sighed. "I guess he's pretty upset, huh?"

With a nod, Vlad frowned. There had to be something he could do to help Henry out, short of reading Melissa's thoughts, anyway. And why hadn't Henry told him about Melissa flaming him in public like that? But then, he was probably pretty embarrassed by it. Who wouldn't be?

Meredith squeezed his hand and said, "You're sweet, Vlad. Henry's lucky to have you for a friend. And I'm lucky too."

"Why?"

"Because I get to do this." She leaned closed and brushed her lips against his cheek.

Vlad's skin warmed at her touch. He smiled and gave her hand a squeeze back. Then he reached up and gently wiped the green makeup from her lips with his sleeve. "I'm the lucky one."

After exchanging blushing glances, they headed up the steps together and immersed themselves in Matthew's living room-turned-graveyard, complete with moss-covered tombstones and eerie fog. The room wasn't as crowded as last year, and as they moved through it, Vlad realized that most of the guests were heading downstairs. He and Meredith made their way to the basement, which had been decorated like some kind of medieval torture room. There was even a robotic half-dead mutant strapped to the stretching rack that screamed every time somebody walked by. Vlad grinned. Now *this* was a party.

The music was pretty loud, mostly Top 40 stuff. Matthew's dad manned the stereo, dressed like a Hawaiian tourist. Vlad had seen him wearing that same shirt all through last summer. It wasn't so much a costume as an excuse to don his immensely ugly orange, teal, and yellow flowered shirt.

Matthew's mom was dressed like Glinda from *The Wizard of Oz*. She was busy force-feeding cupcakes to any guest that came within a four-foot radius of the buffet, but not before asking them in a shrill voice if they were a good witch or a bad witch. Matthew, understandably, kept to the other side of the room and pretended they weren't related.

Vlad was shaking his head at the scene in front of him when he suddenly realized he was no longer holding Meredith's hand and that there was a girlish squeal-fest going on to his right. He looked over at Meredith, who was hugging Melissa and jumping up and down a little. Melissa was dressed as a fairy, complete with large, sparkly wings, which smacked Mike Brennan in the face as Melissa bounced in girlish glee.

Vlad couldn't help but frown. Mike wasn't wearing a costume. In fact, as he looked around, he saw that just a handful of guys were dressed up as anything this year. And while Vlad certainly enjoyed donning a costume and having fun, it was a lot better when everyone else did it too. He nodded at Mike, and to his satisfaction, a glint of jealousy flashed in Mike's eyes as he pointed to Vlad's outfit. "That is one sweet costume, Vlad. How'd you convince your aunt that you weren't too old to dress up?"

Vlad smiled, relaxing some—so that's why Mike wasn't wearing a costume. "Nelly's pretty cool about that kind of thing, actually. She was the one who found the rubber bolts for me."

Mike groaned. "My parents are so lame. I've been arguing with them for weeks about whether or not dressing up for Halloween is something reserved for little kids."

"You lost, huh?"

Mike nodded sullenly. "I wanted to come as the Crypt Keeper."

Vlad flicked a glance at Glinda and back. "Well, if you're interested, I'm pretty sure Matthew's mom has a ton of old costumes lying around. I mean, every year they go all out, y'know? I bet she'd let you borrow one."

Mike bit his lip, watching Matthew's mom as she waved her light-up wand over a fresh batch of cookies. As she did so, she said, "There's no place like home!"

He groaned, but the costume must have been pretty important to him, since he muttered that he'd be right back and crossed the room toward the mound of pink crinoline that was Matthew's mom.

Meredith and Melissa stopped squealing at last, and Vlad forced a smile. "Hey, Melissa. How's it going?"

Melissa's smile was warm, but guarded. "I'm good, Vlad. Just you and Meredith tonight?"

Vlad's insides twitched a little. "If you're asking whether or not Henry is here . . . no. He made other plans."

To Vlad's dismay, she visibly relaxed. Meredith started asking her about her hair or something—Vlad wasn't listening any longer. Instead, he crossed the room to the punch bowl. Even drinking sugary stuff that wouldn't alleviate his thirst was better than standing around listening to Melissa bad-mouth his best friend. After all, what exactly was her problem with Henry anyway? So he made out with a lot of girls. So he'd never really had a serious girlfriend, despite tons of dates. It didn't make him a bad person.

On the other hand, Vlad wasn't entirely convinced that Henry's intentions were honorable. What if the only reason Henry wanted to go out with Melissa so badly was because she didn't want to have anything to do with him? Maybe it was a clear case of "forbidden fruit." Or not. Vlad was pretty confused about the entire situation . . . and he'd never really understood that expression anyway. All he knew was that his best friend was hurting, and Melissa was the one causing him the hurt, intentionally or not.

Matthew's mom was blissfully absent from the buffet, so Vlad poured Meredith a cup of punch and grabbed a handful of cookies for them to share. By the time he got back to his girlfriend, Melissa was nowhere to be found. He managed a smile. "Want a cookie?"

They stood there talking for a while, taking in the scenery and just enjoying the evening, until Matthew's dad got a limbo contest going. Vlad joined in, losing to Mike—who was now dressed as a caveman—but not from lack of skill. He was laughing so hard that he fell flat on his butt just as he passed under the bar. His laughter was short-lived, of course, because at the scent of blood pumping through all those teenage veins, Vlad had to take a break to get his fangs back under control. He retired to a couch in the corner of the room, but not before assuring Meredith that she should keep playing without him.

The thing was, he wasn't really bothered by the necessary break. Without Bill and Tom around, Vlad was having a really good time. And he wondered if at least part of the reason why was because he was now dating an immensely popular (not to mention breathtakingly beautiful) girl. Who knows? Maybe people were just starting to like him, for no apparent reason at all. Whatever it was, Vlad was pretty happy about it.

The fake ficus tree to his left shook as someone bumped it from the other side. A girl's voice—one Vlad didn't instantly recognize—shook with laughter. "Did you see him? I mean, talk about a loser."

Another girl snorted with derision. "Yeah, I don't know what she sees in him. One thing's for sure, she's scraping the bottom of the social barrel by even being seen in public with a guy like that."

Vlad squirmed in his seat, overwhelmed by empathy for whoever the two girls were talking about. He ran the tip of his tongue over his fangs, which had shrunk back into his gums almost completely. He was beginning to stand when he heard one of the bodiless girls say, "I know. I mean, Vlad Tod? Seriously? Is she part of the Dork Outreach program, or what?"

Vlad sank back in his seat. He was tempted to leap up

and defend himself, to say that maybe Meredith thought he was sweet (she'd told him that a number of times), that he wasn't like other boys (couldn't argue with that), and that he was a great kisser (something that sent Vlad nearly floating up to the ceiling after hearing). But instead he listened, wanting to know just what the other guests at the party really thought of him.

"I bet she's just trying to make Henry McMillan jealous. It's been obvious for years now that she likes Henry."

"Yeah, but Henry's not exactly a challenge." Then the girl squealed, "Oh my gawd, I know why she's dating him!"

Together, they voiced a single word—one that Vlad knew would haunt him for the rest of his life. "Pity!"

Vlad sank deeper into the couch cushions. Suddenly he wished he'd followed Henry's lead and stayed home.

"Did you see him during the limbo contest? He has no idea that everyone's laughing *at* him, not *with* him."

"What a geek." The girl's voice trailed off as she said, "Hey, let's go get some punch. I'm thirsty."

Vlad remained on the couch for a good long time. Finally, he reached up and removed the rubber bolts from his neck and the fake scar from his forehead. He rubbed away the makeup onto his sleeve, staining it green, and stood. The room around him was very full, and people were laughing, dancing, playing all sorts of games. Maybe they were playing more games than he'd realized.

Vlad felt like he was moving in slow motion as he

crossed the room and slipped up the stairs. He stepped out the back door, closing it quietly behind him.

There was no reason for him to be here. He'd never be accepted anyway. He was a loser in a sea of winners, a complete and total freak. And a pretty girlfriend and a couple of laughs would never change that.

He had crossed the yard, aiming for the sidewalk, when the back door flung open behind him. He glanced over his shoulder at a breathless Meredith and paused, but didn't speak.

Meredith's bottom lip trembled. "Weren't you even going to tell me you were leaving?"

Vlad shrugged. He still felt like he was moving in slow motion. His heart ached. "I don't think I'm very welcome in there."

Meredith frowned and crossed the yard until she was standing in front of him, blocking his path. "What happened? I thought we were having a good time."

He shook his head, not wanting to go into any details that would further prove what a loser he was. "It doesn't matter. I'd just rather go home, okay?"

"But we were gonna dance." Her lips formed an adorable pout.

Vlad's heart raced to see it. He shook his head and ran a hand through his hair, brushing his black bangs from his eyes. "I'm sorry, Meredith. I wanted to. It's just—"

"So let's dance." She smiled and placed her hands on Vlad's shoulders.

Music drifted from inside the house. Vlad hesitated, and then put his hands on her waist. He pulled back just enough to look her in the eye. "Meredith . . . why are you with me?"

A small line creased her brow. "What do you mean?"

Vlad sighed. "I mean . . . that you're popular, and smart, and beautiful, and I'm . . . not. I hardly have any friends. I'll be lucky if I manage to pass geometry this year. And I'm not exactly a football hero."

She was quiet for a moment, then she said, "Do you remember when we were in Ms. Moccasin's class together in the fourth grade? Henry was relentless that year, chasing me, pulling my pigtails. Then one day he went so far as to stick gum in my hair."

Vlad remembered. That was the year Henry decided that girls weren't quite as icky as he'd thought. But he hadn't quite figured out how to treat them.

Meredith's eyes shone in memory. "But on the playground that day, you knocked him down and sat on his chest until he apologized. You stood up for me. You became my hero that day. You're still my hero."

Vlad's vision blurred with the threat of tears. But he couldn't think of anything to say. Sometimes, silence says it all.

They swayed slowly to the music. Cool, blue-tinted

moonlight covered them, blanching their skin. Meredith closed her eyes and moved closer, laying her head on Vlad's shoulder. Vlad slipped his arms around her, and they danced. Her hair smelled like lilac. Her skin felt like silk. And Vlad was dangerously aware of how close she was to him. His heart swelled up like a balloon until Vlad thought it might burst.

In his mind's eye, they were dancing together on the moonlit widow's walk of his old house, just as he'd seen his parents do countless times before. A small tear escaped his closed eyes, and Vlad squeezed Meredith closer. It wasn't the memory of his parents that had brought on his tears. It was the realization that he loved Meredith. Really loved her. Deeply and truly. He loved her, and he would do anything in his power to make her happy and keep her safe.

The song ended, and they lingered there in quiet closeness for a while. A brisk breeze swept over them and they both shivered, parting at last. Meredith reached out and took his hand in hers. "How about I walk you home?"

Vlad smiled. "I'd like that."

Never mind the fact that it was the polite thing for him to walk her home, or that they'd have to pass her house to get to Vlad's. Meredith's dad had a prime dislike of Vlad going on, so whenever possible, she kept her dad out of the mix. Besides, it would mean more time together.

They moved down the street, hand in hand, slinking past Meredith's house. The walk was blissfully Eddie-free. Only too soon they came to stand on Nelly's front porch. Vlad exchanged shy smiles with Meredith, the way they always did right before they kissed. Vlad could feel the moment coming, his entire body warming with sweet anticipation. Then he leaned in and pressed his lips to hers. She tasted like sugar, spice, and everything nice, with a side of strawberry lip balm. When he pulled away at last, she slipped her arms around him, hugging him close. Vlad nuzzled her neck, marveling at how sweet she smelled. So sweet, he could almost taste it. . . .

"Vladimir!" Nelly's voice, high-pitched and fearful, rang out into the night. She was standing in the open doorway, her eyes wide, an afghan wrapped around her shoulders.

With a horrific shock, Vlad realized that his mouth was open, his fangs elongated, poised over the delicious-looking blue vein in Meredith's neck. He snapped his mouth shut and stepped back.

He'd almost bitten her. He'd almost fed from Meredith. And if Nelly hadn't intervened . . . he could have killed her—would have killed her. Vlad shuddered at the thought. Suddenly the cold air dropped another twenty degrees.

He'd almost killed her. He'd gotten too close.

Nelly's voice dropped to a frightened whisper. "You should go home now, Meredith."

Meredith looked from Nelly to Vlad and back, shaking her head, completely oblivious to what had almost transpired. "It's not what it looks like, Nelly. We were just hugging, not making out or anything."

Nelly spoke again, her voice firm. "Still, it's getting late. I'm sure your parents will be worried."

Meredith blinked, and then glanced at Vlad. As she passed him and headed down the steps, she said, "See you tomorrow, Vlad."

But Vlad couldn't reply. He was still horrified over what he'd almost done.

As Vlad slipped by Nelly and into the warm comfort of the house, he shook his head. "Anything you're going to say can't even measure up to how I'm feeling right now, Nelly. So please . . . don't say anything. I need to be alone."

To her credit, she didn't speak.

Vlad ran up the steps to his room. He closed the door, not bothering to turn on the lights. And when he lay on his bed, he opened his mouth and lightly touched his fangs with the tip of his finger. He was a monster—Joss had been right about that. And if he'd had just a few more seconds, he might have become a killer too tonight. He might have murdered the girl who meant more to him than anything in this world. He might have stolen her away from himself, all because he couldn't control his growing hunger.

He bit down hard, slicing his finger deep. Immediately, it began to heal, but not before a large drop of blood managed to escape. As it coursed down his finger, Vlad swallowed hard. A single tear rolled down his cheek, matching pace with his blood.

With a shuddering cry, Vlad realized that that was all the future held for him. Blood and tears.

8
STANDING UP

V LAD SLIPPED HIS JACKET ON, cursing the chill of the mid-
November air, and flung his backpack over his shoulder, wincing as the corner of his health book caught him in
the small of the back. He threw a glance at the clock, even
though he didn't need to look at it to know that he was running very, very late. Lesson #456 of high school life: Never,
ever trust an alarm clock. Even after you've checked it to
make sure the alarm was set for the right time. Twice. Especially when your best friend won't be there because of
an early dentist appointment.

He bolted out the door and across the street, whipping
past houses, until finally he could see the school looming

up ahead. Relaxing some, still he cursed under his breath at the absence of students outside—a sure sign that there were less than five minutes before the detention slips started flying. He hurried up to the building, determined not to miss the first bell. He hadn't had a tardy yet this year, and didn't plan on getting one now.

To his right, he heard a small whimper, which drew his attention. Bill and Tom were hulking over a small thin boy dressed in black from head to toe. Vlad instantly recognized him as Sprat—one of the goth kids he'd seen hanging out on the front steps of the school at night while he was up in the belfry. He paused, knowing that there was likely nothing he could do to stop their assault. If he intervened he'd not only be late to class, but he'd also likely walk away from his heroism with several bruises. The smart, safe thing to do would be to count his blessings that they'd found someone else to pick on and walk away.

But he didn't pause for long.

He slinked along the school wall and slowly, quietly slipped his backpack from his shoulder. Flitting through the forefront of his mind was every instance Bill and Tom had ever picked on him, every horrible moment he'd ever witnessed them put one of his classmates through. It filled him with anger and a hunger for justice. As he arched his arm back, he called out, "Hey, Klingon!"

Tom looked back just as Vlad flung the bag forward, catching Tom in the face. Tom stumbled backward, cursing loudly and cupping his eye with both hands. Bill leaped toward Vlad, but he ducked away and brought his bag down on Bill's back. Bill screeched. As Bill hit the ground face-first, Vlad positioned himself between Sprat and the bullies, fully expecting them to come out swinging. Tom bent to help Bill up off the ground, blood slowly oozing from the fresh cut above his eye. To Vlad's immense surprise, they bolted away. Vlad smiled. Score one for the little people. He hadn't suffered so much as a scratch.

He looked back at the small goth boy and offered a hand to help him stand. "You okay, Sprat?"

"Yeah, I guess." He brushed dirt from his black pants, glancing toward where Tom and Bill had run. "Thanks."

"No problem. I'm getting really sick of those two. They've been giving me the same treatment for years." Vlad shook his head and flung his backpack over his shoulder again. For some reason, this time it felt lighter. He turned and hurried back out the alley, knowing he was going to catch hell for being tardy, as the first bell had rung just about the time he was whacking Bill's back with his book bag.

Sprat called out, "Hey, how'd you know my name?"

But Vlad kept walking. After all, he wasn't about to mention the fact that he'd been sharing Sprat's company a few nights a week for several years now, from about four stories overhead, up in the belfry—something that would probably freak him out at least a little, and would definitely raise too many questions about Vlad's nighttime activities.

He rushed through the front doors and down the hall until he finally came to first period, where he slowly opened the door and tried to slip inside unnoticed. But so much for the idea that vampires had any kind of skill at stealth— Mr. Cartel looked up as Vlad opened the door and smiled. "Ah, perfect! It looks like Mr. Tod has volunteered to offer an explanation on the function of g-g-g-gonads. Thank you, Mr. Tod."

Vlad rolled his eyes and moved to the front of the class. It was going to be a very, very long day.

By the time he finally walked out of health class and headed toward his locker, Vlad's face felt like it was on fire. It wasn't the subject matter that bugged him—after all, it seemed like important stuff to know. But it was the way some of the girls in class giggled, and the whispers that some guys had been exchanging, always accompanied by low laughter. He just couldn't shake the feeling that they weren't laughing at the mention of genitals and reproduction so much as they were laughing at him for merely existing. Sometimes Vlad wished that he were home-schooled. At least for health class.

Vlad shook his head. Strike that—the last thing he wanted was to listen to Nelly explain where babies came from. With puppets. Again.

Standing next to his locker, Henry was chatting with

Chelsea Whitaker, a.k.a. Cheerleader Snob Supreme. Vlad raised an eyebrow, slowing his steps. Henry glanced over at him and said something like "See ya" to Chelsea before she disappeared into the hallway crowd.

Without a word to Henry, Vlad opened his locker door and dropped his backpack inside, retrieving a few of the books he'd need for the next part of his day. His insides were burning with questions: Since when were Henry and Chelsea pals? And what was up with his gloomy, party-skipping attitude anyway? And why did the conversation stop just as Vlad approached? He bit his bottom lip and forced the questions to remain hidden in his throat, throwing Henry a casual smile. "What's up?"

Henry shrugged. "Not much. What about you?"

Not much? As if Henry hanging out with cheerleaders and dropping years of partygoing tradition at the last minute were things that could easily be ignored. The questions inched their way up his throat once more, but Vlad swallowed hard, forcing them back down. He parted his lips, and when he spoke, his voice came out in a near whisper. "Not much, I guess."

Henry nodded casually.

Vlad closed his locker and looked him in the eye. It was time to find out what was going on with his best friend. "I think we should talk, Henry."

But just then the tardy bell rang out through the halls,

cutting Vlad off. Henry offered a relieved shrug, looking very much like he'd literally been saved by the bell.

Vlad hurried down the hall to geometry. He'd have to deal with Henry later.

Not that it was really any of his business why Henry had ditched the party, or why he was hanging out with Chelsea. After all, it was Henry's life, not Vlad's. But still . . . Vlad couldn't help but wonder what was going on with his friend. And why they weren't talking about it.

Geometry lasted just short of an eternity, and chemistry seemed twice as long. By lunchtime, Vlad was ready to head home and spend the day in front of the television with a bag of potato chips and about five hundred bags of O positive, trying to defend the fate of the Earth against whatever evildoers were currently lurking inside his PlayStation. But unbelievably, he still had half a day of school to trudge through. What was it about Mondays that made them last forever? Vlad wagered it had to do with the space-time continuum or a cruel joke played by Fate.

He slid in beside Meredith and slumped forward, resting his forehead on the table.

Meredith rubbed his shoulder gently with one hand and said, "It can't be that bad."

Vlad mumbled, "Is it time to go home yet?"

"Three more hours to go."

"Then it's that bad." He sat up, offering her a meek smile. "How's your day?"

Meredith launched into a long, detailed, enthusiastic account of her day in typical girl fashion. Vlad tried to pay attention, but he was enormously distracted by Henry, who was lingering near the so-called "popular table" a bit too long for Vlad's taste.

But then, what business was it of Vlad's if Henry decided to hang out with the "in" crowd? It's not like he and Henry had a signed contract of friendship that prohibited Henry from being friends with anyone else. Or that Henry was bound to him at all.... Vlad sat up straight. Oh, wait. Actually, that was the case. But still, it didn't give Vlad the right to pick and choose Henry's friends.

Did it?

Being the vampire who made Henry into a drudge, just what powers did that give Vlad? What rights? Vlad wasn't sure. He was sure that he didn't much care for the kinds of friends that Henry seemed to be associating with of late. But did that give him the right to change it, to stop Henry from making that choice?

Vlad chewed his bottom lip thoughtfully for a moment. Knowing that his drudge could not disobey a direct order, he called out, "Henry! Come here."

Unable to resist, Henry furrowed his brow and crossed the cafeteria toward Vlad, tray in hand. When he got there,

Henry stood for a moment, looking almost pained and ab-solutely angry. Vlad nodded to the empty seat across the table from him, trying hard to keep his tone light and friendly. "Have a seat. Eat your lunch."

Henry sat with an air of indignation. Vlad was only slightly bothered by the fact that he was ordering his best friend around like some kind of human slave. Meredith had grown incredibly quiet. The three sat and ate in utter si-lence for several minutes.

Halfway into his peanut butter, jelly, and blood-capsule sandwich, Vlad noticed that as much as Henry and Mere-dith seemed to be making an effort not to look at him, somebody else was trying to catch his attention. A goth girl, whom Vlad recognized as another of the kids who sat on the front steps of Bathory High at night, nudged the thin boy named Sprat forward, muttering, "Just do it!"

Sprat stumbled toward Vlad's table, looking more than a little uncomfortable. When Vlad smiled at him, it seemed to put him at ease. Sprat said, "I wanted to thank you."

Vlad was about to say that if he was talking about the thing this morning with Bill and Tom, it was really no big deal, but then they were joined by the other goths: a raven-haired girl with black fingernails, a silver-haired boy who always seemed aloof, and a tall, thin boy with black eye-liner. The girl spoke. "Actually, we all wanted to thank you. It was pretty cool of you to stick up for Sprat like that."

Vlad's smile grew. "Hey, no problem. It was really no big deal."

The girl said, "Well, it is to us."

"If you ever feel like hanging out—" Sprat began, but the girl cut him off.

"Yeah, if you ever want to, we're cool with that, okay?" The corners of her mouth lifted in a small smile as she glanced at Meredith and Henry. "We don't bite. And contrary to popular opinion, we don't dance around graveyards and raise the dead either."

Her smile grew as she turned her attention back to Vlad. "I'm October, by the way. You know Sprat. The guy with the raccoon eyes is Andrew, and this silver-haired soul is Kristoff."

Vlad nodded to each of them, and October continued. "So anyway, there's this goth club in Stokerton called The Crypt. Maybe we could hang sometime."

Vlad responded at first by blinking. The very idea that people he hadn't known since kindergarten wanted to hang out with him weirded him out, but in a strangely cool way. Still . . . he wasn't sure Nelly would be too keen on the idea of him spending time in anything that remotely resembled a nightclub. Vlad smiled sheepishly. "I'm not really much for clubs. But thanks anyway."

October frowned, then flashed a fake smile to mask her disappointment. "Suit yourself."

The goths turned collectively and were about four steps

away from the table when Henry muttered, "Thank God the trick-or-treaters left. I'm all out of candy."

Vlad couldn't snap his eyes to his drudge fast enough.

Henry smirked. "I mean, c'mon. Halloween's over, guys."

To his disgust, Meredith chuckled at Henry's cruel quip.

Eyeing both of them, wondering exactly what made them think they were better than kids who chose to dress in black, Vlad released a tense breath and turned back to the goths, who turned around at the sound of his voice. "Hey, you guys. On second thought, I've been meaning to get out more, meet new people. . . . I'd love to check out The Crypt with you guys sometime."

October, Andrew, and Sprat met his eyes with smiles. Kristoff just kept on walking.

Henry and Meredith grew quiet. Vlad let them. Sure, maybe he was only agreeing to go with the goths to prove a point to his friends, to show them that they shouldn't judge people based on whether or not they wear thick black eyeliner. But it was a point he needed to drive home, that different didn't automatically equal bad.

He picked up his peanut butter, jelly, and blood-capsule sandwich and took a bite, ignoring their guilty glances.

The rest of lunch passed in tense silence.

Vlad strained against his leather bounds, but they were fastened tightly to his wrists, and there appeared to be no possibility of escaping. He strained his neck, but could barely see the room that he'd been trapped in. But he did recognize it.

The nightmare was always the same.

Above him hovered a dark figure, and out of the shadow that surrounded it appeared a silver blade. Moonlight glinted off its razor-sharp surface, and Vlad shivered with fear.

He closed his eyes tight. It was just a dream. Just a dream.

The man plunged the blade downward, ripping it through Vlad's stomach. Pain lit up his body, and Vlad screamed.

Vlad's screams continued until he rolled off his bed in a sweaty, tangled mess; his sheets were wrapped around his legs like boa constrictors. He scanned his dark bedroom and breathed a sigh of relief.

Just a dream.

He clutched his side and winced at the pain it caused him, then crawled back into bed.

It had to be a dream. What else could it be?

He lay awake in the dark until his legs jumped with energy. Maybe a moonlit stroll would calm his nerves.

Dressing quickly, he found his way down the stairs and past Amenti, who was curled up asleep on the corner of the couch, nestled in Nelly's favorite sweater, shedding all over it in blissful kitty contentment.

He stepped out the door and buttoned his jacket, shivering in the cool air. He wasn't exactly sure where he wanted to go; he only knew that he needed to move around until the nightmare had shaken completely from his mind. He headed north, content to walk the edges of Bathory until he was feeling a bit more like sleeping.

There was no sign of Eddie, something that improved Vlad's troubled mood.

He passed houses, a small creek, and eventually found his way to Requiem Ravine, where the cops had found the body of Mr. Craig, Vlad's English teacher. He paused, mourning the loss of such a great mentor and friend, before continuing along the town's borders in an effort to quiet his mind. Within minutes, he'd found his way to an extremely familiar clearing.

Vlad looked around, remembering how D'Ablo had waited for him and Joss here last year. The images of that encounter, and of Joss's betrayal, flooded his mind like dark water. He still couldn't believe that Joss had staked him, or that one of his closest friends would purposely cause him such agonizing pain, and almost take his life. But Joss had. Worse still, he couldn't believe how much he missed Joss's company.

Getting staked had been a hard lesson in choosing one's friends wisely, that was for sure.

The chill of autumn snaked its way inside Vlad's jacket, and he shivered briskly before turning to head home. But on the ground, lying amidst dead leaves and half immersed in muddy earth, Vlad spied a coin. He plucked it from the ground and wiped the dirt away. It was bronze, and on one side had two large initials, written in calligraphy: *S.S.* He flipped it over and noted the symbols on the other side. A crescent moon on the left, the symbol for eternity on the right, and at its center, a wooden stake. Along the top, curving along the crest of the coin, was *Slayer Society*. Along the bottom it read *for the good of mankind.*

Vlad frowned in disgust. Joss must have dropped it that night, the night he'd tried unsuccessfully to rid the world of another vampire, the night he'd tried to murder Vlad with a sharp hunk of wood. Furious, he read the inscription again and swore under his breath. As if the Slayers' murderous actions could be so easily disguised as being "for the good of mankind." As if betraying your friend's trust and putting him in the hospital could make you a humanitarian. Psychotic jerk, maybe. Humanitarian? Not so much.

Vlad almost threw the coin into the ravine, but then he squeezed it tight and placed it in his pocket. It would be a good reminder never to trust anyone so easily again.

He turned on his heel and headed home, the nightmare of Joss staking him replacing the one he'd been trying to forget.

9
THE PERFECT GIFT

VLAD TWISTED THE BLACK RIBBON around the knot of an inflated red balloon and tied it before letting the balloon go. It flew up toward the ceiling and then bobbed pathetically at the end of its tether. "How many of these did Nelly say to fill?"

Henry emptied one of the helium-filled balloons into his mouth. When he spoke, he sounded like a deranged Mickey Mouse. "I think she said fifty."

Vlad shook his head. The room was already so stuffed with balloons, streamers, and party favors that he was pretty sure once they opened the door to let any guests in, the house would explode, draping the entire neighborhood in his favorite colors—black and red. Which, now that he thought of it, wasn't such a bad idea. Bathory could use a bold splash of color. Or two. Or twelve. He called out, hoping his aunt could hear him well enough over the sounds of food preparation. "Nelly, just how many people did you invite? I mean, this seems like a pretty big deal for just me, you, Meredith, and Henry."

Nelly's voice drifted in from the kitchen, so full of parental pride that it made Vlad's eyes roll. "Vladimir, it's not every day that a boy turns fifteen."

She was right. But, Vlad noted with a hint of terror rushing through his veins, she also didn't answer his question. Dropping the bag of empty balloons, he rushed into the kitchen and was greeted by warm, sugary smells . . . and enough food to feed an army of teenagers. He stared suspiciously. "Exactly how many people did you invite to my birthday party?"

Nelly glanced at the calendar on the wall, where November 21 was circled in red. Scribbled on the square was *Vlad's B-Day: 38 RSVPs*. She stirred something creamy and brown and smiled. "Around forty. Why?"

Vlad's jaw dropped. "Nelly! I don't *know* forty people!"

"Sure you do. You know Henry's family, some of the nurses from the hospital, and the rest are your friends and teachers."

It took every ounce of his brain to process the fact that

she'd invited his teachers, and a small shudder shook through him. "You invited my *teachers*?"

She looked at him, completely oblivious. "What's wrong with that?"

He stared at her, mouth agape. It was like the real Nelly had been abducted by little green men with a fondness for registered nurses who couldn't cook. "Nelly, I spend all day with them. What makes you think I want to see any of them at my house?"

Nelly tapped the spoon on the side of the bowl and rested it on the counter. "Some of your teachers are very nice."

"Yes, and some of them are descendants of Hitler himself." Exasperated, Vlad threw his hands in the air. "Besides, do you have any idea what a high school faux pas that is? You might as well knit me a sweater that says KICK MY BUTT on it."

Nelly cast him a knowing look. "Need I remind you that last time I invited your teacher over, he turned out to be your uncle?"

Vlad huffed quietly. "All right. But if I find out I'm related to Mr. Cartel, I'm going to g-g-g-go jump off a bridge."

Nelly sighed. "Well, I wouldn't worry too much. Most of your teachers didn't RSVP anyway. It'll mostly be all of your friends."

Vlad raised an eyebrow. "How long have you been my guardian, Nelly?"

"Five years, this spring. But what does that have to do with—"

"And in all that time, haven't you ever noticed that I only have one real friend? Henry?" Saying it aloud made Vlad's stomach shrink. Suddenly he felt incredibly pathetic. And he wasn't just saying it aloud. He was saying it loudly—his voice had risen until he was almost yelling. And he wasn't even sure why, apart from the fact that the one person who should know him better than anyone didn't seem to know him at all.

Nelly met Vlad's eyes, her voice dropping to a tone that was sweet, calm—patient, even. "Henry is not your *only* friend. He's your *best* friend. You've had others, Vladimir. Like Meredith. And that nice Joss boy last year."

Her expression darkened. "Well, up until that unfortunate wooden stake incident, anyway."

Oh yeah. Joss had been a great friend. If Vlad ever wanted to become a pincushion, he knew just who to call. "That's not the point."

"The point, Vladimir, is that you have a terrible habit of comparing everyone to Henry, and if they don't measure up, you don't give them a chance to even be your friend. Not everyone can show you the loyalty that Henry has, you know. You boys have a special bond. It's unfair to compare other people to that. They don't have a fighting chance to even come close to offering you the friendship that Henry has."

Vlad bit his lip, quieting down. If only she knew that Henry was bound by an act of teeth and blood to be Vlad's loyal slave, his drudge. Maybe she wouldn't be so keen on the idea of their friendship then. And what about that other stuff? Did she have a point? Vlad mulled it over for a bit before deciding she was wrong. It wasn't that he had avoided close friendship with other people besides Henry. It was as if, deep down, they knew he wasn't like them. They knew he was different. And maybe, in a weird way, they were afraid of that.

Her eyes brimmed with concern. "I realize the guest list might not be exactly what you'd have come up with, but could you please just allow me a little time to dote on you and brag to the world that my s . . . well, that you're turning fifteen?"

All the tension melted out of Vlad when he realized what Nelly had been saying. Not about making friends or doting on him or any of that stuff. Nelly had been about to call him her son.

His heart throbbed until it had squeezed its way up into his esophagus. When he met her eyes, he didn't know exactly how he should feel. On one hand, Nelly had been every bit like a mother to him, ever since the day the fire had brought them together as a family. On the other, no one could or ever would replace his real mom.

Vlad cleared his throat and did the only thing he could. He nodded, turned, and walked out of the room.

When he got back to the living room, Henry sucked in another lungful of helium and said, "What's wrong, dude?"

Vlad shook his head, clearing away his troubled thoughts. Well, most of them anyway. "Nothing. Let's just get this crap cleaned up so we can cut the dumb cake and throw the stupid confetti and celebrate the fact that I've survived fifteen years."

"Hey, for most people, that's not such a feat. But for you . . . well, let's see. In the past few years, you've managed to outwit a psychotic vampire who chased you down with the help of thugs the size of dump trucks, as well as a stake-wielding slayer, bent on your demise, who actually stabbed you through the chest. Not to mention various math classes and the great feat of getting the girl of your dreams to go out with you." Henry smiled, slapping Vlad on the back. "I think we definitely have reason to celebrate."

He knew Henry was right, but he still wasn't in much of a celebratory mood. After all, Otis had made it clear that he likely wouldn't be visiting until after he'd located that ritual, so the odds that he'd see Otis tonight were small. And with Vlad's present troubles reaching his uncle by telepathy, right now a conversation with Otis was all he wanted to be having—not some lame party where he was expected to be nice to people he didn't necessarily know or even like. But . . . there *was* Meredith . . . and he couldn't deny that the allure of presents was pretty enticing.

Henry scooped up the extra decorations and placed

them in the big cardboard box on the floor. Vlad followed his lead, his thoughts never too far away from the evening ahead, and the fact that Nelly had very nearly referred to him as her son.

Less than an hour later, the doorbell rang.

Vlad and Henry exchanged glances, and Nelly called from the kitchen. "Vladimir, answer that, please. It could be your guests!"

Vlad snorted. He was fairly certain it was his guests, but that didn't make him get to the door any faster. However, he was thankful when he did, because he could see a very familiar outline standing on the other side of the frosted glass. He smiled and opened the door to Meredith, who was bundled up in her fluffy pink coat, the faux-fur collar pulled up to her ears. Meredith's lips looked almost blue. "It's f-f-freezing out here."

But there was no time to think of a witty retort, because soon the porch was full of people and Vlad was busy greeting them all and taking their coats. At one point, he couldn't even see the people he was greeting anymore, and the coats were stacked so high that he resembled a walking pile of laundry. Henry took over and Vlad stumbled his way up the stairs to lay the coats on Nelly's bed. Afterward, he raced back down the stairs and stared in awe at the gifts that were piled in towers on the coffee table, looking like a city in miniature. He moved through the crowd, searching for the one gift he really, really wanted for his birthday, but he couldn't see Otis anywhere. Finally, he located Nelly in the kitchen and asked, "Have you seen Otis yet, Nelly? I thought maybe..."

But the expression on her face was all the answer he needed. Otis hadn't come, wasn't coming. Vlad's heart sank down to his stomach. He wasn't angry, just disappointed. He put on a fake smile. "That's okay. I'm sure we'll see him over winter break."

Nelly smiled too—hers looked just as doubtful as Vlad's felt. "I'm sure we will, Vladimir. Why don't we cut the cake and you can open your presents?"

That did cheer him up, because any sentence that has "cake" and "presents" in it is worthy of a smile. Nelly gathered as many people as she could into the kitchen, including Meredith and Henry, who sat on either side of Vlad at the long plank table, and they all sang "Happy Birthday" off-key until Vlad's ears had blushed so deeply they turned purple. Then Nelly cut the cake and started serving. Vlad and Henry and Meredith talked and laughed and devoured three slices each of Nelly's fluffy, sweet cake until finally, Meredith said the magic words. "You should open your presents, Vlad."

Vlad grabbed Meredith's hand and led her back into the living room, through balloons and streamers and a crowd that looked like much more than forty people, stopping now and again to say hello to people he knew. By the time they reached the coffee table, the towering city of gifts had doubled in size. Vlad gawked. "I don't know where to start."

Meredith smiled sweetly and plucked a thin blue box from the bottom of the stack. The tower wavered, but remained standing. "This one's from me."

Vlad squeezed her hand once before letting go and ripping through the paper. He lifted the lid and gasped. Inside was a lovely leather journal. On the cover was inscribed *The Chronicles of Vladimir Tod.* Vlad met her eyes. "It's perfect. How did you know?"

Her cheeks flushed. "Well, I noticed that composition notebook you're always scribbling in is looking pretty ratty. So I thought you could use a new one. It's refillable."

If Nelly hadn't been standing a few feet away, Vlad would have kissed Meredith on the spot. Instead, he blushed and said, "Thank you."

Nelly slid a large box out from beneath the coffee table, and Vlad knew he must be dreaming. He tore open the wrapping, and sure enough, Nelly had gotten him an Xbox 360. "Nelly! This is so cool! Thank you!"

Henry grinned and shoved a box into his hand. It looked like it had been wrapped in a grocery sack and tied with twine. "Open this one. It's from me."

Vlad beamed at him and tore off the paper, revealing something that made his jaw drop. There were two Xbox games. One was *Race to Armageddon 3: The Final Lap* and the other was a game called *When Vampires Attack!* A quick glimpse of the back of the box revealed that players assumed vampire roles, and whoever attacked the most victims won. Vlad laughed loudly, and Henry joined him. Nelly chuckled. Along with the rest of the crowd, Meredith simply smiled, not understanding just how hysterical it was that Vlad would be playing a game as a vampire.

For the next two hours, Vlad opened gifts and thanked guests and ate food and laughed. And finally, once he'd said good night to Henry and Meredith and the other guests and closed the door behind them, Nelly approached him with one final present. It was a thick parchment envelope. On the front in Otis's scratchy handwriting was *For Vladimir on his fifteenth birthday.*

Nelly smiled a sad smile. "Otis left this with me at the end of the summer. He said he'd try to be here in person to give it to you, but if he couldn't, he still wanted to make sure you got it."

Vlad didn't open the letter right away. In fact, he tucked it into his back pocket. As he and Nelly cleaned up the aftereffects of the party, he took it out every few minutes to look at Otis's handwriting and wonder where his uncle was and if he was thinking about the party that he had missed. More so, if he was thinking about his nephew, who missed him more than he could say.

Finally, after Nelly went to bed—not before reminding Vlad that it was okay to stay up late on his birthday, but to remember that he did have school to face in the morning—

Vlad slipped on his jacket and stole out into the night, clutching Otis's letter to his chest.

He zipped by trees and houses, casting careful, scrutinizing glances all around him, trying to make certain Eddie and his new camera were nowhere to be found. And once he reached the belfry, he floated effortlessly up to the ledge and stepped inside, staring at the envelope as he plopped down in his dad's comfy leather chair.

The envelope was wrinkled in several places, and torn slightly on one end. Vlad read Otis's handwriting once more before opening it slowly and withdrawing the letter inside. With the moonlight acting as his candle, he read.

Dearest Vladimir,

It is with great regret that you are reading this letter, because it means that I was unable to return to Bathory for one of the most important days in a young man's life—your birthday. Please accept my deepest apologies and know that I am thinking of you always. If my tone reads as a troubled one, it is because, at the moment I am writing this, you are upstairs, fast asleep, and in but a day I shall leave you yet again. It pains me, you see, as I have grown accustomed to our time together. But D'Ablo will not stop until he finds and performs this insane ritual that he spoke of last year, and so it is up to me to stop him by finding it first.

I won't lie to you. It may be a long search. Very long, indeed, as I haven't the slightest inkling where to start.

It has been years—if I am honest, it has been centuries—since I celebrated a birthday. Such celebrations are largely human in nature, you see. And it has been even longer since I celebrated a teen age, so I was lost on what gift I could give to you that you would truly enjoy. Initially, I had decided to purchase you something thrilling, like a dirt bike or perhaps a car, though your driver's license is yet a year away. But upon Nelly's input, I have decided to gift you with the one thing your life is truly lacking.

I shall gift you with the story of how your father and I met ... and how we became vampires.

Vlad tore his eyes from the page long enough to release an anxious breath. At first, he was disappointed that Nelly had talked Otis out of that car—not that he could drive it yet— but this present was much, much better. He grabbed the lighter from the bookshelf and lit the candle next to the chair, illuminating the belfry with a soft glow. Then he sank deep into the chair and continued reading.

Your father was born in a small shire just outside of London in 1709. I was born in a small French village just a year later. Our friendship began in the Bastille prison in Paris, France, in 1743.

Now, if you've managed to stay awake during history class, you probably realize that only prisoners of stature were held in the Bastille. No, your father and I were not notable in any way, really. He was the only surviving son of a wealthy English aristocrat, and I was a French horse farmer. But upon being accused of a crime—and to this day, I know not which crimes we were accused of—we were brought to France, to the Bastille, to await death. We lived there for three years and spoke every day, though we could not look each other in the eye. Our cells were side by side. But when Tomas stretched his hand between the bars I could glimpse the signet ring on his little finger. It was made from black onyx. When I asked him about it, he said that the ring was a symbol of his heritage and all that he was. It was all that he had, and though our imprisoners might take our freedom and our dignity— and eventually, our lives—they could never take that from him.

Then, on the eve of my thirty-fourth birthday, a man came to visit. He offered Tomas and me our freedom. But so much more. He offered us eternity. Suspicious, I refused at first, but then Tomas agreed. The man went into Tomas's cell, and all I heard was a scuffle, then slurping sounds, then silence. It was all I could do not to faint from fear when our visitor entered my cell.

He'd killed Tomas, I was certain, and so I had nothing else to live for. If not this man, it would be another to take my life, and I no longer had endless conversations with my new friend to keep me from losing my mind entirely. Let death come. Let it be quick.

But he didn't attack. Instead, he asked me again if I would come with him into forever.

From the next room, I heard Tomas's voice. It was but a whisper. "Come with me, Otis," he said.

Though I hesitated, I eventually nodded to our guest and he leaped on me, biting into my neck. The rest is a blur. I passed out, but when I came to, I was in Siberia, and Tomas was at my side.

Fast-forward many, many years, to the day he told me of his plans to flee Elysia for the love of a human. The last thing he said to me was, "This ring is all that I am, Otis. But as it is a part of me, so are you."

Then he handed me the signet ring . . . and walked out of my life forever.

Please take care of this ring, Vladimir. It belonged to your father, and it meant as much to him—and to me—as I am sure it will to you.

Yours in Eternity,

Otis

Vlad picked the envelope up again and tilted the open end over his cupped palm. Out tumbled a black ring made of stone, with a crest as its insignia. With tears brimming in his eyes, he slipped the small ring onto his pinkie. Despite the fact that he wasn't sure whether or not his uncle could hear him, Vlad reached out with his mind and said, *"Thank you, Otis. This means more to me than any stupid car."*

Then he doused the candle, closed his eyes, and cried.

10

Close Enough to Touch

IGNATIUS TIGHTENED HIS JAW AS HE WATCHED Tomas's son step out of the shadows near the high school and make his way down the sidewalk toward his home. He'd lost the boy for several hours, and only half expected he'd broken into the school—for what purpose, he neither knew nor cared. What was important was that he'd found the boy again, and the sky was overcast, protecting him from the rays of the sun as they reflected off the moon.

He moved in behind the boy, licking anxious lips. As he'd done with his last prey, he'd grab him by a handful of hair and drag him into the darkness, taking his time peeling back the boy's flesh with his blade, making him suffer. It would be exquisite, and he could hardly wait to begin.

With every step, he closed the gap between them. The boy moved along at a casual pace, occasionally glancing to the left or the right, never seeming to think to check behind him. His posture screamed of awkwardness. Ignatius stretched his hand out, his fingers brushing against the boy's soft black hair.

But as the tresses slipped between his fingers, the clouds shifted, uncovering the moon. Ignatius moved as quickly and silently as he could, flying with vampiric speed, to the safety of a nearby shed. Cursing, he watched out the small window as the boy brushed the back of his head with his palm and looked back in wonderment, as if trying to identify just what or who had touched him. After a nervous pause, he hurried his steps. In a moment, he was out of Ignatius's line of sight.

Bitter fury boiled within the hunter. Fury that would only be tamed by Vladimir Tod's suffering.

11

The Price of a Stolen Moment

EDDIE WAS IN AN UNUSUALLY CHIPPER MOOD as he waved a photograph in front of Vlad's nose.

Vlad snatched the picture and took a look, bristling at the fact that it had come from Eddie. The image was dark but crisp. Vlad making his way down the sidewalk at night. Behind him by a matter of feet was a man. Vlad shrugged. It was no one he knew, probably some drunk out for a sobering stroll after a night at the town's only bar. "So?"

Eddie spoke in a singsong voice. "So it looks like I'm not your only shadow."

Henry slammed his locker door and plucked the photo

from Vlad's hand. He tossed it down the hallway Frisbee-style and glared at Eddie. "Fetch."

With a scowl, Eddie walked off, stopping only to pluck his beloved picture from the floor.

Henry turned back to Vlad. "Anyway, you were saying?"

Vlad sighed and leaned up against his locker. He clutched his new journal in his hands. It had become his constant companion since his birthday a week and a half before. "Nelly seriously thinks I'm going to have Meredith for dinner."

Henry shook his head. "That's ridiculous."

Vlad groaned. "I know!"

"Meredith is way too small for dinner. If anything, she'd be lunch, or maybe a big breakfast."

"I'm serious, Henry. What am I gonna do?"

But suddenly Henry didn't seem very invested in the conversation. Melissa Hart walked by them, and with every step she took, Henry's frown deepened. Finally she disappeared into a nearby classroom, and Henry shut his locker, his shoulders sagging, his jovial demeanor subdued. "I don't know, Vlad. I really don't."

Vlad deliberated for a moment whether Henry was answering his question or simply musing about his troubles with Melissa, but he didn't have long to speculate. Meredith stepped into view at the end of the hall, looking pretty as ever, and, with a wink, she gestured with a bent finger for him to follow her.

With a glance at Henry, he headed down the hall, barely taking the time to breathe. "See ya."

Meredith opened up the janitor's closet. Raising an eyebrow, Vlad followed her inside.

It was dark, but Meredith's hands found his shoulders. "Hi."

Vlad smiled. "You brought me into a broom closet to say hi?"

"No. I brought you here so I could do this."

She pressed her soft lips against his, and Vlad felt like he was floating. In a blink, he realized that he was. No more than an inch or two off the ground, but still. He was thankful for the darkness. Bringing himself back down, he kept kissing Meredith until the sound of her heartbeat and her warm proximity became too much to bear. He pulled back, gently but quickly, glad once more for the darkness—and not just because of his fangs. He was also blushing furiously. And his hunger . . . his hunger was crying out, begging to be satiated.

Vlad slowed his breathing, but it hardly helped. Much longer in such close proximity and Meredith would be in very real danger. And the sick thing was that part of Vlad wanted to keep her in the closet with him. Maybe Nelly was right. Maybe he was viewing Meredith as a food source more than a girlfriend.

He shook his head. There had to be a way to protect her, to keep her safe without pushing her away.

First step: Get out of the closet.

He could almost hear Meredith smiling. "That was nice. Between my dad and your aunt, we hardly get any time alone together."

The door flung open, revealing a rather perturbed-looking Principal Snelgrove. "I certainly hope it was, Ms. Brookstone. Because it may be your last."

Vlad gulped and snapped his mouth shut, covering his fangs. He and Meredith exchanged startled glances. Meredith looked shocked and embarrassed. Vlad was both of those, but also immensely relieved.

Principal Snelgrove barked two words that made them both jump. "Office! NOW!"

Principal Snelgrove had turned purple by the time they reached his office, and as he paced back and forth behind his desk, his shade of purple deepened. Vlad sank down in his seat, amazed that a person could look so much like an eggplant. Meredith sat in the chair to his right, staring straight ahead, wide-eyed. He doubted she'd ever had the misfortune of ending up in the Chair of Doom—Vlad's nickname for any chair in the principal's office that didn't belong to the principal. He wanted to squeeze her hand, to reassure her in some small way, but he was almost certain that Snelgrove's skull would split open if he touched Meredith at all.

The purple color lessened as Snelgrove drew a deep

breath before speaking. "I would expect this type of behavior from Mr. Tod here. But you, Ms. Brookstone, are one of our best students. And to pull a stunt like this . . . I must say, I'm very disappointed. You should be careful of the kind of company you keep, Ms. Brookstone. It may lead you down a road that it would be unwise to follow."

Vlad resisted rolling his eyes, but it wasn't easy.

Snelgrove clasped his hands behind his back and twitched his nose—all the rat was missing were whiskers. "I should suspend you both."

Vlad stiffened in his seat. That was the last thing he needed. But he wouldn't have to fret about it for long, because Nelly was going to murder him. If anyone could prove that the Pravus could be killed, it was an angry guardian who found out he'd been suspended for making out in a broom closet at school instead of learning about the joys of worm dissection. He sank down in his seat and silently hoped for a miracle.

"Detention. Both of you. That much is obvious and warranted. Thank your lucky stars I'm such a kind and forgiving individual." Snelgrove slanted his little mouse eyes. "I'll be calling your parents, Ms. Brookstone, absolutely. And Mr. Tod, you can bet your bottom dollar that your guardian and I will discuss this situation at length."

Vlad wasn't aware that he had a bottom dollar, or even a top dollar for that matter, but he did know that he'd like to be cremated, if at all possible, once Nelly heard from Snelgrove. It seemed like a nice blending of human and vampire funerary traditions.

Snelgrove seemed to be waiting for them to speak, but neither did. Vlad mused that he'd like Henry to give his eulogy.

"Ms. Brookstone, you'll have detention this Tuesday and Thursday for two hours after school. Mr. Tod, your detention will begin today after school, and continue on Wednesday." Snelgrove snorted before waving them away. "And I do not want to see a repeat of this type of behavior in the future. Am I clear?"

Meredith mumbled, "Yes, sir."

Vlad simply held the door open for her in silence. He wasn't about to give ol' rat face the satisfaction of a reply.

Plus, he couldn't exactly focus on there actually being a future anyway, what with his imminent demise on the horizon.

The remainder of the school day passed by in a haze of homework assignments, headaches, and an assortment of mind-numbing quizzes—all of which seemed to be pop quizzes which were pretty much like the regular quizzes except that when they were given, they made your eyeballs pop out of your head and explode. By the time the final bell had rung, Vlad had mentally prepared his last will and testament. He decided to bequeath Henry his video games.

And, if she survived her own set of parental wrath, he'd leave Meredith his favorite hoodie and every last one of his books.

Speaking of Meredith . . .

Vlad looked up and down the hall but didn't see her anywhere. Maybe her parents had picked her up early. Or maybe she was avoiding him, for fear of more detention-inducing kisses. Or not. Vlad highly doubted he was that irresistible.

He dropped his physical science book inside his locker and sighed before grabbing his backpack and slipping his homework inside. When he closed the door, he nodded to Henry, who'd been high-fiving him since he'd heard about his and Meredith's closet adventures. Vlad's hand was practically slapped raw, and he blushed every time Henry did it. Whoever had invented the Neanderthal celebration of the high five needed to be dragged out into the street and slapped to death by someone with elephantitis of the hand.

Okay. That might be a bit extreme. But Vlad wasn't exactly feeling celebratory at the moment.

He slunk down the hall through the thinning crowd to the library, opened the double doors, and went inside. He stopped the passing librarian and said, "Excuse me. I'm not sure I'm in the right place. I'm here for detention."

The librarian, Mrs. Moppet, smiled warmly and pointed

to a table near the computer section. "Right over there. It looks like you'll have company today."

"Thank you." Vlad moved to the table and stopped in his tracks before dropping his backpack on the table. He sighed, low and loud, resisting the urge to swear really loudly at the predicament he was in. Not the thing with Meredith or how Nelly was going to kill him when he got home. Oh no. What had Vlad's stomach in knots was . . . his company.

Eddie Poe threw him a glance, and Vlad would have guessed that Eddie was just as displeased about sharing a detention if it wasn't for the eager glint in Eddie's eyes.

The two sat in stony silence until Mrs. Moppet joined them a few minutes later. "Well, boys, it looks like it's just the three of us today. Principal Snelgrove had an afternoon appointment that couldn't be missed."

Vlad imagined that that appointment included a stop at the cheese store, but he kept his humor to himself, allowing only a small smirk to crack his features.

Mrs. Moppet said, "I trust you boys can keep it down to a dull roar over here while I finish cataloging some new books? You can do homework or study, if you'd like. I'm not really sure what the principal had in mind."

As she walked away, Vlad and Eddie exchanged bewildered glances. Eddie looked just as surprised as Vlad felt. Present company excluded, this looked to be the most pleasant detention ever experienced by mankind. Further proof that librarians should run the world—or at least be in charge of detention at Bathory High.

Vlad pulled his new leather notebook from his backpack and began a new journal entry—nothing even remotely vampiric, on the chance Eddie caught a glimpse. Instead, he wrote about him and Meredith, and just how much he'd enjoyed their stolen moment. He left out his urge to bite her and made a mental note to write that in later, in private.

The entire time, he could feel Eddie's eyes on him.

Vlad shot Eddie a look of irritation. "Don't you have something better to do than stare at me?"

To his immense surprise, the corners of Eddie's mouth rose in a smirk. "I was just thinking . . . it's pretty amazing how well you blend in with humans."

Vlad's stomach sank. His fingers fumbled over the pen he was holding and it tumbled to the ground, but he didn't bend over to retrieve it. He held Eddie's gaze in fearful surprise. Maybe it was stupid, but he had really thought Eddie would have let go of that whole Vlad-is-a-monster thing by now.

He parted his lips to offer up his usual protest, but Eddie shook his head with an air of confidence that made Vlad squirm. "No need to deny it, Vlad. I'm quite convinced that you're not human. And after some long nights of research and watching you . . . I think I know what you are."

Vlad's heartbeat picked up its pace, and he had to struggle to calm his panicked breathing. "Why are you doing this, Eddie? You used to be an okay guy. But now . . . you're just obnoxious."

Eddie tightened his jaw. "I wasn't an okay guy. I was a loser. But I'm done being a loser, Vlad. And if you get hurt on my way to becoming a winner . . . well, that can't be helped."

Vlad shook his head. "You're not a loser, Eddie. You're not what people say you are. You're whatever you make yourself out to be."

"I wish that were true. But it's not." Eddie shook his head sadly. Eventually the corner of his lips rose in a small smile. "Luckily, I've found the road to success. It's paved with your secrets."

Vlad stuffed his notebook inside his backpack angrily. "You'd better back off, Eddie. I'm getting really tired of all of your bizarre theories."

Eddie chuckled. "I can't believe I didn't see it sooner. Your pale skin, the way you always bring your lunch to school . . ."

Vlad's heart was racing in panic. Eddie knew. How could he know? Somewhere, somehow Vlad had royally screwed up, and now this determined little weasel knew what he was. He stood up and threw his bag over his shoulder in a frightened huff. He was leaving detention early, and he'd happily deal with the consequences, no matter what Nelly or Snelgrove or anybody else had to say about it.

Eddie leaned back in his seat, arms crossing his chest, not so much as a thread of doubt weaving through his soft-spoken words. "You're a vampire, Vladimir Tod. And I'm going to expose you to the world."

Vlad didn't think. He reacted with all the anger, hurt, and shaking fear that was coursing through his veins and pushed into Eddie's mind, shoving the boy back as far as he could. He slipped out just in time to watch Eddie tilt back in his chair and hit the floor, whacking his head against wood. Eddie yelped. Vlad all but ran out the door.

As he pushed open the front door of the school, he noticed that his hands were trembling. He wasn't sure what he was more afraid of—that Eddie knew that he was a vampire or that he'd wanted to hurt Eddie far worse than he had.

He brushed the threat of tears from his eyes, shoved his still-shaking hands into his pockets, and headed for home.

12

A DRUDGE'S LOYALTY

HENRY DROPPED HIS VOICE to a horrified, but confused, whisper. "A knife? Or a dagger?"

They'd been talking the entire walk to school about Vlad's recent rash of nightmares. Doing so had somehow brought Henry out of his weird shell, something that Vlad was enormously grateful for. Maybe Henry had been flaking out lately, but when Vlad needed him, his drudge was there. Vlad had told him all about Eddie's accusations last week, and Henry had been absolutely sympathetic. Things seemed completely back to normal.

Vlad wrinkled his forehead in uncertainty. "What's the difference?"

Henry shrugged, as if it were obvious. "One's for eating; one's for stabbing."

"I don't . . . know. It was a blade, double-edged with a cylindrical handle. I think it was ivory or bone or something." The image of the weapon glinting in the candle's low light flitted through Vlad's imagination, sending a shiver down his spine.

"That's a dagger. No question about it."

"Whatever. Anyway . . . then he stabbed me in the thigh. But the weird thing is, before I woke up, my leg *really* hurt."

"Huh." Henry pulled the door to the school open and held it for Vlad. After they entered, he said, "Are the nightmares always the same?"

"Pretty much." Vlad hesitated, then moved down the hall, offering Henry a one-shouldered shrug. "Well, I mean, it's always some guy torturing me with a knife—"

"Dagger."

"*Whatever.* Like I was saying, the dreams are about a guy torturing me with some *dagger*—"

Henry smiled.

"—but not always the same kind of torture."

Henry was quiet until they reached their lockers. His insightfulness was astounding. "Dude. That's messed up."

Vlad bit his bottom lip for a second. If it were anyone else, he wouldn't even consider sharing his theory. But this was Henry. "Do you think maybe it could be a glimpse of the future or something?"

Henry seemed to mull this possibility over for a moment, then shrugged. "Weirder things have happened. At least, they have to you."

He punched Vlad lightly in the shoulder. "But Vlad, who would want to tie you to a table and torture you? Aside from Snelgrove, I mean."

After exchanging brief glances, they sighed simultaneously and said, "D'Ablo."

Henry tossed his backpack in his locker rather roughly. "Man, what is that guy's problem, anyway? It's like he got picked last for dodgeball when he was a kid and is taking it out on you for the rest of your life."

Vlad shook his head and reached for his health book. "I don't know. He mentioned some ritual last year, some crazy idea of how he could become the Pravus by killing me. Otis and Vikas both said he was nuts, but just in case, they're looking for the ritual pages he spoke of."

Henry closed his locker and twisted the lock. "No offense, Vlad, but your life sucks."

Vlad sighed and muttered, "Tell me about it."

Henry nodded and gestured behind Vlad with his eyes. Vlad turned and met Eddie's crooked smile with a glare. Eddie raised his camera and snapped a picture. He'd been photographing Vlad at every opportunity since they had detention together, no longer bothering to lurk in the shadows. It was getting really, really annoying.

Luckily, Nelly had been understanding about why Vlad

had ditched detention that day and explained to Snelgrove that he had been feeling under the weather. But that didn't stop her from grounding him for two weeks after the little closet meeting with Meredith. His prison sentence was lifted as of this afternoon, and he wasn't about to have it ruined by a close encounter of the obnoxious kind.

Vlad squeezed the book in his hands. "Eddie, when are you gonna knock it off and leave me alone?"

Eddie smirked, looking somewhat anxious. "When are you just going to admit what you are?"

Henry stepped between them, looking Eddie in the eye. Offering a nonchalant shrug, he said, "What, a vampire?"

Vlad's heart stopped. He was pretty certain he'd died of shock and that only the aid of his locker was keeping him in a standing position.

Eddie looked almost as surprised as Vlad felt.

Henry put an arm around Eddie's shoulders and coaxed him away from Vlad. "It's not exactly a secret that Vlad's the equivalent of a giant mosquito, Eddie. In fact... he's not the only one. The whole school is full of them. And you're their next meal."

Eddie had grown even paler than Vlad was. Henry whipped open a classroom door and shoved Eddie inside, closing the door behind him.

Vlad threw Henry a glance. "What the hell are you doing?"

Henry smirked. "Just trust me, Vlad. Maybe we'll scare

some sense into the little weasel. Nobody messes with my friend."

"When did you set this up?" Whatever *this* was. Vlad cast a nervous glance at the door after Eddie's screams echoed into the hall.

Henry shrugged. "Dude. I'm a McMillan. It's not like it takes a lot to get people to help me out. Especially when it comes to messing with a worm like Eddie."

Eddie burst back out the door. The students in the room, each of whom had donned a pair of cheap plastic fangs, laughed loudly at Eddie's abrupt exit. Eddie, realizing he'd been had, shoved Henry as hard as he could. Henry barely moved. Eddie looked furious. "What makes you so loyal to him? You know what he is!"

Henry set his jaw and tightened his muscles—he'd never liked being shoved. "Yeah, he's a monster. Just like Dracula and Frankenstein. Just like the boogeyman in your closet, Eddie."

Eddie lowered his voice to a growl, but didn't retreat. If anything, he moved closer until he was right in Henry's face. "Why are you protecting him?"

Henry cracked his knuckles, dropping all of the joking tone from his voice. "He bit me when we were eight—we bonded."

Eddie paused, then tilted his head and smiled. "So what? Now you're some kind of vampire's pet?"

Henry's shoulders lowered slightly. For a moment Vlad

thought that Henry was about to walk away, that he was going to let Eddie win. But then Henry grabbed two handfuls of Eddie's shirt and slammed him into the lockers. "Listen to me very carefully, you little speck. Vlad isn't the dangerous one here. I am. And unless you back off and stop harassing my friend, you're gonna find out just how dangerous I can be. You got me?"

Henry pulled him away from the lockers and slammed him against them again. When he spoke, it was more of a growl than actual words. "I'm nobody's pet. Now get lost before you make me angry."

After Eddie disappeared out the front doors with wide, terrified eyes darting back to Henry with every step he took, Vlad gave Henry's shoulder a squeeze. "Dude, that was awesome. Thank—"

Henry shook him off. "Yeah, don't mention it. Just leave me alone."

13
THE MANY FACES OF FRIENDSHIP

VLAD BUTTONED THE BOTTOM BUTTON on his black vest and regarded his reflection in the mirror. While Nelly had fought him tooth and nail on wearing skinny black pants, a white dress shirt with black pinstripes, a black vest, a black jacket, and tennis shoes adorned with tiny skulls to the Snow Ball, Vlad thought even she would agree that he looked pretty good. He slipped his jacket on and brushed his black hair from his dark eyes. He was cloaked in shadows from head to toe. This was going to be a night to remember.

Downstairs, the doorbell rang out in an ominous tone. Moments later, there was a soft knock on Vlad's door. Vlad checked his jacket pocket for ChapStick and said, "Come in."

Henry opened the door, and Vlad's smile deflated. He was dressed in the same outfit he'd worn to school that day.

Unwilling to entertain the notion that his best friend was ditching him again, Vlad said, "Dude, you do know that this is a semiformal dance, don't you? Snelgrove will never let you in wearing that."

"That's okay." Henry cleared his throat against his fist, then took a deep breath, as if whatever he was about to say required an enormous bout of bravery. "I'm not going."

Vlad stiffened—it wasn't like Henry to miss a dance, let alone this dance, and they'd been talking about going as recently as last week, the day he stood up to Eddie, the day Henry had stormed out in a huff. The Snow Ball was a huge deal to everyone—from the goths to the jocks. It was just about the only time the two groups could mingle in the same room without any snide comments being tossed around. Vlad couldn't imagine Henry missing out. "What about Kylie McAuliffe?"

Henry shrugged vacantly. "I called her a couple of hours ago and canceled."

Vlad just about choked. "Why?"

Henry stood there for a long time, despondent. He seemed to be bursting with things to say, but holding them in, as if he didn't want to taint Vlad's mood with his own. Finally he sighed and dropped his gaze to the ground. "It's just a stupid dance, Vlad."

Vlad tightened his jaw, resisting the temptation to read Henry's mind. "Is it because of Melissa?"

Henry shoved his hands in his front pockets, his eyes still on the ground. Finally, in a gravelly tone, he said, "If you really wanna know, it's because of you."

Vlad blinked. He wasn't entirely certain he'd heard Henry right. He squeaked out, "Me?"

Then Henry's hands were out of his pockets, his eyes blazing, his face red. "I'm so sick of it, Vlad!" he yelled. "You think you're so special because you can float through mid-air and read people's minds. You think you're so great because you can order me around and I have no say at all. I'm sick of it! I'm sick of you!"

Vlad was shocked into complete silence. Every word slashed through his heart like a knife, until his insides were nothing more than a pile of goo. It hurt to hear these things—but it hurt a thousand times more to hear them from Henry.

Though it pained him to do so, Vlad took in a slow, deep breath, licked his dry lips, and forced his mouth to form words. "For one, I don't think I'm all that special. Most of the time, my abilities just make me out to be some kind of freak. And since when do I order you around?"

"At lunch a few weeks ago. And there were other times." Henry's eyes were red and shining, as if he were fighting back frustrated tears. "I don't get a choice. You made me your drudge and didn't even ask me, didn't even tell me what it would mean."

Vlad's own eyes filled with tears, and he shook his head, hoping the action would clear his vision. "How could I have told you? I didn't know, Henry! Not until Otis told me two years ago. This is nuts. You're acting like a crazy person."

Henry met his gaze. His words were crisp, cold. "I'm tired of being your slave. I want out."

Vlad felt as if every ounce of air had been sucked out of his lungs, and he nearly staggered in an effort to catch his breath. He couldn't believe what he was hearing. It was like his best friend had been replaced by one of the pod people. He shook his head, confounded. "You ... you really don't want to be my drudge anymore?"

Henry didn't reply. Vlad fought the urge to weep uncontrollably and instead pushed his anguish deep down, where he could pretend it didn't exist. He didn't speak for a very long time.

Then finally, once his heart had completed its explosion, throwing shards of itself up against the walls of his rib cage, he choked out, "I read something about releasing a drudge in the *Compendium of Conscientia.* If you're serious—"

Henry's glare said that he was.

"—I'll brush up on the details."

Henry stood there silently. Vlad was beginning to wonder if he'd ever speak again, when he blurted out, "Do it soon."

Something inside Vlad snapped, and his anguish turned to fury. "If I didn't have a dance to go to with my girlfriend, I'd do it right now!"

"Good!"

"Fine!"

Henry stepped out of the room and slammed the door. Vlad could hear him as he stomped down the stairs and banged the front door shut. Tears were streaking Vlad's face when another soft knock came at his door. Not meaning to, he snapped, "What now?"

Nelly cracked the door open and peered at him with a look of pity that made Vlad's tears fall faster. She rarely came to his room, so he knew she'd overheard at least part of the argument. "Henry seemed pretty upset when he left," she said softly. "What happened between you two?"

Vlad wiped his tears with the back of his hand. When he spoke, his voice shook with exasperation. "Have you ever thought you knew somebody better than anyone and then they just changed out of the blue into somebody else entirely?"

Nelly slipped inside and sat on his bed, nodding with understanding. "Your mother, actually."

Vlad flashed her a curious glance and sank down onto the mattress beside her. "Really? What happened?"

Nelly sighed, as if the memory was almost too much to bear. "One day we were sharing all our secrets and spending all sorts of time together. The next day she needed time alone and couldn't tell me what she was doing when she was away. It was a horrid period in our friendship. We argued a lot. I shed more than a few tears, convinced I'd lost my best friend forever."

"But you made up, right?"

Nelly smiled, but her smile was tainted with a strange sadness that Vlad wasn't sure he would ever understand. "Eventually. One day, Mellina came to visit me, and she brought with her the man of her dreams—that's what she called your father, the man of her dreams. Once she and Tomas explained the situation—that he was not human, and that they were expecting a child—I understood her reasons for secrecy. Everything was fine after that, and our friendship was as close as ever."

She met his eyes, her gaze aching with concern for him. "My point is, Vladimir, that there is almost always a reason for people to act as Henry is acting. Your job as his friend is to be kind, to be available when he needs for you to be, and to understand, no matter what those reasons may be. That's what a good friend does."

Vlad chewed his bottom lip for a moment. "What if he told me the reason, and now he wants me to do something for him that I don't want to do? Only . . . the reason I don't want to do it is because I'm scared we won't be friends anymore after that."

Nelly paused notably before narrowing her eyes in suspicion. "Is whatever he's asking you to do illegal?"

"Nope. Nothing like that."

"Just checking." She smiled, this time more naturally. At least her bloodsucking ward wasn't a criminal. "Well, I suppose you'll just have to decide if Henry's needs, and his happiness, are important enough to you that you can take that risk."

It seemed simple enough. But applying that logic to actual actions seemed more daunting to Vlad than hang gliding in a blizzard.

Nelly patted his hand. "But the most important thing that you need to do right now, Vladimir, is put this out of your mind and have fun at the dance. Are you ready to go?"

Vlad sighed, his shoulders slumping. "I guess so."

Nelly gave his hand a squeeze and stood up to leave his room. She stopped at the door just long enough to tell him, "By the way, you look very handsome."

Alone once again, Vlad adjusted the signet ring on his pinkie, and tried to put his argument with Henry in the back of his mind. He took a deep breath and left his room, heading downstairs. He had a dance to get to.

Nelly had insisted on driving Vlad and Meredith to the dance—partly, Vlad thought, to lessen his and his girlfriend's alone time. They had just backed out of the driveway on their way to Meredith's house when Nelly started in. "If you get hungry, just give me a call. I can always stop by with a few blood bags. Better safe than sorry, you know."

Vlad rolled his eyes. Nelly was seriously blowing things out of proportion. It wasn't like Vlad had tried to bite Meredith intentionally or anything. Besides, it had only happened once and not recently. Just that one time, after the Halloween party, and that teensy little moment in the broom closet. So, twice. It was no big deal, really. Looking back, Vlad could almost forget the horror of that moment when he realized he'd been poised to snack on the girl of his dreams. Almost.

They came to a stop in front of Meredith's house. Vlad opened his door and started to get out, but Nelly stopped him. "Hey, you might need this."

She handed him a clear plastic container. Inside was a wrist corsage of white roses and black feathers. Vlad had completely forgotten about flowers. "You picked this out?"

She nodded.

"Good choice. Thanks, Nelly."

Nelly smiled, and Vlad closed the door behind him, making his way up the icy sidewalk to the front porch of Meredith's home. He rang the bell, and a large shadow appeared on the other side of the door. The door opened to reveal Meredith's father. He had the broadest shoulders that Vlad had ever seen. He glared at Vlad and kept his voice low. "No funny business, and have her home by eleven. You hear me?"

Meredith's sweet voice lilted from within. "Daddy, let Vlad in. It's cold out there."

Meredith's mother, a thin woman with warm brown eyes and strawberry blonde hair, appeared by Mr. Brookstone's side. "Really, Harold, let the boy in."

She smiled at Vlad as her husband retreated back into the house. "Don't mind him, Vlad. He's a big teddy bear. Come on in. Oh, what a lovely corsage!"

Vlad was quite certain Mr. Brookstone was a bear of some sort—maybe a grizzly or a Kodiak—but definitely not a teddy. And his diet absolutely consisted of boys that dated his daughter. He moved inside and closed the door, and when Meredith drifted down the stairs, Vlad's heart choked him into speechlessness.

She wore a long, white satin gown, with embroidered black snowflakes adorning the bodice. In several spots, the snowflakes seemed to cascade down her dress. Her chocolate hair was in ringlets, and pinned up so that the curls barely brushed her shoulders. She looked more beautiful than any girl Vlad had ever seen.

As she left the bottom step, Vlad found his voice. Taking a step forward, he said in hushed awe, "Meredith . . . you look amazing."

Behind him, the bear growled.

Mrs. Brookstone smacked her husband gently on the

arm and picked up her camera. "Come on, you two; let's get some pictures so you can be off to the dance."

Vlad opened the corsage box and slipped the corsage on to Meredith's wrist. As he did so, he noticed the tiny snowflakes painted on her fingernails. Meredith gasped. "Oh Vlad, it's perfect!"

Vlad beamed. "I picked it out just for you."

She leaned forward, like she was going to kiss him on the cheek, and then faltered, as if remembering her boyfriend-eating father was in the room. Vlad smiled gratefully.

After posing for approximately five bajillion pictures, Vlad helped Meredith with her coat, and they moved out the door and down the sidewalk to the car. Vlad held her hand over the icy parts, not wanting her to slip and fall. He was keenly aware of the bear's eyes on him the entire time. Once they were safely in the car, Nelly gushed over Meredith's gown. Vlad stayed quiet for most of the drive, allowing Nelly and Meredith their girl-focused conversation while he mused about how lucky he was to be dating a girl like her. But overshadowing his thoughts was tonight's argument with Henry . . . and what it would mean if he was no longer Vlad's drudge.

Their friendship, Vlad wagered, would be a memory. Vlad would be alone, lacking that bond of blood and promises that he'd had since he was eight years old. What would it be like to be without a drudge? Would he make another? No. No, he didn't think he was even capable of such an act.

After all, if Henry weren't his drudge, what was the sense in creating another?

Vlad bit his lip. The thing was . . . he wanted Henry to be happy. And if breaking that bond would give him a chance at happiness, then Vlad had no choice. What it came down to was the fact that Vlad would do anything for his best friend—even if that meant losing him forever.

Meredith squeezed his hand, and when he met her eyes, it was clear she was wondering what was wrong. But how could he explain that part of his soul was breaking off, all because of eons of vampire tradition? He couldn't. So instead he forced a smile and squeezed her hand in return.

At the school, Nelly took pictures of them standing in the snow. She insisted the photographs would be memories they would cherish for a lifetime, but Vlad was pretty sure the memory-retaining part of his brain had been frozen solid by the time she finished snapping pictures.

At last, Vlad led Meredith up the snow-covered steps and into the school. Soft light filled the halls, and silver snowflakes glistened all over the floor, guiding them into the gym. Meredith covered her mouth in awe. Vlad's eyes went wide. The room had been transformed into a winter palace in honor of the annual Snow Ball. The punch and snack table was disguised to look like a snowbank. Silver, white, and blue snowflakes hung from the large arched ceiling. An ice sculpture of a giant snowflake stood next to the food. And the DJ's booth had been completely wrapped in silvery paper, giving it a frosty exterior. It was the coolest dance theme that he had ever seen.

Melissa bounded up to Meredith, and they squealed over each other's dresses. Mike nodded to Vlad like they were old pals. "What's up, Vlad?"

"Not much." Vlad beamed. It was hard not to smile on such a magical night. A night, he noted with a quick glance around, that didn't include Eddie's stalking or Bill and Tom's bullying.

A song that Vlad knew by heart pounded from the DJ's speakers, and the girls dragged him and Mike onto the dance floor. Vlad froze for a moment, because he really had no idea what he was doing. But eventually, he figured out a way of shifting his feet around that almost, sorta, kinda felt like dancing. After two songs, Meredith excused herself, and Vlad took refuge by the punch bowl.

It was nice to attend a dance where Bill and Tom were nowhere to be seen, and even nicer to have a date—especially the girl of his dreams. In fact, if it weren't for the dark cloud that had been hanging over his head ever since Henry had made his big I-don't-want-to-be-your-drudge-anymore speech, the evening might have been a pretty good one. For once, Vlad felt like a normal, human teenager.

He was wandering past the gym doors on his way to find Mike when he overheard Meredith's voice coming from the hallway outside. "No, I won't stay away from Vlad. How could you even suggest such a thing, Kylie?"

Peeking around the corner, Vlad saw Kylie whisper to Meredith. Whatever she said put an irritated crease in Meredith's forehead.

Meredith shook her head. "Well, I don't believe it."

"But Henry McMillan told me—"

"I don't care, Kylie. If it didn't come straight from Vlad's lips, I wouldn't believe it. What a crazy, stupid rumor to spread! There's no such thing!" Meredith stormed off in the direction of the girls' bathroom. Kylie stood there, looking wounded but determined.

Vlad's stomach had twisted into a million knots.

Henry wouldn't. He couldn't. Could he?

Vlad quickly ran through every order he'd ever given Henry. None of them had included "Don't tell people I'm a vampire."

A wave of nausea washed over him. It was quite possible that Henry had broken his trust in a moment of blind fury, and had spilled his most valuable secret to the girl he was supposed to take to the dance. Vlad shook his head, unwilling to believe it, but also unable to deny the possibility that Henry might have slipped up in a moment of anger.

And all at once, Vlad was a freak again, and the dance was all but ruined.

Kylie almost bumped into him as she reentered the

gym. Vlad forced a smile, not wanting to cause any more damage or to do anything that might substantiate any possible claims that he was a bloodthirsty monster. "Hey, Kylie."

Kylie's face went white and she stepped backward, away from him. "Henry told me about you. Stay away from me!"

Vlad forced himself to remain calm, even though he was in full-on panic mode inside. "What did he say?"

"Leave me alone!" Kylie bolted across the room and started talking to a group of kids, gesturing wildly at Vlad.

Vlad swallowed hard and glanced about the room. The only thing missing from this scene were torches and pitchforks. From behind him came a familiar voice, warm, sweet. Meredith. "Don't worry about Kylie. She's just a little worked up over something stupid Henry told her."

He turned to face her, not wanting to see fear in her eyes. Thankfully, he didn't. "What would that be?"

Meredith furrowed her brow. "Are you okay? You look sick or something."

Vlad shook his head, indicating that nothing was wrong. Meredith didn't look like she believed him, but went on, "Anyway, he told her that she should stay away from you, that close contact with you would be dangerous or something. Are you sure you're not sick, Vlad?"

Vlad felt like vomiting. So Henry really had betrayed him. Apparently, you can't even trust your best friend.

"I'm fine. Just wondering why Henry would say something like that."

Meredith shrugged. "No clue, but he told her that you're the reason he was too sick to bring her to the dance tonight. He said he caught something called Contagidiginosis from you. Apparently, it eats away the lining of the stomach like acid and comes from cross-eyed antelopes in Africa."

Vlad's jaw dropped. Henry hadn't exposed him. Henry was just being stupid. Completely, ridiculously stupid "Antelopes?"

Meredith chuckled. "You look better already. How's your stomach?"

Vlad smirked. "Still intact. Guess I must be on the mend."

A slow song started playing, and Vlad swept all of his fears away, turning to face Meredith. He smiled. "Wanna dance?"

In moments, they were on the dance floor.

Meredith placed her hand on his shoulder, and Vlad shivered as he clasped her free hand in his. He still wasn't sure exactly what to do with his feet, but when he looked into her deep chocolate brown eyes, he realized that it didn't matter whether he could dance or not—all that mattered was that he was here with her, that they were together, that it was the Snow Ball, and he wasn't alone. He was in the gym with his girlfriend instead of in the belfry with his thoughts.

They moved in slow circles, and snowflake-shaped confetti and silver glitter lazily drifted down from overhead, covering the dance floor and everyone on it. Meredith tilted her head back and closed her eyes, laughing softly as the glitter graced her cheeks. Vlad smiled, blinking away confetti. She was so beautiful that his heart ached.

The music drifted through the room. Vlad brushed a snowflake from Meredith's cheek. They weren't dancing anymore so much as standing in the center of the room, holding each other close to the tune of gentle music, covered by the decorative splendor of an unusual high school dance. Vlad met her warm gaze and was transported back to Halloween night, when he'd realized how much, how deeply he loved Meredith. Only tonight, his feelings seemed even deeper somehow, bigger, more real. He placed his forehead lightly against hers and closed his eyes.

So this was how his dad had felt about his mom. Vlad got it now. It was love, real and true. And it didn't matter that one of them wasn't entirely human. It didn't matter that technically, they were predator and prey. Or that when Vlad inhaled, he could detect the subtle, sweet scent of her blood as it moved from artery to vein and had to force his thoughts away from the danger of her close proximity. None of it mattered.

The only thing that truly mattered at the moment was that Vlad loved Meredith, and that he always would.

14

UNFAMILIAR GROUND

VLAD DREW HIS SHOULDERS UP in an effort to block the freezing early-January wind from his ears. It didn't work. The wind picked up and pushed against his chest with all its might, slowing his already slow steps to the school. Snow drifted over his shoes as he made his way down the sidewalk, soaking his socks and chilling him to the bone. His ears were completely numb, as were his gloved fingers. Winter break was over, but clearly, winter was not.

And whose sick idea was it to have school today anyway?

At the top of the steps, tucked safely inside the warm school, stood Principal Snelgrove, eyeing each student with his distrustful, rodentlike stare. Vlad rubbed his numb hands together and swore under his breath. Of course. Snelgrove. Rat-man extraordinaire. Next time the weather got this fierce, somebody had better distract the principal with a maze and the promise of cheese. Maybe then school would be canceled for the day.

He climbed the steps and went inside, thankful for the heat of the building, even if it was school. It took him a minute, but he fumbled with numb fingers to unlock his locker, then looked around. Henry was nowhere to be seen, something that deeply troubled Vlad. He hadn't seen Henry since before winter break, since the day Henry had told him that he no longer wanted to be his drudge. Vlad was hoping he'd cooled off by now and maybe changed his mind. After all, Henry was the only human in the world besides Nelly who knew what Vlad really was. Except for Eddie. And his were only unconfirmed theories. So far anyway.

Vlad drifted impatiently through his morning classes, with no sign of Henry between classes. By the time he got to lunch, Vlad was beginning to wonder whether or not Henry had called in sick, despite the fact that Henry hadn't called him to bemoan his various aches and pains. Deep down, Vlad knew he was kidding himself. But the possible truth was far more upsetting to consider.

Vlad's stomach rumbled angrily. He'd been so anxious to get to the cafeteria that he'd forgotten to stop by his locker and grab his sack lunch. But at the moment, he didn't care. All he could think about was finding Henry and righting whatever was wrong between them.

Winter break had given him plenty of time to consider why Henry might feel suddenly put off by his drudge status. And while Vlad had only recounted a handful of instances where he'd ordered Henry to grab him a Pepsi, and maybe two where he'd told his best friend to back off and let him win a video game, clearly those moments had meant a lot more to Henry than he'd realized. And though he hadn't at the time, recalling each of those things now filled Vlad with a burdening guilt. Maybe Henry was right— maybe Vlad had been acting more like a vampire overlord than a best friend. Whatever it was, he had to make things right, and hope that Henry would abandon the insane notion of leaving his position as Vlad's drudge.

As he approached his usual table, he smiled at Meredith before scanning the room for any sign of his best friend. Just as he was about to count Henry as absent, he spied him seated at the "popular table," a table that made the tiny hairs on the back of Vlad's neck stand on end. Vlad's shoulders slumped in confusion as he made his way across the cafeteria toward him. The air grew thicker with every step he took. Vlad was most definitely uninvited here.

Chelsea Whitaker was the first to detect the intruder. She flipped her hair and wrinkled her nose, as if Vlad didn't smell very good. And though she was looking right at Vlad, she spoke to Henry, who was sitting to her right. "It looks like we have company."

Vlad's jaw tightened. He managed to squeak out, "Henry?"

But Henry wouldn't look at him. He just slumped down in his seat and said, "I'm sitting with Chelsea today, Vlad."

Vlad spoke through clenched teeth. He didn't like standing this close to the popular table any more than Chelsea liked him doing it. "We need to talk about something. It's important."

Henry picked a French fry off his lunch tray and swirled it around in a pile of ketchup. "I haven't changed my mind, if that's what you're wondering."

"Can I please talk with you?" Vlad moved his eyes briefly to Chelsea and raised his voice slightly for emphasis. "Alone?"

After a moment, Henry nodded and left the table with him, directing him to a quiet spot near the Pepsi machine. "Look, Vlad . . ."

"No, you look!" Vlad paused and got a firm grip on whatever part of him was still in panic mode. This wasn't going to be easy, but it would be a lot harder if Vlad approached with the wrong attitude. "I mean, Henry . . . I'm sorry, okay? I was thinking about what you said, and if I have been treating you more like a slave than a friend lately, I'm really sorry."

Henry looked as if a weight had been lifted from his shoulders. But he didn't speak.

Vlad did. "So do you accept my apology?"

"Of course."

A rush of relief filled Vlad—a rush that was cut short by Henry turning back toward the popular table. "Wait. Where are you going?"

Henry shrugged, as if it were the most obvious thing in the world. "I told you. I'm sitting with Chelsea today."

A thousand words ran up Vlad's throat, but only a few managed to escape. "Chelsea Whitaker is quite possibly the most obnoxious person on the planet. Why would you want to hang out with her?"

Henry paused. A good long pause too. At least he had to take a second to think about it. "We have stuff in common."

"Like what, other than the fact that you're both human? And I'm still not all that sure about Chelsea." Vlad snorted at his wit, but when he looked in Henry's eyes, all the humor drained out of his body. That was it. Exactly it. Chelsea was human. Henry was human. And Vlad . . . Vlad was not.

His mouth went dry from the sudden onset of shock and anger. "You know, you're a real piece of work, McMillan. I guess you're more like your cousin Joss than I realized."

Henry scowled with contempt. "Are you done? Or are you planning on ordering me to sit, stay, and roll over for your amusement, *master*?"

Vlad stepped closer and jabbed his finger into Henry's chest. "I'll give you an order. You do whatever you want to do. But you'd better choose right now—either me or Chelsea."

"Fine."

To Vlad's horror, Henry turned and rejoined the popular crowd.

Vlad turned in a huff and left the lunchroom. He slammed the school doors behind him, and was halfway across town before he realized where he was going.

His old house looked exactly as it had the last time he'd visited—cold, dark, empty, haunted. Not haunted by ghosts, but with thousands of happy moments and memories, all spoiled by the horrific reality of his parents' passing.

He moved around to the back door, knowing it would still be unlocked, and opened the screen. Before he went inside, he took a deep breath—both for bravery and to bring with him a little piece of the outside world, the world where he was slowly getting past the pain of their demise, the world where he was beginning to feel safe once again.

The floorboards creaked slightly as he made his way inside, and that familiar acrid stench of smoke invaded his nostrils. He wasn't exactly sure why he'd come here, only that he needed to be somewhere alone, somewhere that reminded him of who he was. He climbed the stairs and walked into his father's office. Papers still littered the floor from when he and Henry had searched the office two years before. A fine layer of dust now covered them. Vlad sneezed, and the sound of it echoed through the house.

He ran a hand over the surface of his father's desk, then whispered angry words that only his father could answer. "Who am I, Dad? What am I? Am I a vampire? A human? Both?"

He hesitated a moment, choking back horrified tears, then added, "Neither?"

His concern, the same concern that haunted his dreams, was that he would never really fit in anywhere. And he couldn't help but wonder if Henry's recent detachment was just another reminder that he wasn't one hundred percent anything, only two halves . . . incomplete.

Sometimes he wondered if he would ever be whole.

Disgusted at the mess he and his potentially-former best friend had made, he knelt on the floor, plucked several papers from the floorboards, and stacked them neatly in an empty file box. The least he could do was put everything back in order. Besides, he was technically skipping school, so he needed something to do while he was hiding out until the last bell rang. With any luck, the school wouldn't call Nelly. After his recent detention, he was pretty sure she'd come down hard on him for walking out in the middle of the day. Normally Vlad would have stuck it out, but today's events called for truancy. After all, it wasn't as if it would have done him any good to sit through physical science with Chelsea after Henry had chosen her over him.

Most of the papers Vlad had gathered up were boring— old tax returns, receipts for furniture, photocopies of various things that Vlad didn't recognize. But then he came upon something he very much did recognize—his father's handwriting. All it was was a simple list of things to buy, but what made the corners of Vlad's mouth lift in a small smile was the note at the bottom: *Buy roses for M, bring chocolate for V.* Whenever his dad had to go into Stokerton to make purchases that weren't available in Bathory, he'd always bring Vlad's mom a dozen of the sweetest blood-red roses he could find, and he'd bring Vlad a small gold box of delicious milk chocolates. It was just one of those things, one of those tender things that had made Tomas such a loving and attentive husband and father.

Vlad folded the note and was about to tuck it into his pocket when he noticed a single word scribbled on the back of the list.

Pravus.

He read the word again, silently wondering what that word was doing on a list that had belonged to his father, let alone scribbled in his own handwriting. But then, maybe that was what Tomas had meant in his journal when he'd written that he had "suspicions" about his son. He must have known what an oddity it was for a human and a vampire to procreate, so of course he would have wondered if Vlad was the Pravus.

Tomas wasn't the only one. Vlad couldn't help but wonder if the story was true, if he were some subject of ancient prophecy.

But there was no way to know, as Vlad wasn't too keen on the idea of testing out the checklist of traits that only the Pravus would have. Sunlight? No, thank you. Immortal? He wasn't touching that with a ten-foot stake.

But one thing was for sure.

He had to learn as much about that prophecy as he could.

15

THE FEAST BEFORE THE KILL

IGNATIUS STARED UP AT THE SKY in blissful contentment. Not only was it a new moon, but the sky was overcast with thick black clouds, ensuring that his hypersensitive allergy to the sun's rays would not emerge tonight. It would make for a luxuriously long ending to his hunt for the boy, and he would take his time with every stroke of his blade. The boy would bleed quickly, but the cuts would be oh so slow.

Nothing could stop the hunter tonight. No glinting of the sun's light off the surface of the moon. No concerns about the boy's human ward witnessing his actions. Ignatius had listened to her thoughts as she left the house an hour before—a double shift at the hospital would keep her away all night.

Now there would only be the boy, and the delicious slicing of his pretty skin.

But he had to be careful. He was famished, which always made for a better hunt, but it also increased the temptation to feed off the hunted during his cutting sessions. And he'd be damned if he was going to taint his palate with the bitter crimson of an arrogant half-breed. Better that he should complete his hunt on a full stomach than run the risk of draining his flawed captor.

As if in answer to his needs, a girl passed him on the sidewalk, her skin pale, purple streaks through her dark hair. Ignatius recognized her at once as one of the human children who frequented the front steps of the local high school each evening. Her name stuck on his tongue. It was a time, not a name, and had reminded him instantly of the smell of autumn and cool breezes. October.

He turned, following her quietly, daydreaming about the moments following his meal. He'd steal into the boy's home stealthily and make his way up the stairs to his bedroom. Then, with a turn of the knob, enter the boy's resting place.

October turned the corner, oblivious to the vampire following her.

Once he was in the boy's room, Ignatius would unsheathe his favorite blade and, with its tip, draw the covers down, away from the sleeping boy's form. And then...

"What are you doing?" A voice from the shadows. Ignatius hung back, lost in his fantasy, but not so lost that he would expose his presence and lose his meal.

October slowed her steps, but by her posture it was clear she'd been expecting the intruder. "I'm going home. What's it look like?"

Another human, a boy with silver hair, stepped from the shadows, his lips pursed. "It looks like you've been inviting a dork like Vladimir Tod to hang with us without even asking my opinion."

She shrugged coldly. "I don't need your permission, Kristoff. If you don't like him, you can find other people to hang out with. Besides, he's not a dork. I think he's interesting."

Kristoff snarled. "Interesting? He's boring. And about as far from being goth as you can get."

"I don't choose my friends because of labels. I choose them because they intrigue me." She raised a stark eyebrow, her posture suddenly very defensive. "You used to be so open-minded, Kristoff. What happened to you?"

After a long, silent moment, the boy shrugged, sighing. "There's just something about him. I don't know what it is. But I don't like it."

"So don't like it. But give him a chance. The way I gave you a chance, *David*."

Kristoff winced at the mention of his non-goth name and walked away without another word.

In waiting, Ignatius's thirst had become dire. He had to

feed, quickly, and get to his task. The sun would be up in five hours. He would need at least a quarter of that for the journey back to Stokerton. It wasn't as much time as he'd hoped for, but his recent fast had weakened him, making waking from rest a drawn-out chore. But that was about to end.

He closed the gap between himself and the girl, and with a quick glance around them at the darkened windows of the houses that lined the street, he closed his hand around her arm. To his surprise, the girl threw her arm up, slamming her elbow into his Adam's apple. Ignatius stumbled back for a moment, recoiling from the shock of pain. As he recovered, she spat out, "Don't even think about it, pervert. I've been in self-defense classes since I was five."

Ignatius considered engaging her in conversation, toying with her until the moment of her demise, but there was no time. He needed her blood far more than he needed her fear. With vampiric speed, he moved close to her, knocking her off her feet. He could smell her blood rushing through her veins in excited fear, and his hunger raged through him. He leaned closer, opening his mouth, exposing his fangs. The girl's eyes were squeezed tightly closed. She kicked and thrashed uselessly, completely unaware that her life was about to be stolen away by a creature she'd only seen in her dreams. Ignatius brushed his lips against her throat, ready to bite down, savoring the moment for all its worth.

A bright light blinded Ignatius's too-sensitive eyes. It was false light, but too bright for his vision to handle. He stumbled, then ran blindly into the darkness, hoping he was heading in the direction of the Tod boy's home. Let it be finished then, hungry or not. Behind him he heard what sounded like a human police officer comforting the girl.

By the time he reached the boy's home, his vision had cleared. He stood across the street, watching for a moment, hoping to savor his duties at least a little. He stepped forward, beginning to cross, but that same light that had assaulted him flickered in the corner of his eye. Down the street, a police car shined its searchlight between houses, seeking him out.

Begrudgingly, Ignatius turned from the boy's home and fled. It would be safer to wait, and give the boy who would be Pravus one more night of peaceful rest. Or at least, a few more hours.

As he whipped through the town, it occurred to Ignatius that a more direct approach would be called for. And that the next time he encountered Vladimir Tod, his violent tactics wouldn't just be fueled by a sense of duty and justice . . . but by revenge for having made him wait this long.

16
A Restless Night

THE DARK FIGURE STABBED THE BLADE into Vlad's side and
forced it as deeply as he was able, inciting an anguished
scream from Vlad. But when the man twisted the dagger,
forcing the wound to open further, Vlad began to think he
would lose his mind. He could barely see now, practically
blinded from the pain. Pain that was unending, unyielding,
and could only be measured by peaks and valleys of
torment.

The smell of his own blood—sweet, metallic—filled his
nostrils. He would die on this table, of that there was no
doubt. But death would be a tender release at the end of
this boundless torture.

The man leaned closer, but Vlad could not make out his face. His words weren't a voice so much as a sizzle, like bubbling liquid on hot steel. "I will never stop."

At his final spoken word, he twisted the blade again, this time wrenching it until it pulled through Vlad's flesh.

Vlad shrieked, and edged ever closer to the thin line between sanity and madness.

Vlad gasped and sat up in bed, bathed in sweat, his throat raw as if he'd been crying out in his sleep. The nightmares were getting worse.

He sat there for a few seconds, shuddering breaths shaking his already trembling body. It took him a moment to realize that he wasn't tied to a table somewhere but in his soft, warm bed, safe and sound. He turned on the lamp beside his bed and glanced around the room, just to be sure. But somehow, knowing that his dreams were not his reality didn't make him feel any better.

Before the details slipped from his memory, he grabbed his journal from the nightstand and scribbled down every last moment he could recall of the horrific nightmare, as he had almost every night since his birthday party. As he scribbled the last words down, a picture flashed in his mind—too similar to the weird, external camera view he'd experienced with Otis. A dark figure, standing outside in the snow, watching his house. Vlad tensed as the image left his mind.

Vlad moved to the edge of his bed and slipped on a pair of jeans. Shirtless, he moved out his bedroom door and down the stairs as quickly as he could. Pulling back the curtains, he searched the scene outside, but no one was there. Vlad frowned. Maybe his vampire abilities were on the fritz. Or maybe it had just been his imagination.

He walked into the kitchen and pulled open the freezer. For some reason, he was famished. He grabbed three blood bags, bit his lip, and reached for a fourth, then a fifth.

As he sat at the table, biting into the bags with his razor-sharp fangs and gulping down mouthfuls of blood, Vlad's thoughts turned to Henry. Could it have been him lurking outside in the blowing cold? Maybe he had changed his mind. After all, Vlad could slip into Henry's thoughts. . . . Perhaps the bizarre camera trick wasn't a vampires-only kind of thing. Maybe he could see anyone with it.

And on the chance that Henry hadn't come to his senses, Vlad desperately needed to read through the *Compendium of Conscientia* and see just what lay in store for him and his drudge.

Tossing the empty bags into the biohazard container beneath the sink, and ignoring the still-hungry rumble of his stomach, Vlad hurried to the living room and slipped on his sneakers, tying them haphazardly. He was just slipping his coat on over his bare torso when he noticed a parchment envelope lying on the small table next to the front door. His heart jumped with hope . . . hope that he would spy Otis's familiar scrawls when he flipped it over. It didn't surprise him that Nelly would forget to give him his mail when she was working double shifts all week, but it did fill him with disbelief that she wouldn't give him a call to say that Otis had written.

When he flipped the envelope over, his hopes swirled down the drain, but not for long. The postmark was Siberia, and the handwriting belonged to Vikas.

That was something, at least.

He pocketed the letter and opened the front door, stepping out into the bluster of a midwinter night.

17
PROTOCOL

VLAD SANK DOWN IN HIS CHAIR in the belfry, shivering. It had been a quick walk to his secret sanctuary, and one ended by the horrible task of learning just how to release his drudge. He stared, bleary-eyed at the tear-spotted page, rereading the words he'd hoped to never find.

> To rid oneself of one's drudge, one need only perform a blood cleansing. This can be accomplished by administering a second bite and feeding the vampire's intent into the wound. However, it is crucial that the vampire restrain him or herself from imbibing any of the drudge's blood, lest the ritual become tainted and ineffective. It is

important to remember that once a human's drudge status has been removed, it can never be successfully restored.

Beyond anything, he wished that he hadn't been able to locate the passage, or that it had ever been written. But there it was, in black and white. Henry's salvation.

The temptation to ignore the page, or even to rip it from the book and burn in it the flickering light of the candle, overwhelmed Vlad, but he remained vigilant and reread the passage so that he would know exactly what he was doing the next time he and Henry had a moment alone. After all, he had sworn last year never to treat Henry the way Vikas treated his drudge, Tristian. Henry was more than a servant. And Vlad had vowed that cold, crisp night in Siberia that if Henry ever asked for his freedom, Vlad would find a way to give it.

And here it was. On a piece of parchment. Ripping Vlad's soul to shreds.

Candlelight flirted with every corner of the belfry, brightening his gloom against his will. Vlad pinched the wick, dousing the candle's flame.

So this was it. With a bite, Henry would be free. And Vlad would face the world alone.

He couldn't be angry at Henry anymore. After all, finding out that your will is lost to that of your vampire master would put a damper on anybody's day. So anger was no longer a part of what he was feeling. Just sadness. Deep, immense sadness that he was losing his best friend, that Henry didn't want to share that bond with him any longer.

It was agonizing. And Vlad's heart felt like it had shattered into a million pieces, only to break away within him, jabbing at his insides with every splinter.

And because that pain couldn't be made any worse by any other, Vlad withdrew Vikas's letter from his pocket and read it over again.

Vladimir—

I must say that I am greatly confounded by your recent letter, as I have not shared the company of your uncle in many months. Nor have I received any sort of communication from him since August. It is deeply troubling to me that you cannot seem to reach Otis by telepathy, as I am experiencing the same troubles. Please stay in touch, Mahlyenki Dyavol. I will do all that I can to locate your uncle.

   In Brotherhood,
   Vikas

Vlad sat back in his chair, sinking deeper into the soft, worn leather. It was bad enough that his uncle had been missing in action for over five months now, but losing

Henry as a friend and a trusted drudge was unbearable. What's worse, Vlad had absolutely no one to turn to for advice. Nelly wasn't aware of Henry's drudge status, and Vikas didn't share his view of drudges. Vlad was alone in this. Alone and confused, with no way out but through.

He had to release Henry as his drudge, and trust that their friendship would be strong enough to survive the change. And if it wasn't . . . well, then he'd deal with it. He had no idea how, but he would. After all, he didn't have much choice in the matter.

He trusted Henry . . . or rather, he had, before he'd mistakenly thought Kylie had insinuated that Henry had divulged his deepest darkest secret. He'd just have to trust him on that too, and maybe everything would turn out all right.

Or . . . it would all go horribly wrong, and Vlad's world would fall into a dizzying array of pain and loss.

Either way, it had to be done. Vlad would have to release Henry, and soon.

At the thought of once more tasting Henry's blood on his tongue, two things happened almost simultaneously. Vlad's heart shrank with guilt and sorrow and his stomach growled. In a burst of self-directed fury, he threw the *Compendium* across the room with all the force he could muster. The tome slammed against the wall and dropped with a loud thud to the floor. Vlad glared into the darkness, wishing it away, wishing it all away.

He closed his eyes and pushed as hard as he could with his mind, calling out to his uncle, wherever he was. *"Otis, if you can hear me, please talk to me. Everything is so screwed up right now, and I desperately need your help. Please, please answer me. I need you."*

To his immense disappointment, only silence followed his plea.

After several minutes, Vlad dried his tears on his sleeve and stood, making his way slowly to one of the open arches. He stepped onto the ledge and closed his eyes momentarily, letting the breeze brush his hair from his eyes and gently dry his still-moist cheeks. When he was certain he had pulled himself together, he stepped forward and floated nimbly to the ground.

Soft voices found their way around the corner of the building. Vlad paused and, after a moment, made his way around to the front of the school.

October was the first to notice him. She smiled, her pale skin almost blue in the moonlight. "Out stalking the shadows tonight, Vlad?"

"You might say that." He stepped closer, nodding in greeting to the skinny boy called Sprat. "What are you guys up to?"

October shrugged. "Just hanging out, as usual. Some creep attacked me on my way home earlier, so we were thinking of going after him."

Vlad furrowed his brow. "Somebody attacked you?"

She nodded, adopting a casual tone, but her still-frightened eyes betrayed her. "Yeah, but lucky for me, Officer Thompson showed up in the nick of time."

Vlad's memory reached back a few years, to the officer who had questioned Nelly about Vlad's nighttime activities. "I hate that guy."

He blinked apologetically at October. "I mean, I'm glad he was there for you. I just don't like him."

October smiled. "Who does?"

Kristoff glared in their general direction. "Are we going after this psycho or not?"

Vlad wondered briefly what they would do once they caught up to her attacker. He mumbled, "Bad idea, following some crazy guy like that."

October seemed to mull this over for a minute before looking at Kristoff. "No. Not tonight. I think we'll let the cops handle this one."

She met Vlad's eyes, whispering, "He really cares, y'know? It might not seem like it, but Kristoff is a real sweetie. He just wants to watch out for his own kind."

Vlad raised an eyebrow. "Is that why he's always glaring at me?"

She chuckled. "You're catching on."

Sprat bounded up to Vlad with such a spring in his step that Vlad wondered if he had been downing sugar packets all night. His speech was equally overflowing with boundless energy. "Hey, do you think you might wanna check out The Crypt in a couple of weeks? They're having a Blood Ball in honor of Valentine's Day."

Sprat's eyes were eager, and try as she might to hide it, so were October's. Vlad glanced at Andrew, who managed a halfhearted shrug. Kristoff didn't react at all to Sprat's invitation. Vlad chewed his bottom lip for a moment and thought it over. Thanks to Meredith's dad, she was going to be busy that weekend, so it wasn't as if his plans with his girlfriend were standing in his way. He wasn't sure why he was hesitant to hang out with them. Maybe it was because, for as long as he could remember, only Henry wanted to be his friend. Maybe he'd been scarred forever—both literally and figuratively—by the one time he'd befriended someone who wasn't his drudge. His experience with Joss last year had left him once staked, twice shy. Still . . . they seemed harmless. And how many nights had he spent watching them in curious fascination? Here was his chance, and he felt obligated to take it.

"Sure. What time?"

Sprat grinned broadly, and October squealed. Andrew managed a half smile. Kristoff snorted and said, "Valentine's night, nine o'clock. Don't be late or we'll leave without you."

"Don't worry. I'll be here." Vlad turned toward home, flashing a small smile at Sprat. On his way, he stuck to the sidewalks.

It was a strange thing for Vlad, hanging out with people other than Henry or Joss or Meredith. And Vlad was beginning to wonder if the kids at school had kept their distance over the years because of his staunch unpopularity or because they could detect his differentness on some level. Was that why the goth kids seemed drawn to him now? Or was it something else, an obligation of some sort to repay his good deed of rescuing Sprat? Whatever it was, Vlad didn't want to analyze it too much. He desperately needed the distraction from Henry and Otis for a night.

He made his way down the sidewalk, past houses with dark windows. Everything was shrouded in a cloak of black tonight, as the moon was new. Only fireflies lit his way.

A shadow amongst shadows shifted, and Vlad paused. It was a man, that much he was sure of. But he wasn't sure if it was human or if D'Ablo had returned.

The man chuckled, low and gruff. "No. Not D'Ablo."

Vlad furrowed his brow, doing his best to block his thoughts. "Then who are you and what do you want?"

The man moved again, pulling up his sleeve. The tattoo on the inside of his left wrist glowed a cool blue, illuminating his face for a moment. "To talk for a moment."

Vlad stepped back, uncertain. He recognized the man from Eddie's photograph. So he'd been following Vlad. But why? "Did D'Ablo send you? Are you here to ... hurt me?"

The man laughed again. "It is clear that you have not been raised around your own kind, boy. You have no manners. It is customary to show your mark before we discuss things that pertain to Elysia. We must follow protocol, or hasn't your uncle taken the time to teach you the finer points of vampire society?"

Vlad's jaw tightened at the mention of Otis—Elysia, it seemed, knew too much about him these days. He pushed his sleeve up, revealing his own glowing mark, his eyes never leaving that of the strange vampire. "Answer my question, please."

"I have been awaiting this moment for a long time. In fact, it wasn't until recently that I actually believed you existed." He slid his sleeve down, his features darkening once again. His voice was a harsh whisper. "Tomas always had his own agenda. I just never dreamed he would actually manage to mate with a human. Not to mention, how he could stomach the touch of one without devouring every drop of her."

Vlad bristled. Before turning to walk away, he said, "I don't have to stand here and listen to you insult my parents. If it's the journal you want, you can tell D'Ablo that the answer is still no."

Then the man appeared before him, quicker than Vlad could blink. He growled, "I know nothing of the journal you speak of, boy. I've only come to see what *thing* Tomas has created, before dragging your lifeless body back to the council in Stokerton."

Vlad swallowed the frightened lump in his throat and said, "Well, I guess that answers the question about D'Ablo. But you still haven't told me who you are."

The man's hand shot forward, clutching Vlad by the

throat. His raspy voice was surprisingly rich in tone, as if he were enjoying himself. "I am Ignatius. And to you, I am the end of all things."

Ignatius threw Vlad back, and Vlad hit the ground hard. Before Vlad could stand, Ignatius was there in a blink, grabbing Vlad once again by the throat. Vlad pulled at his fingers, to no avail.

"The Pravus." Ignatius laughed.

Vlad shivered inside.

"Isn't that what they call you? The halfling boy who will come to rule over vampirekind and enslave the human race. Yet you can't even manage to escape an old vampire's grip."

Ignatius effortlessly tossed Vlad several feet through the air. As Vlad flew, he gasped. It felt like it wasn't happening—a weird sensation, almost like he was watching a movie rather than truly experiencing it. Then Vlad collided with the trunk of a large oak tree, and reality sank in. The air left his lungs in the form of a yelp. He had to get away, far away, but the moment he stood, Ignatius was on him once again, gripping his throat and choking him into silence. For a moment, Vlad thought he might pass out.

Ignatius's lips were so close to Vlad's ear that they brushed his skin as he spoke. "I have spent over eight hundred years walking the earth as a vampire, and you are nothing more than a mistake made by an idiot daydreamer. I shall take great pleasure in introducing you to my blade. After all, I wouldn't compromise my palate by tasting the filth that runs through your veins. Be glad your parents are already dead, boy, or I'd kill them myself tonight, and you along with them."

Fury boiled through Vlad, and as he met Ignatius's eyes, he saw a grim flicker, as if his attacker had witnessed something he hadn't expected. Vlad bet that his eyes had flashed that weird iridescent purple again, and for once, he was glad. With all the anger he was feeling, Vlad peeled Ignatius's hand from his throat, leaving Ignatius a bit stunned. But Ignatius wasn't the only one. Vlad marveled silently at his sudden onset of vampiric strength and continued to twist his attacker's hand back, forcing the man down on one knee. The pained expression on Ignatius's face reassured Vlad that his words would be heard. "Don't you ever talk that way about my parents. My mother was a saint, and my father was a far better man and far better vampire than you ever dreamed of being." He shook his head. "Whatever you want from me, you're not getting it."

Vlad released the man's hand at last. "I suggest you leave."

Ignatius stood and loosened the leather strap that bound his curved dagger to his thigh. He met Vlad's gaze with clouded eyes. "I'm not going anywhere until I get what I came for."

Vlad tightened his hands into fists and growled, his fangs long and bare like that of an animal. "Then come and get it already."

Ignatius moved so quickly that Vlad didn't see the raised dagger till it had nearly pierced his side. He swung around and picked Ignatius up, then tossed him several yards. Ignatius slid to a stop in a catlike pose, poised to strike again. He sprang forward, and Vlad mustered all his strength. He punched Ignatius as hard as he could in the chest. Ignatius fell again, this time losing his balance and meeting the pavement with the side of his face. As Ignatius began to stand, Vlad could see the scrapes on his cheek beginning to heal. Vlad moved. He wasn't sure how, but he moved with a speed that he hadn't known before. Ignatius had managed to make it up onto one knee before Vlad appeared next to him. The surprised expression on the old vampire's face mirrored the thoughts in Vlad's mind. Vlad struck out with his foot, making contact with Ignatius's side. He felt ribs breaking. Ignatius got up and flew down the street, crashing down on the hood of a parked car. Again, Vlad found himself standing next to this older, more experienced vampire. He was winning. He didn't know how, but he was winning.

He grabbed the collar of Ignatius's shirt and moved in until their faces were mere inches apart. "It looks like you're gonna have to leave here empty-handed."

As Vlad pulled back his fist, ready to plant it in the face of his foe, the first rays of the sun peeked out over the horizon. Before Vlad's fist had the opportunity to fall, Ignatius let out a howl of pain, and his fist met Vlad's chest. Vlad flew back, coming to land in his own front yard. He braced for the next blow, but Ignatius was nowhere to be found.

Vlad was alone. He stood and began to make his way up the front steps. He reached out with his mind to Otis, but as expected, no answer came. Vlad was beginning to think that his uncle had abandoned him.

Once inside, he climbed the steps to his bedroom, where he would find no rest.

18
THE CRYPT

VLAD SHUT THE RUSTY CAR DOOR behind him, thankful that it didn't fall off its hinges, and followed Andrew to the sidewalk, where the other goths were waiting. They'd ridden in Andrew's car. Andrew was the only one among them with a license, and also the only one with what could possibly pass as a vehicle. But it didn't matter that Andrew's car was rusty, loud, and unlikely to survive the winter. It didn't matter that the chill of mid-February couldn't be kept out by its metal frame as it barreled down the highway. It didn't matter that the outside was four different colors, and that the inside smelled like old milk. Vlad—and the rest of Andrew's friends, he was certain—was incredibly envious that Andrew even had a license, let alone a car. Truth be told, Vlad was dying to own anything that he could refer to as a car—even a piece of crap like this. A car meant freedom. A car meant cool.

The outside of the club didn't look like much. In fact, it resembled all sorts of places Vlad had seen in movies— mostly, places people ended up dying in. It had no windows, and but for the spray-painted sign above the door that read *The Crypt* in large, swirling letters, Vlad would have no idea that this was the club his new friends were taking him to.

October smiled at Vlad, her lip piercing glinting in the streetlight. "You okay, Vlad?"

Vlad shrugged. He was actually pretty nervous about tonight, but he wasn't about to give the goths any reason not to like him. "Yeah, I'm cool. This is it, huh?"

"Wait till you see inside. It's Goth Heaven." Sprat grinned and tilted a handful of open Pixy Stix up, filling his mouth full of flavored sugar. He offered some to Vlad, but Vlad shook his head. His stomach was already jumping from nerves. The last thing it needed was sugar.

Kristoff brushed his silver hair from his eyes, lined thick with black, and pulled the dull black door open. Music, heavy with bass, poured out from inside the club, reverberating through Vlad's chest in a strangely familiar way, even though he didn't recognize the tune at all. Suddenly, Vlad was seized by a warning sensation in his chest. It was something he couldn't explain, but he was overwhelmed by nervousness inspired by the unfamiliar. And there was no way out of this ... not that he was necessarily against the idea of hanging out with the goth kids. After all, hadn't he wanted to do this for a while now? To connect with them? Just what was he afraid of?

Kristoff gestured inside with a snort. "Come on already."

October led the way, followed by Andrew, who couldn't seem to stop staring at his shoes. Sprat tugged the shoulder of Vlad's jacket until they were heading down the hallway. Behind them, Kristoff kept his distance, as if signaling to anyone who might see that he wasn't a follower. The door closed, sealing them all inside the long hallway that led, presumably, to the club. The walls were painted a deep blood-red. The carpet matched. The floor slanted downward, and as they walked, Vlad felt like they were descending deep into the earth. The sensation was discomforting.

They turned a corner at the bottom of the hallway ramp and entered the club. Vlad gasped.

The walls and floors of The Crypt were painted black. There were no windows, but the corners of the room were home to long velvet drapes in rich eggplant purple. Along the walls, there were hundreds of empty picture frames.

October caught his eye and smiled again, straining to be heard over the music's pumping vibes. "Empty picture frames are supposed to catch the souls of any ghosts that might be lurking around."

Vlad raised a sharp, disbelieving eyebrow. "Really?"

She shrugged and moved out of Kristoff's way as he walked to one of the fluffy velvet sofas in the corner of the room. "That's what they say."

"Who?"

"You know . . . *they*." She laughed softly and pointed to a long black counter, lit by black lights. The entire room was fairly dim, but the bar seemed to be its heart. "They have juice, soda, glow jewelry, candy, coffee, tea, this vampire energy drink, and a bunch of other stuff, if you're interested."

Vlad bit his tongue in surprise at her mention of the V word. "Vampire energy drink?"

She nodded and wrinkled her nose. "It's way too sugary for me, but Sprat loves it, says it's better than Red Bull. Come on, I'll introduce you to everybody."

She led him across the room to the group of velvet couches in the corner. On the wall above one couch hung an oversize mirror that looked like it had seen better days. Between the couches, which were covered with several throw pillows—each one more tasseled and velvet than the last—sat an old trunk that had been painted black and acted as a coffee table. October gestured to the group that was sitting there. "Everyone, Vlad. Vlad, everyone."

Several kids nodded at him. Some found their way to the dance floor. A few excused themselves to unknown destinations. Vlad took a seat at the end of one of the couches. Its cushions were worn and well-loved. He sank into its fluffiness and slipped off his jacket. He still couldn't shake the feeling of impending doom, but attributed it to the fact that outside of Henry, Joss, and Meredith, he'd never really hung out with anyone for an extended period of time. He wasn't sure how to act. Or what to say.

Sprat flopped down on the couch beside Vlad. From the way he couldn't seem to stop moving, Vlad thought the sugar rush from all those Pixy Stix had probably finally hit him. The lapels of Sprat's many-buckled jacket were covered with buttons. Most of them belonged to bands, but a few were pretty funny. Like the one that read MY FAMILY'S A FREAK SHOW WITHOUT A TENT and the one that boldly proclaimed I (HEART) BEING AWESOME. Vlad pointed to the one that read I'M SO GOTH PEOPLE ASK ME TO AUTOGRAPH BOXES OF COUNT CHOCULA and smirked. "Where'd you get that?"

Sprat looked down at the button and beamed. "You want it?"

But before Vlad could insist that he wasn't goth, Sprat had removed the button from his lapel and pinned it to Vlad's shirt. Vlad nodded his thanks, but he wasn't sure Sprat saw, as Sprat had all but run onto the dance floor.

October returned from the bar and thrust a plastic goblet into Vlad's hand. The thick red liquid inside sloshed against the glass, almost spilling. Vlad sniffed, but it was hard to discern what he smelled in the glass. At first, he thought it might actually be blood, but then he realized that not only would that be ridiculous—after all, why would a human hand him a cup of blood?—but also that the scent of blood pumping furiously through veins as the teens danced behind him was throwing off his sense of smell. He took a sip. It was sugary sweet, and nothing at all like blood, except for its appearance. Vlad wrinkled his nose but drank it anyway. He didn't want to be rude.

Kristoff lounged on the couch across from him, one leg flung over the lap of a very pretty girl with raven black hair and pale china skin. The girl shoved his leg away and leaned forward, smiling at Vlad. "You have such lovely eyes."

Vlad swallowed, shifting uncomfortably. He'd never been smooth at taking compliments. "Uh, thanks."

She extended a hand, her silver bracelets clinking together on her wrist. "I'm Snow."

Vlad took her hand in his, and the moment their skin touched, he inhaled a whiff of her scent, the blood pumping through her veins. It was almost dizzying. He managed a smile. "Cool name."

Snow smiled, parting her burgundy lips. "Thanks."

Vlad took another drink of the red, slushy liquid, hoping to distract himself from the delectable scent of Snow's blood. It was almost irresistible. AB negative, he was certain.

As if tiring of not being the center of attention, Kristoff eyed Vlad with an air of indifference, and said, "Just so you know, I'm a vampire."

Vlad nearly spit out a mouthful of "blood" and resisted

the urge to laugh. Kristoff was no more a vampire than Principal Snelgrove.

Kristoff opened his mouth, revealing pretty realistic fangs—they'd probably been made by a professional costumer. They were impressive. But not real.

Vlad dropped his eyes momentarily to his glass, suddenly cautious of the strange feelings that were boiling up within him. He was tempted to reveal that he was one too.

He mulled over the idea, all the while sipping the sickly sweet concoction that October had given him. On one hand, he knew that Kristoff was pretending. On the other, he had an edge, an insight to what vampires were really like—not to mention the urge to one-up the guy who seemed to think he was so much better than everyone else. Besides, as far as Kristoff knew, Vlad was pretending too. Trying hard not to think about possible repercussions, Vlad forced himself to swallow and met Kristoff's serious gaze with a knowing smirk. "Then we have more in common than I thought."

Snow grinned and moved from Kristoff's side to Vlad's. The scent of her was maddening. "I knew it! The moment I saw you, I was all 'That guy's a vampire.' How long have you been playing?"

Playing? Vlad blinked. He had absolutely no clue what she was talking about, but if she didn't keep her distance, he was going to make a seriously bad first impression. Vlad scooted over half a cushion. The distance wasn't much, but it was something. "For as long as I can remember."

"Liar." Kristoff's voice was low, but ragged. He glared at Vlad, then looked aghast at the rest of the group. "What? He's clearly lying. *Vampire: The Masquerade* has only been in existence for like a decade."

As if a lightbulb had flickered on over his head, Vlad relaxed. "Oh, I don't play that game. I'm just . . . well, a bloodsucking monster. You know."

Snow smiled brightly. October and the others were all looking at Vlad as if he were the coolest person on the planet. Kristoff sulked.

It didn't matter that they were pretending, that they didn't really believe that they were in the presence of a real, actual vampire. What mattered was that he had confessed, had come out with the truth, and not one of them—well, except for Kristoff, but he didn't count—had balked at the idea. Rather than fear him, they seemed to respect him. Even if it wasn't real to them, it meant a lot to Vlad.

Snow and October exchanged glances—they seemed to be speaking in that weird telepathic way girls have. Vampires might be good at carrying on conversations with their minds, but all of Elysia couldn't hold a candle to the female population.

The girls each grabbed one of Vlad's hands and dragged him out to the dance floor. Horrific images of spinning in slow circles at school dances flitted through his mind and Vlad dug his heels into the floor, shaking his head emphatically, but it was useless. They tugged harder until finally he was immersed in the crowd on the dance floor. The music was a heavy techno with bass so loud that Vlad could feel it pounding in his chest. As if in response, his pulse began to race.

Snow put her arms in the air, swaying slowly even though the music was pretty fast in tempo. October moved her feet like crazy and jumped up and down. Vlad closed his eyes and listened to the incredible blend of music, chatter, and beating hearts. If he listened close enough, he could almost make out the rushing of blood through veins. With a smile, and his eyes still closed, Vlad danced to his own music.

A long, long time later—Vlad couldn't tell just how long, as the music and the blood seemed to pump nonstop—he opened his eyes and realized he was having the time of his life. He grinned at October, who grinned back, and then he shouted, "This place is so cool! Do you think next time I could bring Henry?"

October burst out laughing. "Henry McMillan? I don't think he'd like it like you do, Vlad."

Vlad yelled over the music, "Why not?"

"Because you're goth and he's not." She shook her purple-streaked head. "He wouldn't get it."

Vlad's feet slowed to a stop. "But I'm not goth."

Both Snow and October stopped in their tracks and stared at him. "Wow, Vlad!" Snow shouted. "You're so goth you don't even know you're goth."

Vlad shook his head, bewildered. "I'm gonna take a break, okay?"

The girls nodded, and Vlad headed back to the couch, where Kristoff sat scowling into a goblet of the syrupy red "blood" mixture. Vlad took a seat across from him but didn't say anything. He had a strong feeling that Kristoff didn't care very much for his company.

Kristoff met Vlad's gaze. "Don't you have better things to do than go slumming with us?"

Vlad raised an eyebrow. "Did I do something to offend you? I wasn't aware we hated each other."

"Just stay out of my way. And keep away from October."

Sudden realization hit Vlad, and he smiled inwardly. Kristoff had a thing for October and thought Vlad was trying to edge his way in. He couldn't have been more wrong. "It's not like that, man. I have a girlfriend."

Kristoff grew very quiet. Subdued. Almost calm. After several minutes, they were joined by a girl who looked like a china doll. Kristoff stood when she approached and took her hand in his. "Ah . . . dinner has arrived."

Vlad couldn't imagine biting through all that makeup just to get to her veins, but hey . . . whatever does it for you.

Then Kristoff swept the girl into his arms and, once she moved her hair to the side, he bit her on the neck. The fangs weren't real. Vlad knew that much. But seeing something that resembled his own fangs sinking into flesh—not breaking skin, but biting nonetheless—sent Vlad's fangs shooting from his gums, and suddenly it was all he could do not to rip the girl from Kristoff's arms and indulge in every last delicious drop of her. Vlad clutched the couch cushion and forced his eyes away.

But it wasn't enough to keep him from thinking about what he'd seen, or to stop his stomach from rumbling.

Moving as quickly as he could, Vlad hurried toward the nearest exit, which opened up to a back alley. The music blared into the night until the door swung shut, muffling the trance-inducing beats. Vlad leaned against the building's outer brick wall, resting his head back. His fangs were fully elongated and, try as he might to will them under control, they wouldn't shrink. The gums beneath them pulsed with hunger.

In hindsight, he should have known better than to come to a club full of humans without bringing a backpack full of blood—not that he thought it would have been enough to prevent this. His bloodthirst had grown to obnoxious levels, and lately, just the scent of blood and adrenaline coursing through a group of humans' veins was enough to bring his fangs out and set his stomach rumbling. He was losing control, and he had to find a way to rein himself in. And fast.

The side door swung open, and out stepped Snow. Vlad

eyed her for a moment, her porcelain skin, that perfect blue vein that ran up one side of her neck. It moved slightly, pulsing with life—oddly, in sync with Vlad's gums. Vlad tore his eyes away and slid his thumbs in his front pockets, making certain his lips were covering his fangs at all times. "It's cold out here. You should go back inside."

Snow cast a timid glance back at the door, her eyes shimmering, the black eyeliner under her left eye smudged. "I can't. My dad's in there."

And that's when Vlad noticed the red mark on her left cheek . . . about the size of a hand. "Did . . . Snow . . . did someone hit you?"

Tears poured from her dark eyes and she nodded, drawing her arms around her small frame. "My dad. He's drunk again. He's always doing this."

The door swung open again, and a burly man with a swagger in his step stumbled into the alley. His words were slurred. "You better get home like I told you. Hanging around these freaks—didn't I raise you better?"

Vlad stepped in front of Snow, ready to defend her. She was, after all, such a tiny girl, and her father a hulking mass of muscle and flab. "I'll make sure she gets home okay, sir."

The man shoved Vlad aside and, closing the gap between him and his daughter, started to unbuckle his belt. "This time I'll knock it right out of you. Teach you a lesson you won't forget."

Snow backed up against the wall and squeezed her eyes shut, as if she knew she could no longer run from his abuse. Her cheeks, coated with tears, glistened in the streetlight.

Vlad didn't think. He didn't have time to think about what was right and what was wrong, about who might see and who might not. He grabbed the man and pulled him back, then shoved him as hard as he was able.

Snow's father hit the ground several yards away. He groaned in pain, stood, and ran off. To where, Vlad didn't know. But at least he was gone.

And Vlad was left with the understanding that shoving Tom that hard last year hadn't been a fluke. Apparently, another skill Vikas and Otis had yet to mention was vampiric strength. He flexed his fingers and turned back to Snow, who looked beautiful despite her tears. "Hey. He's gone now. You can open your eyes."

Snow looked down the alley, then blinked at Vlad, confused. "Where did he go?"

Vlad shrugged. "Let's just say I convinced him to go home and sleep it off."

She met his eyes, and understanding filled them. Then she wrapped her arms around him and hugged him, nice and tight and close. Her skin smelled like roses and Vlad drank in her scent, so sweet. He couldn't resist placing a small kiss on her pretty cheek, still moist from tears. And then another, on the smooth, pale skin of her jawline. And one more, just one, as he inhaled her sweet, irresistible scent, on her neck. He could taste the salt of her tears as he placed each kiss, and when he kissed her neck, they flowed into his mouth and over his tongue. They weren't salty anymore, but sweet, like her scent, like her. And she tasted ... *so* ... good.

Vlad's jaw tightened, bracing her neck against his jaw even tighter. He knew he was drinking from her, swallowing mouthfuls of blood, but he couldn't stop, no matter how he tried. He swallowed and swallowed, feeling terrible that he was feeding from her, but not caring that he couldn't seem to stop. He couldn't recall when he'd started. The kiss on her neck, he surmised. But there was no stopping, no walking away now. There was just her blood and his hunger. Nothing more. Nothing else seemed to matter at the moment.

Vlad slipped his arms around her, cradling her body as she trembled, then weakened into his embrace. Her heartbeat was fluttering against his chest, each beat sending a splash of crimson onto his tongue. And he swallowed, drinking it down, so much better than anything he'd ever tasted before. He wanted more, so he took it, ignoring the fact that her heart was rattling at a dangerous rate, that he was probably killing her, that she was a human and he'd vowed not to do exactly what he was doing right now, never, never, never. But he was doing it. He had to. It was so sweet and tasty and filled his muscles with an energy he'd never felt before. And she tasted ... so ... *good.*

And finally, his belly was full, but Vlad kept drinking, just to taste her, just to have her blood coursing through him just a little bit longer. The idea that she was dying sent an excited chill through him . . .

. . . and that's when Vlad's stomach clenched. He shoved the girl away from him, not caring that she was going to fall onto the hard pavement, only that she'd be away from him, and safe . . . safer than she was in his arms. His fingers were trembling, a twisted blend of fear, excitement, and insatiable need. His face felt warm and flushed. His feet refused to remain still, so Vlad paced the alley, his dark eyes locked on the nearly unconscious girl lying next to the Dumpster.

He'd almost killed her.

He'd almost taken her life, all because he couldn't control his hunger.

And what had set him off? The taste of her tears? Vlad retched at the thought.

It had been too easy. He'd gotten too close. And it could never, ever happen again.

The girl stirred, as if waking from a dream. She sat up, bruised from her fall and weak from Vlad's feast, but the glazed expression in her eyes said that she likely didn't recall exactly what had happened. She rubbed her neck and stretched, looking around the alley in confusion. When her eyes met Vlad's, he took a step back, as if the distance would help.

It wouldn't.

He knew that, just as sure as he knew that the only thing keeping him from crossing the alley and drinking the last of her blood until she'd slipped into death's arms was his dire fear of enjoying such a terrible, disgusting act, his utter terror of himself.

Snow blinked at him, still dazed. "Vlad?"

Vlad swallowed hard, the taste of her crimson still on his tongue.

"What happened? Did I fall?"

Vlad paused, then nodded slowly.

Then, because there was nothing more that he could do, Vlad turned and walked away, down the alley, down the street, until he was blocks away from the club, from the girl with the salty sweet tears, from the part of him that he couldn't bear to be near. Along the way, he tried once again to reach Otis with his thoughts, but Otis still wasn't answering, so Vlad kept his head down and walked until he'd found a pay phone. He dialed Henry's cell number, cursing Nelly for not letting him have one, and waited for the rings to cease. Finally, they did. "Yeah?"

Vlad licked his lips, took a deep breath, and squeezed the phone closer to his mouth. "Henry? I need your help."

He could almost hear the irritation in Henry's breath. For a long time Henry didn't answer. When he did, his voice was tense. "What makes you think I'll help you? Going to order me to?"

"Henry..." Vlad's eyes brimmed with tears. "I just fed on a human."

And he broke. The sobs came quickly, his body shook. And his stomach, so full of irresistible blood, ached as it had never ached before.

Henry's tone softened, once more the friend that Vlad had always had, once more his loyal drudge... but more, he was Henry. He was Vlad's number one. "Tell me where you are. I'll be right there."

19
THE OTHER'S GOLD

ENRY'S ROOM WAS DARK, LIT ONLY BY THE GLOW of the moon through the open curtains. Vlad was sitting on Henry's bed, trying desperately not to look at Henry, who watched him from his desk chair across the room. They hadn't spoken since Henry had pulled up in Greg's car. It had been a long, quiet drive.

Henry would probably catch hell from his brother for taking the car, but Vlad was pretty sure Greg wouldn't clue their parents in to Henry's theft—or his driving without a license. Some secrets were important to keep. Luckily, Greg recognized that. Even if he had no clue what Henry's secret was. Vlad gripped the edge of the mattress, trying to get ahold of his insatiable thirst.

Henry ran a hand through his hair and sighed. "Do you want to talk about it?"

Vlad's eyes moved to his friend's neck. Otis was right. There was nothing like feeding from the source. And now that Vlad had had a taste, he knew he would always yearn for another. He gripped the mattress tighter and forced his eyes away. "Not yet."

Henry nodded thoughtfully. "Hungry? I can run to your house and grab something."

"It's not that. My stomach is full. It's just . . ."

"You want more."

They exchanged understanding glances, and Vlad eased up on the mattress. He looked at Henry. "It's like I just realized that paradise is all around me, lurking in the veins of people. It's wrong. I know it's wrong. But it's all I can think about right now. As if the moment I swallowed that girl's blood, it woke up this thing inside me. This hunger. This . . . beast."

Henry stood and Vlad winced, blurting out, "Don't come any closer."

Henry hesitated, then crossed the room anyway and sat on the bed beside Vlad. "You won't hurt me, Vlad. I know that."

Vlad wanted to believe that, but he just wasn't sure. "I don't. Not anymore."

Henry went quiet for a while. After a long time, he whispered, "Did you kill her?"

Vlad licked his lips, the taste of her blood still, incredibly, on his tongue. "No. But I wanted to."

The image of Snow's sweet face floated at the front of Vlad's imagination, followed shortly by the feeling of his fangs as they'd sunk into her pale flesh. Vlad broke, and hot tears streamed down his face. "Oh God, Henry! I'm sick. I'm a monster. Joss was right!"

Henry shook his head adamantly. "You are not a monster, and my idiot cousin couldn't have been more wrong. You're just..."

He looked at Vlad, as if trying to determine just what exactly Vlad had become. Finally, he shrugged. "Well, I guess your needs are just changing."

Vlad dried his eyes on his sleeve and took a deep, shuddering breath. "Otis mentioned that. Before he left. He told me that if I didn't start feeding on humans, I could become a danger to the people I care about."

He ran a trembling hand through his hair. The smell of warm, delicious human blood was calling to him from within Henry's veins. He had to get a grip. "What am I supposed to do?"

The room grew silent as they both mulled over the possibilities in their minds. It didn't take long, as there weren't many to be considered.

Henry cleared his throat, and in a raspy voice said, "You

could feed off me. I mean, if you needed to. Just until you release me, y'know?"

"No. I won't feed off a person ever again. I just . . . can't." But glimpsing the vein on Henry's neck told him that he could. And if Henry didn't keep his distance, Vlad would.

Henry gauged his reaction for a moment, then said, "Then we need to find another solution. What about teachers? They're not really people."

Vlad cracked a smile. "Think that would help my geometry grade?"

Henry chuckled. "Nothing can help that, Vlad."

Vlad took a deep breath and let it out slowly. His hunger diminished some, enough to make him feel like maybe he wasn't going to rip into Henry's veins. "Hey, Henry?"

"Yeah?"

"Does this mean we can hang out again?"

Henry looked taken aback. "I never said we couldn't hang out."

"You said it. Maybe not with words, but your actions said everything." Vlad swallowed the large lump that had formed in his throat. "You're sick of me, remember?"

Henry winced. "Vlad, I—"

"Just tell me one thing." Vlad swallowed again, but his throat was still very dry. He glanced at Henry. "If I hadn't bitten you when we were eight, if I hadn't made you into my drudge, would we still be friends?"

There was a long pause. After several minutes, Vlad began to wonder if Henry was ever going to speak—or worse, if Henry's silence was doing the talking for him.

Henry ran his hand through his hair again. He sighed, stood, and crossed the room. He wasn't pacing, but it sure seemed like he was having a difficult time sitting still. And with every sigh, every step, Vlad became more and more worried that his fears hadn't been irrational, that maybe Henry really was only friends with him because of the drudge thing.

Finally Henry stopped moving and shoved his hands into his front pockets. He dropped his eyes to the floor—his tone followed. "How can you even ask me that question, Vlad? How can you doubt that I'd be your friend no matter what, despite some stupid vampire virus that you knew nothing about at the time?"

He met Vlad's eyes, hurt shimmering in his. "Of course we'd be friends."

A strange mixture of guilt and relief flooded over Vlad, and when he sighed, it seemed to make it easier to breathe, like an enormous weight had been lifted off his shoulders. He nodded quietly at Henry, showing his relief that their friendship was real. Henry didn't just hang out with him because of some vampire master's spell. He actually liked Vlad. And that was pretty cool.

Vlad cleared his throat. "So, what's with the distance lately?"

Henry sank into his desk chair again. "To be honest, I've

been really stupid. Questioning why you never gave me a choice about being your drudge. Stuff like that. It's not like you knew what biting me would do. And I was the one who suggested it."

He grew quiet for a long time. When he spoke, his voice was but a whisper in the quiet dark of the room. "I guess I've just been wondering if you'd wander off someday with your vampire friends and leave me behind. I mean, why wouldn't you pick vampires over me?"

Vlad's jaw nearly hit the floor. He never imagined that Henry, Mr. Cool, king of make-out and popularity galore, would be worried about Vlad leaving him behind. He shook his head vehemently. "Because you're Henry. Because you're my best friend, and I can't picture any part of my life without you in it."

Their eyes met. After another long silence, Henry smirked. "So should we hug now, or . . . ?"

Vlad chuckled, putting a hand up. "Hey man, I missed you. But I didn't miss you that much."

Henry grinned, then grew more serious and said, "It would be easier to be your drudge if you didn't order me around."

"Sometimes it's just easier to tell you to do something instead of ask." Vlad shrugged as a wave of guilt crashed over him. "I know that's wrong . . . but it's true."

After a moment, Henry cleared his throat and said, "So, have you heard anything from Otis lately?"

Vlad shook his head, pulling the letter he'd just received from Vikas from his back pocket. "Nothing yet. But I'd written to Vikas to see if he knew what was going on with Otis and he wrote back a couple of weeks ago, said he had no idea but would check into it. I wrote him again, and just got a letter back this morning."

"What did he say?"

Vlad unfolded the parchment, revealing Vikas's perfect cursive, and read aloud.

Vladimir—

I was both elated and disappointed to receive another letter from you. I had my hopes raised that by now you might have been able to overcome the distance between us and reach me by telepathy. But regardless, it was wonderful to hear from you, Mahlyenki Dyavol.

But I return your good tidings with sad confusion, as I am still unable to locate your uncle. The last I heard from him, he had planned to visit, but when he did not show, I took it to mean that his plans had changed. Regarding your concerns, please allow me to put your fears to rest. Your uncle has not been arrested. If he had been, I would have learned of his arrest immediately, as I have friends in each of the councils. You may call them "spies."

You asked about the relationship between your father and D'Ablo—a question I admittedly find most curious.

It is true, Tomas and D'Ablo were friends. But they were not friends in the same way that Otis and Tomas and I were friends, or that you and your drudge are friends (something that, I admit, boggles the mind). They were friends in the way that a mentor and one who is mentored are friends. D'Ablo looked up to Tomas, and rightfully so. Your father was an ingenious man. And D'Ablo desperately wanted to be like him.

As for your nightmares, I am convinced that those are brought on by the stress of your uncle's absence. Do not worry, Mahlyenki Dyavol. I am certain Otis has his reasons for such silence, and that he will be in touch shortly.

In Brotherhood,
Vikas

Henry spoke quietly, his words sending a shiver down Vlad's spine. "So, they were friends?"

"More mentor and mentored, it seems, but yeah." Vlad folded the note and returned it to his pocket. "I wonder what my dad would think of his onetime friend trying to take his son's life."

"Repeatedly." Henry met his gaze, his eyes brimming with concern. "Why didn't you tell me you were still having nightmares?"

Vlad shrugged. "You were distracted. But yeah, I'm still

having them. Not to mention the weird visit I got from a vampire named Ignatius."

Henry gave him a look, and Vlad poured his guts out, filling his friend in on all of the details that he'd missed out on. After he finished, Henry hesitantly said, "Listen, Vlad. About me not wanting to be your drudge anymore . . ."

"It's okay, Henry." Vlad wet his lips. His mouth felt horrifically dry. "I get it. I do. And it's okay. But releasing you involves another bite—"

A momentary flash of fear crossed Henry's eyes.

"—and right now I'm just not sure that's such a good idea."

"Okay. But we'll talk about it later, right?"

Vlad winced at his friend's reaction, but understood it completely. "Of course. I should get home. Nelly's going to be irate that I was out so late."

Henry shrugged, as if the solution were obvious. "Why don't you just crash here for the night?"

"And tell her what?"

"Tell her it was my fault you got in so late, and I begged you to sleep over."

Vlad mulled this over for a minute. It wouldn't be the first time he'd stayed at Henry's house without letting Nelly know in advance. Of course, there was the maddening scent of Henry's blood to be considered. . . .

"You'll be safe. I promise," he said. "I won't attack you or anything."

Henry frowned and grabbed one of the pillows from his bed. He tossed it to Vlad. "Who are you trying to convince, Vlad? Me or you?"

Vlad bit his bottom lip and lay down on the floor, curling up on his side. He was too terrified to admit that he didn't know the answer to Henry's question.

Vlad tried desperately to tug his arms free, but the straps held fast, digging into his wrists and ankles, refusing to release him.

The shadowed man lifted the blade over his chest and plunged it deep between his ribs. Vlad screamed, howling from the pain. As his torturer pulled the knife out and stabbed him again, he lost his voice, unable to express with mere shrieking how unbearable the pain was. Blood gushed from his torso, spilling onto the floor below.

His torturer leaned forward, into the light, and Vlad was not at all surprised to see his face, which was twisted in an expression of immense satisfaction.

D'Ablo.

"Vlad! Vlad!" Henry shook him awake from his nightmare.

Vlad sat up, eyes wide. His hands were trembling as he combed back the hair from his sweat-drenched face.

"You were screaming. Are you okay?"

Vlad shook his head. It was his nightmare again. His never-ending nightmare. "The journal, Henry. He wants the journal. And he won't stop sending me these nightmares until I give it to him."

"I thought you were convinced the dreams were a vision of the future."

"I think maybe I was wrong. I think they're a threat." Vlad gasped, trying to calm his nerves, and failing miserably. "I'm giving it to him. I just can't take this anymore."

Henry's tone softened. "Are you sure you want to do that? You know he probably has some pretty twisted reasons for wanting it."

Vlad lay back down, phantom pain still lighting up his chest. "I don't think I have much of a choice."

Henry paused, then said, "Well, do what you gotta do, man. Now get some sleep, okay?"

Vlad curled up on his side, his fingers still trembling. That was it, then. The decision was made. He had to hand over the journal to D'Ablo.

He tried to comfort himself with the knowledge that he'd memorized every page and there was nothing within it that D'Ablo shouldn't necessarily see. But still sleep came very slowly. And when it did, it was filled with more nightmares.

The worst Vlad had yet experienced.

20
GROUNDED

NELLY'S VOICE HAD RISEN SO HIGH that it had left the realm of hysterical about five octaves ago. "Vladimir, I don't know what's gotten into you lately. First, you nearly bite Meredith. Then you get detention for skipping class and kissing in the supply room—"

"It was a broom closet, and I wasn't skipping class."

"—and now you're hanging out with a new set of friends who keep you out all hours of the night, with no explanation of where you've been or what you've been doing."

Vlad took a deep breath, buying time to go over his and Henry's story once more in his mind before speaking it out loud. "I told you, Nelly. We went to this club in Stokerton, and afterward I ran into Henry. He said he'd give me a ride home, but he got distracted by a girl, and then I stayed over at his place so I wouldn't wake you up."

Nelly shook her head. "And just how long did it take you and Henry to come up with that feeble excuse?"

Vlad pursed his lips. Nelly was smarter than he'd been giving her credit for.

When she spoke again, her voice cracked. "And exactly why is the front of the shirt you wore last night covered in what looks like dried blood?"

Vlad stared at the shirt for a moment, trying to find the right words. There was no way he could tell her the truth, no way he could burden her with his horrific, beastly act. Meeting her gaze, he saw suspicion lurking in her eyes. He replied with a blatant lie, mostly so they could both go on pretending that he was a normal teenager. Better that way. Let Nelly have her delusions. "I got sloppy with a snack pack, okay?"

The hurt expression on Nelly's face cut Vlad deep, but it was better than telling her the truth and seeing fear there instead. She dropped his shirt back into the laundry basket and lowered her voice, as well as her eyes. "You're grounded. One week for doing whatever you were doing last night. And one week for lying to me about it. Now go upstairs."

A lump formed in Vlad's throat. Nelly had never spoken to him that way before, or sent him to his room. He knew he deserved far, far worse for what he was putting her through. But it was better to lie and hurt her some than tell the truth and break her heart completely.

With a slumped posture, Vlad made his way up the stairs to his room, closing the door softly behind him. Before the door closed entirely, Vlad thought he heard soft weeping from downstairs. The sound of it made his chest ache. *I'm sorry, Nelly,* he thought. *I'm so sorry . . . for everything.*

He lay on his bed for a while, staring at the ceiling, trying not to think about his conversation with Nelly or the fact that he missed Otis more than ever. He thought a little about Meredith, about his almost uncontrollable hunger, and wondered exactly how he could protect her from his dire thirst. Drinking from Snow had been paradise—a paradise he didn't want to revisit with Meredith. But how could he save her from his hungry advances without distancing himself?

Mostly he focused on how he was going to give D'Ablo the journal. Being grounded complicated matters, but not by much. He contemplated calling Henry, to let him know that he was going to sneak into Stokerton tonight to pay D'Ablo a visit—after all, somebody should know his whereabouts, just in case something happened—but he wasn't entirely sure he would be allowed a phone call. After several minutes, he cracked open his door and slowly made his way downstairs.

Nelly was sitting on the couch, quietly flipping through the pages of a magazine that Vlad was almost certain she wasn't reading. He stood at the bottom of the stairs for a long moment, unsure of what he should say. Finally, he cleared his throat softly. When she didn't look up, he knew she was angry, but he wasn't surprised. She had every right to be. He took a breath and said, "Can I call Henry?"

Nelly blinked up at him, her eyes red from crying. "I don't know. Are you allowed phone calls?"

Vlad sighed and sat on the bottom step. "I don't know. Don't you kinda make up the rules on that?"

"Your mom would know what to do." Nelly's voice cracked. "If she was still here, things would be different. You wouldn't be acting the way you've been acting."

Vlad tilted his head, meeting her eyes. "How have I been acting?"

Nelly reached for another tissue, tears retracing the tracks on her cheeks. "Like a teenager, I suppose. But you have to understand, Vladimir, I've never dealt with a teenager before. Let alone a teenager as . . . special as you."

Special. Vlad's insides shrank a little. What a nice way of pointing out what a freak of nature he was. He was sure Nelly hadn't meant it that way, but that didn't erase the hurt.

Nelly took a shuddered breath. "I have no idea what I'm doing."

Vlad's face flushed, and he felt sick to his stomach. He had no idea he'd been hurting Nelly like that. "Nelly, I've been a teenager for a couple of years now. And you're doing fine. I just . . . there's a lot of stuff going on right now that I can't talk to you about."

Nelly's eyes grew wide with concern. "What kind of stuff? Girl stuff? Friend stuff? Drug stuff? Gang stuff?"

Vlad suppressed a smile. It was sweet how she worried endlessly about him. "More like vampire stuff."

"Oh." Nelly relaxed some, then asked, "Do you want to talk about it?"

Vlad sighed and ran a hand through his hair, brushing his bangs from his eyes. "That's the thing. I want to, but there are these . . . laws. And I'm not exactly sure what I can tell you and what I can't."

Nelly nodded. "Otis mentioned something about vampiric laws. He said that he broke one in telling me he was a vampire, and that that's one of the reasons he can't stay here with us."

Vlad blinked, suddenly curious what else Otis had shared with his guardian. "That's one of them. But there are a ton more, and I have to be careful not to break any more. Because I don't want to put you in any more danger from Elysia just because I couldn't keep my mouth shut."

Nelly was quiet for a good long time. Finally she dried

her eyes and nodded. "That makes sense, I suppose. So what you're saying is, don't ask too many questions?"

Vlad sighed, the sick feeling dissipating. "That's about it, yeah. I wish Otis were here."

"So do I, sweetie." Nelly straightened in her seat. "Okay. But I have to ask one question, or I'll never be able to sleep at night. Did something happen last night that you can't tell me . . . or that you won't?"

Then it was Vlad's turn to be quiet. Finally he shook his head, hoping she'd believe his lie. For both their sakes. "It's not what you think, Nelly. I meant what I said before. I just got a little messy with a midnight snack, that's all."

To his enormous relief, Nelly visibly relaxed. "You should be more careful, Vladimir."

He nodded, the burden of guilt heavy on his chest. "I know. I'll try."

Nelly nodded in return. "Are you going to call Henry now?"

"Am I still grounded?"

She sighed and met Vlad's eyes with a forgiving smile. "I suppose I can't really ground you for trying to protect me."

Vlad shoved his hands in his pockets and turned to walk out of the room, then paused and looked back at his aunt. "Thanks, Nelly."

Before he could reach for the phone, there was a knock at the door. Vlad opened it to reveal Henry, who looked as if he'd just run all the way from his house. Breathless, Henry steadied himself again the doorjamb and managed to puff out, "I thought of a safe way you can hand over the journal."

Vlad hushed him and opened the door, muttering quietly to Nelly as he ascended the stairs that he and Henry were going to hang out in his room for a while. Once safe inside his bedroom with the door firmly shut, Vlad turned to Henry and said, "First off, how did you know I've been making plans all day to return the journal, and second off, what are the odds you'd show up at my house just as I was about to call you?"

"You mentioned giving back the journal last night. And . . . I dunno, I just couldn't shake the idea. What's the big deal?"

Vlad shook his head. He didn't want to bring up how Henry always seemed to show up when Vlad needed him, even without being told. It was like he could beckon his drudge without even thinking about it—something he knew would freak Henry out. "No big deal. I was just curious. What's your plan?"

"We ship it FedEx."

Vlad blinked and tried hard not to look at his best friend like he was a complete and total idiot, but he was pretty sure he was failing. And with good reason.

Henry frowned. "What? It makes the most sense. They'll deliver it straight to D'Ablo and you don't have to share the same air as him."

Vlad shook his head. "So your answer to my problem is to put someone else in harm's way? Henry, what if he killed the FedEx guy?"

"At least it wouldn't be you."

It was touching in an odd way that Henry would rather some poor delivery driver bought the farm than Vlad, but still. "I can't do that. I have to go to Stokerton myself. And I have to do it tonight, after Nelly's asleep."

Henry sighed, scratching his head in frustration. "What time are we leaving?"

"We?" Vlad cocked an eyebrow at him. If Henry thought he was tagging along, he was crazy. It was stupid enough that Vlad was willingly going to face the man that had almost been responsible for Vlad's death . . . twice. He wasn't about to subject Henry to D'Ablo's insane bouts of moodiness.

Henry's eyes widened in shock as realization sunk in. "You don't think I'm letting you go back to Elysia to face that jerk alone, do you?"

"Henry, he could *kill* you. I at least have this Pravus thing going for me, y'know? He could hurt me, but I'll live. I know I will. But in order to protect you, I have to leave you here." Vlad met his gaze and held it, wanting very much for Henry to just drop the subject completely and realize that Vlad was only doing it for his own good.

Henry searched Vlad's face. Then his jaw tightened. "Are you going to order me to stay?"

"Do I have to?"

"Look. What if these dreams you've been having are predictions of the future, like you thought? You're gonna need some backup. If you order me to stay here, you'll be on your own, strapped to some bloody table deep in the heart of the council building, right?" Dire need crossed Henry's eyes. The need to help. "Otis isn't here to save you. I am."

Vlad sighed and ran a careless hand through his hair. He chewed his bottom lip for a moment before meeting Henry's eyes again. "We leave at midnight."

Henry grinned, victorious. "I'll drive."

Vlad shook his head. He couldn't believe he and Henry were going to face D'Ablo together—and he really couldn't believe Henry was stupid enough to think they'd actually survive. "There are about a million things wrong with that, but the top two that come to mind are that you don't have a license and you don't have a car."

"I have a permit and I can borrow Greg's car." Vlad must have looked just as horrified at the idea of Henry driving as he felt, because Henry frowned and said, "What? You rode with me last night."

"Last night I was distracted, and fearing more for your life than my own."

Henry huffed. "I'm a good driver."

"Who says? Your mom?"

"Actually, no. She won't even get in the car with me, says it makes her sick to even think of it."

Vlad laughed first, but after a moment, Henry joined in. Vlad was quite certain the worst thing he'd face tonight wasn't D'Ablo—it was the possibility that Henry would forget where the brake pedal was located.

21

Maybe FedEx Wasn't Such a Bad Idea

A T A QUARTER AFTER MIDNIGHT, Vlad finished placing a protective glyph on the front door of Nelly's house, climbed into the passenger seat of Greg's car, and cringed as Henry gunned the engine to life. For a brief moment, as the car lurched forward into the night, Vlad saw his life flash before his eyes, but then they were on their way, and Henry seemed to know what he was doing behind the wheel. After a few minutes of silence, Vlad reached for the radio knob.

"No music!" Henry almost shrieked. Vlad stared at him, wide-eyed, questioning. Finally Henry threw him a glance.

"Sorry. It distracts me. I can't listen to the radio and concentrate on driving at the same time."

Vlad raised his eyebrows and relaxed back in his seat. The last thing he wanted was to distract Henry from the road. "Okay . . . no radio."

An hour later, Henry finally peeled his hands from the steering wheel. They were parked across the street from that familiar thirteen-story office building deep within downtown Stokerton. They sat there in silence for a long time, Henry no doubt recovering from one of the longest driving sessions of his life, and Vlad clutching his father's journal to his chest and staring out the window at D'Ablo's lair. It looked horrifically ominous, framed by a moonless sky, with only the streetlights illuminating it.

There was no sense in delaying any longer.

Vlad opened the door and got out. Henry followed his lead. They were only ten steps from the building when Henry let out a yelp.

Vlad turned to see what was the matter, and what he saw sent his heart racing. Ignatius, the vampire who'd attacked him that dark night in Bathory, had Henry by a fistful of hair. A sharp, curved blade was pressed dangerously close to Henry's throat. "We have unfinished business to attend to, boy."

Vlad set his jaw, more angry than terrified. "Whatever business we have, it's not with my drudge. Let him go."

Not wanting Ignatius to gain the upper hand, Vlad didn't miss a beat. He pushed hard into Ignatius's mind, and Ignatius released his grip on Henry. Henry ducked down and away, running back to the car, as if he knew this fight was beyond him. Then Ignatius clamped down hard on his thoughts—so hard that Vlad's head throbbed—and said, "That was unexpected. But I won't underestimate you again, boy."

As he spoke the last word, a piece of spittle flew from his mouth. His fangs were elongated, his eyes almost glowing with hatred. In a flash, he cocked the knife back and flung it forward. It whistled through the air, straight for Vlad's right eye.

Terrified, Vlad leaned fast to the left. It was like the entire world was moving in slow motion, except for him. He couldn't explain it, had no idea just how he'd done it, exactly. It was just like the first time he'd faced this monster— vampiric speed took over in a rush of instinct and reflex. Only this time, Vlad had more control over his actions. His abilities were growing.

As he leaned, the blade whistled closer, merely inches from his ear. He reached up with that same mysterious, glorious vampire speed and grabbed the knife as it flew, marveling at his own actions. The edge of the blade sliced the small webbing of skin between his forefinger and thumb, but the wound healed almost instantly. Feeling abnormally powerful, Vlad snapped a glare back to Ignatius and raised a daring eyebrow.

Ignatius exploded.

But not in the now-wasn't-that-convenient blood-and-guts-went-flying-everywhere way. More in the blind-fury kind of way.

He flew at Vlad with fists flying, and Vlad stepped back from each blow, wondering exactly why—whether vampire or human—things always seemed to end in a fistfight. Ignatius's knuckles whispered by his face, but Vlad kept moving, kept dodging every attempted blow. Recalling the knife in his hand, Vlad tightened his grip on the handle and slashed the blade across Ignatius's chest, managing only to catch the fabric of his enemy's shirt. Soon the front of Ignatius's shirt was shredded, and what tiny cuts Vlad had managed to make were already healing.

Vlad took another step backward—he was doing it; he was winning and could hardly believe it—and Henry cried out from his place near the car, "Vlad! Behind you!"

Vlad turned with that amazing speed, dodging another blow, still incredulous that he was capable of such a thing, and saw the ledge behind him. One more step and he'd have fallen backward, thirty feet straight down, into a delivery-truck dock. He kept turning, spinning as fast as he could manage, until he saw his target. Lifting the knife into the air, Vlad brought it down hard. The blade sang as it moved through the air, and then all sound ceased as it sank deep into Ignatius's back. Vlad spun around again, feeling the gums around his fangs pulse at the scent of Ignatius's blood, and kicked Ignatius hard in the back, driving the blade deeper still and knocking Ignatius over the ledge, into the shadows below.

Vlad stood there, catching his breath and searching the darkness for any sign of his attacker, for what seemed like an eternity. But nothing moved below. No sounds echoed up to him. He'd defeated Ignatius in one fell swoop and had barely suffered a scratch.

It had been too easy to trust.

His fangs shrank back into his gums. With careful, troubled steps, he walked over to Henry and said, "You okay?"

Henry's eyes were huge and round. "Am I okay? I'm freakin' *awesome!* How did you do that? You were moving so fast I could barely see you!"

Vlad shook his head, the corners of his mouth rising in a smirk. It was pretty cool, after all. "I figured out that I could do that the last time I saw that jerk. Pretty cool, huh?"

"I'll say." Inspiration lit up Henry's face. "Dude, you should try out for the track team. You'd be a star."

Vlad rolled his eyes. "Yeah, that'll happen. C'mon, we should probably get inside in case he comes back."

Henry slapped him on the back as they turned toward the building that housed the Stokerton council. "Whatever you say, hero."

As they walked, Vlad thought he heard a noise, a small rustle in the distance. He glanced back to the docking area, but all was still. He was about to mention it to Henry when a small breeze brushed against his left cheek. He looked over to his friend, panic rising in his chest. Instantly, he was overcome by confusion.

Henry was gone.

Vlad turned full circle, finally noticing his friend flying through the air, as if he'd been thrown. Henry hit the wall of an adjacent building hard, falling in a heap, as if the force had wounded him terribly. Vlad moved his eyes about the area but saw nothing. Then Ignatius's hand flew forward out of the darkness, connecting with Vlad's jaw. The force of the blow sent Vlad through the air, until his back collided with the car several yards behind. The car alarm blared into the night, alerting the world to their presence. Lightning shot through his muscles and Vlad cried out, both in surprise and in pain.

Then Ignatius was standing before him, his fangs exposed. He planted his foot on Vlad's chest, and Vlad's ribs screamed. With a growl, Ignatius pulled his hand back and let it fly, backhanding Vlad again and again. Vlad tried hard to wriggle free, but it was useless. He was stuck. Small bones in Vlad's face cracked. His cheeks swelled. And with every hit, Ignatius dug the heel of his boot deeper into Vlad's chest.

After he was done with Vlad, he was going to feed off

Henry until Henry was no more than a memory. Vlad didn't need to read his twisted mind to know that. The truth of it lurked hotly in Ignatius's eyes.

Ignatius stood tall, but left his boot on Vlad's chest, pinning him to the car. "Now, boy," he hissed. "We finish this."

Ignatius reached back with one hand and tore the curved blade from his back. He gripped it tightly, his own blood dripping from metal to flesh as he held the knife over Vlad, ready to strike the final blow.

Vlad closed his eyes and thought of his parents. It would be nice to see them again, at least. He tried not to think of Nelly, or of Otis. But his efforts were futile.

He knew he would die, Pravus or not. Because Ignatius wouldn't stop until he did.

"Ignatius, stop." A voice—familiar, cold, somewhat bemused. And then a dark figure appeared, moving closer through the fog-filled alleyway by the building.

D'Ablo met Ignatius's gaze and uttered one word with all the strength of a man who is in complete control of a situation. "Enough."

Ignatius stepped back, fury still lighting up his eyes. But he halted his attack, and that was what mattered.

Vlad gulped for air and scrambled away from his attacker to check on Henry. Henry nodded that he was okay, but Vlad was almost certain he'd sprained or maybe broken his ankle during his fall. He helped Henry to his feet and plucked his father's journal from the ground.

D'Ablo gestured to the office building that housed the council rooms. "Please."

They moved up the steps, Henry, barely able to walk, using Vlad's shoulder for support, Vlad limping slightly. D'Ablo didn't speak, only led the way.

As D'Ablo held open the door for Vlad and his drudge, Vlad gestured back to his attacker with his eyes. "Isn't this getting a little old, D'Ablo? Sending your thugs after me? I gotta say, I'm getting really tired of it."

D'Ablo paused, but just barely. "Actually, it wasn't me. The council voted, and *they* sent him after you."

Vlad furrowed his brow. "But you're the president."

"Elysia is a democracy, Vladimir Tod. And I am but one man." A strange expression crossed his eyes—one that made Vlad feel almost sorry for him. Then D'Ablo cleared his throat. "Inside, please. The elevator."

Vlad supported Henry as they made their way through the lobby and stepped inside the elevator. Once inside, Henry held onto the railing, giving Vlad a break. D'Ablo touched the glyph hidden in the wood and a second panel slid down, revealing additional elevator buttons. He turned, momentarily blocking Vlad's view, and pressed one of them. The elevator began its ascent, to the tune of some Muzak melody that Vlad didn't recognize.

Vlad exchanged glances with Henry, who was wincing from the pain but seemed to be holding up all right. Then he cleared his throat and looked at D'Ablo, who was quietly waiting for the elevator doors to open again. He wanted to say something, to let D'Ablo know that he appreciated his calling Ignatius off, that he was relieved to know that it wasn't D'Ablo who had set Ignatius after him. But the words wouldn't come. They were choked down with too many memories of the pain and fear D'Ablo had caused him.

The elevator doors opened and D'Ablo led them down the hall wordlessly, stopping only to pull open a large, ornate metal door. He held it open and gestured inside with a nod. Vlad helped Henry through the door, mentally kicking himself for so easily following the will of his mortal enemy.

But he didn't really have a choice.

The room was dark, except for one corner that was lit by a single candle. D'Ablo stepped inside, closing the door behind him. As he lit several more candles, he spoke—his voice subdued, almost gentle. "Am I to assume you've had a change of heart about entrusting me with your father's journal?"

Vlad helped Henry to a nearby chair and turned to face his worst enemy, a man whose motives he was no longer sure he understood. He pressed the journal protectively to his chest. "Why aren't you trying to kill me?"

Vlad could make out D'Ablo's smirk even in the dim candlelight. "The Pravus can't be killed."

"Yes, but..." Vlad struggled to find the words. "I mean, why are you being...practically nice to me? It's unnerving."

"It has been my lifelong dream to see the Pravus come into being. And here you are." D'Ablo managed an honest smile and held his arms outward. "And here I am, willing servant of he who shall rule over all of vampirekind and enslave the human race."

Vlad thought he detected a note of sarcasm, but at the same time, he wondered if D'Ablo meant it. "I have a really hard time accepting that my father would have been friends with you."

D'Ablo's gaze dropped—but only for a microsecond, barely long enough for it to register—to the journal. "He was my mentor, my teacher, in many ways. I had the utmost respect for Tomas. Friends . . . yes. I suppose we were that too."

Vlad wet his lips and squeezed the journal to his chest, feeling the comfort of its worn leather against him. "Why the journal? My father had many possessions, hundreds of things you could have to remember him by. What's so special about this one?"

"I'm sure you never knew this, Vladimir, but most of your father's belongings were left behind when he fled Elysia. Items that he had spent centuries collecting. Things that held real meaning for him. The trinkets in your house were not much older than you, my boy. They hold no history, no real worth. When he left, the council ordered all of his possessions confiscated and burned. The journal you now hold is the only thing that remains of Tomas Tod the vampire." D'Ablo's posture relaxed some. He looked conflicted. "From before he was Tomas Tod the traitor."

Vlad furrowed his brow. He couldn't help but wonder if that was really how all of Elysia viewed his dad now.

"And besides, that book holds some sentimental value for me personally. You see, Vlad, I was the one who gave it to him."

Vlad shook his head curtly. "That's a lie."

"I assure you, it is not."

"I don't believe you."

D'Ablo sighed indignantly. "See for yourself. Open the front cover. Lower left corner."

After a doubtful pause, Vlad opened the book as D'Ablo had instructed. There, in the lower left corner of the inside cover, right where he said to look, was a small, ornate letter *D*. Vlad had never noticed it before. He had spent so much time reading the words between the covers that he had never taken the time to look at the covers themselves. He closed the journal and ran his hand lovingly over the front cover. "So I guess you guys were pretty close then, huh?"

"You might say that. And all I really want is something to remember him by. To remember him as I knew him." By the end of his sentence, D'Ablo's voice had dropped to a whisper.

With a shuddered, uncertain breath, Vlad gripped the journal tightly, then loosened his hold and held it out to

D'Ablo. Maybe he was making a grave mistake, but he didn't think he was.

D'Ablo met his eyes and bowed his head slowly as his hand closed over the journal.

Vlad had to fight the urge to rip it away from his grasp at the last second. But he managed to resist. He cleared his throat. "Now that I've given you the journal . . . will the nightmares stop?"

"Nightmares?" D'Ablo raised a questioning brow as he flipped through the journal's pages. Then he smiled. "Ah, so it worked. How delightful to know."

Vlad blinked, confused. "What worked? I thought you sent the nightmares as a way of convincing me to hand the journal over."

"In a manner of speaking, it was your uncle who sent those horrific images to haunt your dreams."

Vlad swallowed the lump that had suddenly formed in his throat. "Otis?"

D'Ablo offered a nod as he flipped through the pages of the journal. Finally he seemed to find what he was looking for and stopped on a page dated September 21. With a distracted voice, he quipped, "Every single bloody thing you saw was by his doing."

Vlad shook his head. He didn't believe a word. "Otis wouldn't."

D'Ablo met his eyes. "Wouldn't he? After all, he takes

his leave of you repeatedly, doesn't he? And hasn't it been difficult to reach him with your mind? Haven't you even once questioned why Otis has kept his distance all these months?"

Against his will, a sliver of doubt jabbed its way into Vlad's mind. His bottom lip shook at the possibility of such treachery. Was Otis capable of such a horrible thing? He hoped not, but then, how well did he really know his uncle? "He said he had to stop you from finding some ritual."

D'Ablo laughed heartily. "He's been working with me this entire time, so to speak."

Then in Vlad's mind an image appeared. It jumped forward, like a grainy reel-to-reel film image—it had to be a memory, like Otis had shared with him last year. The image was a mirror of his nightmare. Vlad was strapped to a table, half naked and bleeding. D'Ablo leaned over him with a blade, cutting. But then . . . Vlad noticed the mark on the inside of his left wrist. Clear as day in Elysian code, Vlad read the name: Otis Otis.

Oh no.

The film stopped, and Vlad glanced about the room. In the corner behind him was the table with leather straps from his nightmares. The floor beneath it was stained with blood. It smelled too familiar. And Otis . . . Otis had been the one being tortured. Actually, physically, painfully tortured. It hadn't been Vlad's bad dreams at all, but Otis's reality, reflected in Vlad's subconscious. Otis had been sending him memories all year, begging for help through nightmarish images. What's more, he was here, somewhere in the building, punching through D'Ablo's hold over his telepathy long enough to warn Vlad that D'Ablo hadn't changed.

Relief and horror swirled through Vlad's veins together in a gale-force torrent. After a brief pause, Vlad regained his composure and said, "Where is he?"

D'Ablo set the journal on the table to his left and turned back to Vlad. "He's here, actually. Would you like to see him?"

At a loss for words, Vlad managed a nod.

D'Ablo seemed to search Vlad's expression for a moment before nodding in grave satisfaction. Perhaps he thought Vlad would finish his own uncle off, saving him from breaking the highest law. Whatever he thought, Vlad didn't care. He just needed to see Otis again. And, somehow, figure out a way to get free.

D'Ablo nodded again and said, "Wait here."

Once D'Ablo stepped through the large metal door, Vlad grabbed the journal and stuffed it into his waistband, then helped Henry to his feet and headed for the second door on the opposite end of the small room. "Come on, Henry. We've gotta get out of here."

Henry muttered, "It's about time you had that idea."

But when Vlad opened the door, he found Ignatius standing there, snarling. As quickly as he could move with

Henry leaning hard against him, Vlad shuffled back to the metal door, which opened to reveal D'Ablo, whose lips were curled in a cruel smile. D'Ablo stepped inside and lifted Vlad's shirt, snatching the journal back. "Now, now, Vladimir. You can't leave without first saying hello to your darling uncle."

Behind D'Ablo was a face that Vlad recognized with a glance—Jasik, the vampire who'd bitten him last year and brought a vial of his blood back to D'Ablo, healing him. But what stopped Vlad dead in his tracks, what almost made him drop Henry, what nearly made him lose it completely, was the sight of the man that Jasik all but carried into the room.

Otis's left eye was swollen, his body broken and bleeding in several places—wounds that could only still be there, unhealed, if the torture had been continuous. Vlad gasped in horror. "Otis?"

Otis struggled to lift his head, but when he did, he met Vlad's eyes and managed a strange, impossible, relieved smile. Vlad wondered if he was thinking that Vlad could save him, save them all.

Or maybe, Vlad thought with a shudder, Otis just wanted to see his nephew one last time before he died.

22
HIDDEN IN BLOOD

OTIS PARTED HIS CRACKED LIPS and, through bloodied teeth, whispered, "Don't . . . listen . . . to him, Vladimir."

As the last word escaped his mouth, Jasik threw him to the floor. To Vlad's astonishment and his uncle's credit, Otis didn't cry out.

Vlad released Henry, who limped back over to the chair he'd been sitting in, and knelt before his uncle. Otis met his eyes, and an unspoken understanding passed between them. Otis hadn't meant to be out of touch for so long. It was D'Ablo and his cronies who'd kept him away. And Vlad hadn't caught on to the nightmare clues, Otis's cries for help—the only bits of communication that D'Ablo had allowed through. "I'm sorry, Otis. I'm so sorry I didn't come sooner. I hadn't realized . . ."

A chilling laugh echoed from D'Ablo. "Ah, what a touching family reunion."

Despite the warning in Otis's eyes, Vlad stood up straight and tall, turning to D'Ablo. "You monster! There was no reason for this. You were just getting your sick kicks torturing him like you did."

The fury within Vlad's chest continued to build. "You knew where I was this whole time. You even stopped by my room. Why not take the journal by force? Or send one of your lackeys to do it? That seems to be more your style."

"I would have, but I confess that after our previous encounters, I'm—pardon the phrase—once bitten, twice shy when it comes to direct confrontation with the Pravus. And that much is true, young Vladimir, you are the Pravus. And there are at least a thousand other vampires who share that belief with me. We have been waiting your coming for a millennium."

Otis managed a wheezing laugh. "You're a fool who believes in fairy tales, D'Ablo."

"Your uncle is among the majority of misguided vampires, those who believe the prophecy to be false, a mere children's story. Despite the fact that you have been born— a miracle in and of itself. You see, before the law was passed, vampires and humans were allowed to intermarry for several hundred years. In all that time not one child was ever born. Not to mention that you have survived a stake through the heart." D'Ablo straightened with pride, clearly pleased with his manipulation of Joss last year. "But it doesn't matter what Otis believes or doesn't believe. You *are* the Pravus, Vladimir Tod. Even you cannot deny it anymore, after all that you have seen, all that you have experienced. Think of it—it would make no sense for the prophecy to be no more than a bedtime story for children. In all of vampire history, there has only ever been *one* child."

Otis managed a single word. "Lies."

But any further words were replaced by a scream as D'Ablo forced his gloved thumb deep into the open wound on Otis's shoulder.

Vlad cried out, "Knock it off!"

To his amazement, D'Ablo withdrew from Otis, but as he did, he licked Otis's blood from his thumb and shivered with delight. "You see, it was the council who sent Ignatius after you. It was they who insisted that he should be given a chance to restore his family honor."

D'Ablo shook his head. "Such fools. Sending a vampire to kill the unkillable. Oh, that's not what they told him—they ordered him to bring you before them, to be tried for your crimes at last. But this is Ignatius, and his temperament has always run a murderous trail. I quite think they were hoping you'd not survive long enough to face them. Most of them would find it a difficult task to punish a child with the brutality of our laws—especially the child of a departed friend."

Vlad looked at Otis, but Otis nodded, as if to indicate that he was fine. Then he looked back at D'Ablo in confusion. "Wait... 'restore his family honor'?"

Otis wheezed, gulping for air between words, as if his lungs had been damaged too. "Vladimir... Ignatius is... your grandfather."

Vlad's eyes shot to Ignatius, who snarled, emitting a low, guttural growl that made Henry slide his chair back several inches. Vlad shook his head, refusing to believe that this monster could possibly be related to him.

D'Ablo chuckled. "Oh yes, it's quite true. Ignatius turned your father and your uncle into vampires. He created them. And, by extension, created you. Something that deeply disturbs him."

In wordless agreement, Ignatius cracked his knuckles, his fierce eyes on Vlad the entire time.

D'Ablo continued in an oddly casual tone. "By bringing you to justice—or death—it would bring honor to his bloodline, honor that was lost by Tomas's and Otis's crimes, not to mention those of his grandson. I didn't want to send him, because Ignatius is a skilled bounty hunter, one of the best there is, despite his intense allergy to the sun—so severe that even the sunlight reflecting off the moon will harm him. You see, he can only venture out under the dark of the new moon."

Vlad swallowed hard. He thought he had it bad by having to slather on sunblock several times a day.

"Alas, due to the proper paperwork being held up, as sometimes happens, and his seeming inability to find you completely alone, as well as his unfortunate exposure to the dawn during your initial encounter, which took an enormous amount of time for him to recover from, Ignatius has hardly had a fair chance at justice. Something that has both embarrassed and infuriated him no end." D'Ablo flicked his eyes to Ignatius and back, a bemused smile on his lips. "I knew that Ignatius would not succeed in killing you, but would bring you before the council—something that would make acquiring the journal difficult, to say the least."

Vlad gulped as the pieces fell into place in his mind. It had been a trap all along. And he'd fallen for it, hook, line, and sinker. "So you kidnapped Otis."

D'Ablo offered him a nod, the smug smile never leaving his lips. "And took great pleasure in causing him pain, knowing that though I blocked his telepathy with a Tego charm, he would be able to send you images of his experiences when your mind was most susceptible."

"When I was sleeping." Vlad almost gasped. He was quite certain that Otis and Henry were going to die, but he had no idea what D'Ablo and his cronies had in store for him.

D'Ablo nodded once more, his lips twisting into a sneer. "Luckily, I am an infinitely patient vampire. Besides, invincibility is well worth the wait."

Vlad threw him a confused glance.

"Through my studies, I have learned that the great vampire philosopher Diogenes once theorized that there is a way to steal the status, the traits, the power of the Pravus. And so he designed a ritual to do so. And you, my boy, have just handed it to me."

Vlad rolled his eyes. "Nice try, nimrod. I know that book from front to back. There's no ritual in there."

D'Ablo held out his hand and in his most gentlemanly voice said, "Your hand, if you would."

"Not a chance."

"Very well."

Before Vlad knew what was happening, he was grabbed from behind by Jasik. He had been so involved in his conversation with D'Ablo that he hadn't even noticed Jasik moving into position. Otis summoned all the strength he could and leaped out to free his nephew, only to be met by D'Ablo's elbow in his face. Otis fell back on the floor in a heap.

From behind his back, D'Ablo pulled a dagger—the same dagger, Vlad noticed with a shudder, that he had used to torture Otis. With a nod, Jasik grabbed Vlad's wrist and offered up his hand. D'Ablo slashed his palm open, and Vlad cried out, but remained still. Blood dripped from the wound, and before it could close, D'Ablo pressed the backs of two of the journal's pages against Vlad's palm, staining them with crimson.

D'Ablo's eyes were locked onto the blood-smeared pages. Vlad was about to use the distracted moment to shove Jasik away and try, somehow, to get his wounded uncle and friend out the door, but then something happened....

The pages began to glow. All of the pages.

And after a moment, flames scrawled across the pages that Vlad could see, burning letters, then full words, into the parchment.

Vlad almost forgot completely about the wound in his palm, which had already begun healing closed. He gasped, "What is it?"

"It's your future, Master Pravus. It is your end." D'Ablo met his gaze with the glowing grin of an empowered lunatic. The three words he spoke next made Vlad's heart skip a beat and his limbs freeze with terror. "And my beginning."

23
THE RITUAL

JASIK RELEASED VLAD AND STARTED HELPING D'Ablo to arrange things on the table. Otis reached a shaking hand up to Vlad's sleeve and tugged him closer. "He believes the ritual contained in those pages will steal the invincibility of the Pravus, and he fully intends to perform it. He truly believes in the story, Vladimir, dangerously so. You must leave. Find a way out while their backs are turned. Or he is going to kill you."

Vlad whispered back, "I'm not leaving without you and Henry."

Otis smiled at him through his tears, grateful for even this final moment together. "Don't you see, Vladimir? Henry and I are as good as dead. I can barely move, and he's just a drudge. You can make another."

Vlad flinched. "He's not *just* a drudge."

"Get out while you can. Get to Vikas. He'll protect you."

Vlad shook his head, tears welling in his eyes as well. "When we were in Siberia last year, I overheard Vikas tell you that I didn't need his protection."

"But you do. Right now, you do." Otis winced in pain. As he spoke, a small amount of blood left the corner of his mouth and trailed down his chin. "Please. Don't make me witness your demise. You're like ... you're like a son to me."

In that moment, Vlad's tears dried, replaced by determination. Because Otis was like a father to him, the same way that Nelly was like a mother to him, and there was no way he was going to lose his entire family a second time. He was getting out of here—they all were—and they were going home, to Nelly.

"C'mon." He took Otis's arm and placed it around his shoulders, helping Otis to stand, despite his quiet protests, then gestured to Henry with a glance. Henry, wide-eyed, nodded in response and carefully stood, wincing as he put weight on his injured ankle. Vlad nodded to the big metal door, and Henry followed his lead. They moved slowly, only a single step every few seconds, hoping that the other vampires—who were engaged in some kind of setup for D'Ablo's insane ritual—wouldn't notice their departure until they were gone, or at least until they had a good head start.

The seconds slipped by, and Vlad counted his blessings with every heartbeat. After what seemed like an eternity, Vlad's fingers met the ornate doorknob.

As if he'd actually heard the subtle sound of Vlad's fingertips lightly brushing metal, D'Ablo stiffened, then turned to face them. "Fools. Did you really think that would work? The three of you are no match for even one of us. Especially given the fact that two of you are injured, one but a drudge. You can't escape."

Vlad's jaw tightened. "Then let's even the odds. You and me. Right now."

"As tempted as I am by your offer, Master Pravus, we have other business to attend to." D'Ablo glanced at his cronies for a moment. "Lock Otis and the human in a cell together. It ought to be quite interesting having them share such a small space, what with Otis's now surely ravenous appetite. How long has it been since you fed, Otis? Nine months? Ten?"

As Jasik helped Otis to stand—much more gently than Vlad had expected him to—a horrified expression crossed Otis's face. One that sent a bolt of terror through Vlad. Otis forced a bitter laugh, as if D'Ablo's twisted plan was of no consequence to him. "I've gone longer without blood."

D'Ablo clucked his tongue. "You shouldn't utter such lies in front of these impressionable youths, my friend."

Otis wrenched his body forward, but Jasik held fast. Otis spat a mouthful of blood, which splattered on D'Ablo's cheek. As D'Ablo wiped it from his face with the back of his glove, Otis growled, "I may be a lot of things, D'Ablo. But your friend is not one of them."

D'Ablo very calmly removed a crisp white handkerchief from his inside jacket pocket and wiped the remainder of Otis's blood from his pale skin. Once it was clean, he met Otis's eyes, his gaze sharp, penetrating. "Enjoy your meal."

Even Jasik seemed troubled by D'Ablo's words. He pulled Otis back and firmly, but gently, took him out the large metal door. Ignatius wasn't so kind. He grabbed Henry by a handful of hair and dragged him out of the room, kicking and screaming and swearing more than Vlad had ever heard him swear.

The door closed, and Vlad was left alone with D'Ablo. He wet his lips, which were suddenly unbelievably dry.

And though he wasn't as sure of his status as Pravus as D'Ablo was, it seemed like a good way to stall for time while he thought about his next move. "So what now? You can't kill me."

"No, but with the ritual you were so kind to provide me with, I can withdraw that which gives you invincibility and imbibe it. And then, once I have drunk enough of your blood to render me immune to the horrors of sunlight, I will give you to Ignatius." D'Ablo met Vlad's eyes and spoke in a matter-of-fact tone. "With your invincibility gone, he will be able to kill you. And in so doing, it will render me untouchable for all eternity."

Vlad's stomach shrank in fear. If he could keep D'Ablo talking long enough, he might be able to think of a plan. At the very least, it might prolong his inevitable demise. "So what now then, huh? Do you really think that all those vampires who truly believe in the Pravus will be very happy to hear what you've done?"

"That fact matters very little to me. You see, the existence of this ritual is not known to many. I myself only discovered it little more than a year ago."

Vlad racked his brain, but couldn't think of anything he could do to escape. He glanced at each of the doors, and a hopeless feeling swallowed him whole. "So, the fact that nobody knows about it makes it okay?"

"Not at all. The fact that nobody knows about it means that by the time they find out it will be too late. The ritual will be done and I will be invincible." The corners of D'Ablo's mouth rose slightly in a pleased smile. "No one would dare challenge me at that point. And those who do will fall before me."

Vlad shook his head. "Dude, you have serious issues. Do you know that?"

D'Ablo laughed, "Is that so?"

"Yeah, it is. And do you know something else? It doesn't matter what you do to me. It doesn't matter if you manage to drain my essence and become invincible. Because there is one thing that you will never be, D'Ablo. You will never be the Pravus." Vlad's eyes narrowed, his stare never leaving that of his foe. "You will never be me."

"Enough of this," D'Ablo snapped. His smile was gone, leaving behind only a bitter grimace. "The hour grows late and my patience wears thin."

The door opened, drawing D'Ablo's attention to Jasik as he entered. "It's done."

"Good." He turned his eyes back to Vlad. "I'd wager the human won't be your drudge for very much longer."

"You son of a—"

"Come now, Vladimir, we must be civil. What would your father think if he knew that you were to meet your end slinging curse words and insults? I'm sure he would want you to die with honor and dignity." D'Ablo bowed his head briefly in respect, as if saying goodbye to the former king of everything. His head still low, he whispered, "Shall we begin?"

Vlad leaped forward and moved with his amazing vampiric speed, grabbing the dagger before D'Ablo knew what was happening. He jabbed the blade upward, sinking just the tip into the underside of D'Ablo's chin. "I don't think so. Now call your cronies off and let my uncle and friend go, or I'll turn your skull into a pincushion."

Cold, metallic laughter ebbed from deep within D'Ablo.

Furious, Vlad jabbed the blade in deeper. "Why are you laughing?"

D'Ablo met his eyes with a bemused smile. "Because I'm going to enjoy every second of this."

D'Ablo gripped Vlad's hand and the dagger's handle at the same time. With one powerful thrust, he yanked it to the side, slicing through the flesh and bone of his own jaw. Blood gushed out, coating Vlad's hand instantly, but D'Ablo didn't bat an eye. Instead, he snapped his hand back, and hot pain shot through Vlad's wrist and up his arm. The cracking sound of bone breaking reverberated through his skull. And faster than he could blink, D'Ablo slammed him in the face with the butt of his gloved hand, knocking him backward. Vlad fell back onto the table, where Jasik was waiting. Jasik strapped Vlad's ankles down, then his wrists. As he tightened the strap on Vlad's left wrist, Vlad screamed obscenities and then growled at the mastermind of his torment. "When I get free, I'm going to hurt you like you've never been hurt before."

D'Ablo smirked. "Child, I have walked this earth for almost five centuries. I have both caused and experienced levels of pain that you cannot even imagine . . . yet."

D'Ablo picked up the journal and began to read from the pages of the ritual. His deep voice was rising and falling like a song as he formed the words of the Elysian code. He circled the table over and over as he read, stopping occasionally to touch Vlad's shoulder, or his foot, or his forehead. Occasionally he would draw a symbol in the air with his finger and then move again.

Vlad squirmed away from his every touch, but it didn't help. He was trapped. Trapped and scared, and not exactly sure what was transpiring. Worse yet, there was no one who could save him. And no way Vlad could save himself.

D'Ablo finally came to rest at Vlad's left side. He started to repeat the same phrase over and over again, his voice growing louder with each repetition. He placed his hand on Vlad's chest, pressing hard into the bone. Vlad struggled uselessly when he saw D'Ablo's other hand, no longer holding the journal, raised high above D'Ablo's head. The hand fell with force, and Vlad cried out. A six-inch needle plunged deep into Vlad's chest.

The pain was like nothing Vlad had ever experienced before. Not even getting staked could come close compared with the agony that ripped through Vlad. He screamed as a fire seemed to blaze to life at his core. It felt like it was burning its way straight through Vlad's soul.

The syringe filled with a liquid—purple in color, and iridescent, reminiscent of that strange color his eyes changed whenever he touched a glyph—and D'Ablo boiled over with cruel, joyous laughter. "Yes! At long last—the essence of the Pravus has been withdrawn!"

He said something else in Elysian code, and Vlad desperately wished that reading the vampiric language and understanding its spoken form went hand in hand. Without warning, D'Ablo bent down, gnashing into Vlad's unbroken wrist. He drank deeply, and Vlad's head swam as he nearly lost consciousness. Once D'Ablo had had his fill, he swallowed one last time and stood, steadying himself against the table as if he were drunk. He whispered, "I've never tasted anything like it."

Ignatius entered the smaller door, his eyes full of an arrogant gleam. At D'Ablo's nod, he lifted a blade—the metal a strange blackish-gray, as if it were made of hematite—over Vlad's chest, and Vlad screamed in terror, knowing that his end had come at last. He would never again see his uncle or Henry, never eat Nelly's cookies or hold Meredith's hand, never catch snowflakes on his tongue, or read another book. His life would be over as soon as that blade fell. A thousand images flitted through his mind in his final moment—pictures of everything that he had ever loved and would never experience again—and Vlad knew that there was nothing he could do to stop his end. Death had come for him at last, wearing the face of his own grandfather, and all he could do was scream.

With his peripheral vision, Vlad saw Jasik, and in a second his plan was formed. He pushed as hard as he could with his mind, invading Jasik's thoughts, embedding his own into the vampire's mind, pushing Jasik to act, act now, stop this horrible moment before it was too late.

At first, he wasn't certain that his mind control had worked, but then Jasik closed a hard hand over Ignatius's wrist and twisted the dagger in his grasp. Jasik's fist fell into Ignatius's elbow, bending his arm and forcing the blade into his stomach. Ignatius staggered back, throwing Jasik a wild-eyed look of confusion. Jasik jumped high into the air, meeting Ignatius's temple with a roundhouse kick, knocking him out cold.

Vlad glared at D'Ablo, the burning sensation within him finally subsiding. "Give it up, D'Ablo. It's over."

Jasik's lips moved, his voice low, echoing the words Vlad had spoken. "Give it up, D'Ablo. It's over."

D'Ablo looked back and forth between them, his confusion slowly dissipating. He shook his head, snarling at Jasik. "You fool! He's controlling your mind."

At Vlad's mental command, Jasik pointed the dagger at D'Ablo with one hand and undid his straps with another. When Vlad's left hand was free, he undid his right. "Know this, you overgrown mosquito. Whatever sick fixation you have with me ends here today."

Vlad unstrapped his feet and climbed down off the table. "I want you out of my life for good. If I have to kill you, I will."

Jasik's muttering caught up, echoing Vlad. ". . . If I have to kill you, I will."

Vlad stood, making certain that Jasik remained between him and D'Ablo at all times. As Vlad made his way closer to the door, clutching his broken wrist to his chest, Jasik sidestepped at his command.

D'Ablo snarled, "You won't get far once I've dispatched your puppet."

Vlad held D'Ablo's gaze as he moved. The door was only a few yards away. "You're assuming I'm not going to make him take your life."

Jasik's voice followed, sending a chill into the air with his muttering. "...make him take your life."

"We've both made assumptions." The corners of D'Ablo's mouth tugged upward slightly. Then without warning, he lunged forward and grabbed Jasik, throwing him to the side. With his fangs gleaming in the candlelight, he rushed toward Vlad, a hungry look in his eyes.

Vlad struggled to make Jasik stand, but couldn't make him move fast enough. In a blind panic, he grabbed one of the lit candles from the table and thrust the candle toward D'Ablo, tossing hot wax into his open eyes.

D'Ablo roared in pain, clutching his face and thrashing about the room.

Finally Vlad coaxed Jasik back onto his feet, causing him to leap onto the still-blind D'Ablo with the blade in his hand. As D'Ablo struggled to keep the blade from entering his chest, Vlad bolted from the room.

It took him a second, but soon he recognized where he was and hurried through the next door to the corridor of prison cells. Vlad pushed hard and reached out, locating Otis in the cell at the end, astonished at his ability to take on two mind-focused tasks at once. What he saw when he reached the cell jolted his entire being.

Henry's head was bent to the side, and Otis's mouth was

firmly fixed to his neck. Henry's eyes were closed—it looked like he was sleeping . . . or dead. Oblivious to anything else around him, Otis drank, swallowing greedy mouthfuls of Henry's blood.

Vlad felt his control over Jasik waver slightly, distracted by the horror he was witnessing.

Otis was feeding on Henry.

A single tear escaped the corner of Vlad's eye and traced a line down his cheek, before falling to the floor with all of his hopes for the future.

24
A DIFFICULT DECISION

O TIS, NO!"

Otis pulled away, and Henry winced as Otis's fangs slipped out of his neck. Vlad breathed a brief sigh of relief that Henry wasn't dead, but he was still horrified at the scene before him. "What have you done?"

Otis stood, strong once again, his wounds completely healed. "Your drudge saved my life."

Then he met Henry's eyes. "Thank you, Henry. I am indebted to you."

Henry nodded weakly and said, "Hey, you needed blood. I couldn't let you starve to death. Besides, you could barely move and, not that I don't have faith in Vlad's abilities, but something tells me we're going to need your help getting out of here."

Otis replied, but Vlad was too distracted to hear it. His breathing had picked up in panic, his eyes blurring with tears. But these things hadn't come from him. He focused on the part of his mind that was still controlling Jasik, pushing a bit more until he saw through Jasik's eyes.

D'Ablo was beneath him, holding the blade at bay, his eyes fierce. "You're weak, Jasik. Letting a boy control you like this. You deserve what fate awaits you."

Jasik was panicking and struggling to regain control—Vlad could sense that much. But he couldn't. Vlad, for once, was too strong—something that pleased Vlad more than he would ever admit to.

But still Jasik struggled, pushing with his mind against the part of Vlad that lurked within him. It was more than Vlad could allow, and he pushed back with all of his might, harder than he ever had before. Jasik lowered the knife momentarily, dazed. Something warm and wet dripped from his nose. It was only when a drop of crimson landed on D'Ablo's hand that Vlad realized Jasik's nose was bleeding. What's more, Jasik seemed dazed, as if Vlad had caused him physical harm, all from pushing with his mind.

In an instant, D'Ablo had wrenched the blade from Jasik's hand and shoved him across the room. Jasik stumbled and fell, only to find D'Ablo atop him with the blade, growling to Vlad through Jasik's ears, "You'll be next, Vladimir Tod."

He shoved the blade forward hard, piercing Jasik's chest and sinking the blade as deep as he could. Jasik struggled to pull it out, but it was too late. Blood poured from his heart, and Jasik's vision blurred, then darkened.

Sharp, horrible pain crashed through Vlad's mind. He staggered, and Otis caught him. "Vladimir, what's wrong?"

But Vlad couldn't speak. The pain . . . the pain of death was too much to bear. He could feel the blade in his own chest, though nothing was there. He could feel his life aching and ebbing from his limbs. He was alive, and apart from his wrist, which was already beginning to heal, in good health, yet he hurt as if it were he who was dying.

And then . . . the emptiness came.

Vlad weakened in Otis's embrace. He could almost feel himself going paler. It was over. Jasik was dead.

But the pain remained, coupled with the terrifying shadow of death that shrouded his being. Vlad was a living zombie now, an echo of what his living self had been. There was no going back. This was penance for what he had done to Jasik, and he deserved every nightmarish bolt of pain. He coughed, the feeling of blood pooling in his throat, and Otis whispered, "You were in his mind. He . . . died before you could withdraw."

Vlad still couldn't make a sound, only nodded feebly. Unbelievably, the pain went on and on, and only Otis's presence brought him any comfort.

Otis blanched, but spoke in a commanding tone—one

that he'd never used with Vlad before. "You have to block these feelings, Vladimir. Or they will haunt you until the end of your days. Now stand up. If Jasik is dead, then D'Ablo will be here shortly. I need you. So stand up."

Vlad stood, because Otis told him to. But it was the only thing that could have made him move through the agonizing sensation of death. Otis needed him.

Otis again spoke in a commanding tone, all business now. "We need to get out of here, and fast. Unfortunately, the escape tunnel we used in the past has been blocked off, so we'll have to leave through the lobby. Stay behind me. Henry, you remain between Vlad and me for protection—I know your ankle hurts, but keep up and move quickly. When I stop, you stop. And don't make a sound."

"Vladimir." Otis met Vlad's gaze, then finished his sentence with his thoughts. "*Sunrise is in twenty minutes, and we are without sunblock. We need to get out of this building and into the cover of darkness as soon as we can. If anyone gets in your way, kill them quickly. We don't have time to be merciful. And we do not want to be in this building when the council members arrive.*"

After a moment, Vlad nodded slowly. He'd had enough of death today, but apparently, death hadn't yet had enough of him.

Otis nodded in return. "Through the door now. Follow me."

Otis led the way and Henry followed. Vlad, very much

on guard and fighting to keep the pain of Jasik's death at bay, stepped in behind them. They moved quickly down the hall and through the open door. Otis led them through several dark corridors, always whispering before they determined which direction to take. "Left . . . now right . . . left again . . ."

As quietly as possible, they descended a long set of stairs that led to a small, dark room. They crossed the room, then Otis listened carefully at the door at the other end. "Here. This way."

The door opened into another small room, this one full of copiers and a fax machine. As he followed Otis and Henry into the room, Vlad paused. Something wasn't right. He reached out, wondering where D'Ablo might be, and then he saw him, actually saw him. The gloved hands, the cane he held, the sinister, sneering face, the curled lip, the fierce fangs. He saw D'Ablo with his mind, as he'd seen Otis earlier this year standing in front of Mr. Craig's old house. Pulling away from his vision, he called out in a whisper, "Otis, don't . . ."

But Otis and Henry were already out the door. Vlad ran to catch up with them just as they reached the lobby doors. He cried out, "Otis, D'Ablo is—"

Otis stopped suddenly, and Vlad caught up. D'Ablo was standing just as Vlad had seen him in his mind, in front of the lobby doors, their exit. "—right there. . . ."

Otis sighed, sounding weary. "So he is."

D'Ablo tilted his head slightly, eyeing them with utter disdain. In stark contrast, he kept his tone light. "Yes. Yes, he is. And he's grateful that you chose to come to him instead of making him come after you."

Vlad saw Otis's jaw tighten. Something told him there was a dark history between them that he knew nothing about. Otis growled, "Even you can't be stupid enough to face two vampires alone, D'Ablo. The odds are against you, powerful as you may be. Let us pass and you can go back to whatever it was that you withdrew from my nephew."

D'Ablo's eye twitched, and Vlad couldn't help but wonder how Otis knew what had transpired during the ritual. Most likely, he guessed, Otis had been lurking around in D'Ablo's thoughts from the moment he had tasted Henry's blood.

Otis took a bold step forward, and Henry followed. Vlad felt a surge of pride. His best friend knew when to follow orders, that was for sure.

"That"—D'Ablo gripped the handle of his cane and twisted, withdrawing a long sword from the belly of the cane—"can wait." The ritual dagger was nowhere to be found—Vlad guessed that a psycho like D'Ablo had deemed its purposes too holy for the likes of killing Otis. D'Ablo stood there, eyeing Otis. Vlad wondered how much of their conversation was occurring in telepathy.

"Then leave them out of this. I'd be happy to take your life on my own."

D'Ablo tilted his neck one way, then another, cracking it. "Then take it. If you're vampire enough."

All Vlad saw was the corner of Otis's mouth twitch, and then Otis flew across the room. D'Ablo swung the sword, slicing a button from Otis's shirt in half, but Otis changed directions before the cold metal could pierce his skin.

D'Ablo moved in a blur, slashing the sword toward Otis, who ducked it, but just barely. Then D'Ablo snarled, his fangs dripping with saliva.

Vlad turned to check on Henry, but he seemed to have disappeared. He wondered if Henry had had the wits to get out while he still could. After all, being a human in the middle of a vampire battle was not a good way to foster one's promising future.

Otis kicked D'Ablo in the chest, and D'Ablo stumbled back. But once D'Ablo regained his composure, he swung the blade around again, catching Otis's cheek.

Otis cupped the gash in his face with a trembling, surprised hand. The look in his eyes was fierce and daring. "I'll heal in but a moment, but you'll always look the fool. What vampire needs a weapon to take down a foe?"

D'Ablo hesitated before throwing the sword across the room. He hissed, "I may look the fool for now, but it is the victor who writes the history books. And you'll be lucky to end up as a footnote."

With dizzying speed, so fast that Vlad almost missed it, D'Ablo darted to Otis, picked him up, and threw him toward the receptionist's area. Otis slid over the desktop, catching its edge with his fingertips, and pulled himself up, so that he landed on the desk in a perch. He grinned at his attacker, the cut in his cheek healing closed. "You're playing with me now. Surely you can't think that maneuver is enough to keep me down."

D'Ablo laughed. "Not at all. But it was enough to put you farther from your dear nephew."

Otis's eyes darted to Vlad, and before Vlad could blink, Ignatius gripped him by the throat from behind, the blade of his knife poised to plunge into Vlad's chest. Ignatius squeezed hard, and Vlad felt his air supply cut off. After a moment, he could no longer tug at the hands that were suffocating him, could no longer fight. All sound seemed very far away. Even the color began to bleed from the room. He thought he heard someone scream, and then Ignatius released his grip. Vlad fell to the floor in a heap, coughing and gasping until air returned to his lungs.

Ignatius was on the floor to his left. Otis was on top of him, swinging his fists so fast they were a blur. Ignatius gnashed his teeth forward at every swing, biting with his fangs into Otis's knuckles. But Otis kept punching, despite the pain. Blood flew from his hands, and the knuckles healed over until Ignatius bit them again. Finally, Ignatius managed to push Otis off him and they were both standing again, circling each other, like territorial felines. The two circled closer as the sun began to rise, shrinking the shadows of the room. Otis's voice was harsh. "The next time you touch him will be your last."

Vlad was watching the scene unfold with great intensity when, out of the corner of his eye, he noticed that D'Ablo had retrieved his sword and was creeping up on Otis. Vlad acted before he could think about it. In a flash he recalled every action movie he had ever seen, every stupid wrestling match that he had been forced to endure on Saturday mornings at Henry's house. He ran as fast as he could toward D'Ablo, jumping high into the air at the last minute. Two size 10 shoes connected with D'Ablo's face. A letter-perfect drop kick that even Hulk Hogan would be proud of knocked D'Ablo off his feet and away from Vlad's uncle.

D'Ablo wiped blood from his already healing lip and pulled himself back onto his feet. "I'm growing very tired of you, boy. I am going to enjoy killing you."

"Oh my God, you broken record. Why don't you get your cronies to write you some new material?" Vlad glanced quickly to check on his uncle, but Otis and Ignatius had disappeared down the hall. Vlad could only hope that Otis was strong enough to defeat his own father. He turned his attention back to D'Ablo, balling up his fists in fury. "Now do you want to go ahead and admit that your little plan has failed and give up? If not, then I suggest we finish this."

D'Ablo cast a condescending smile, "As you wish." His sword having been knocked away when Vlad kicked him, D'Ablo lashed out with his fist, catching Vlad under his jaw. Vlad flew several inches into the air and came down hard on the floor. But he wasn't down for long. When D'Ablo jumped to cover him, he kicked him in the chest with both feet, sending him flying, then did a flip and was on his feet again.

Henry had reappeared, and he yelled Vlad's name. Vlad looked just in time to see a small object flying through the air toward him. He turned his attention back to D'Ablo long enough to deliver a kick to his side that sent the vampire skidding across the floor. He turned back and reached out his hand to catch what Henry had thrown. His friend had one small bit of advice: "Just make sure you don't miss."

Vlad furrowed his brow, and then opened his hand. What he saw there completely explained why Henry had disappeared and very nearly made him hug Henry on the spot. He turned the familiar black cylinder over in his palm, and all he could hope was that what he was holding was the real Lucis, not the copy he'd been tricked with last year. He turned just as D'Ablo reached down to retrieve his sword. Holding his breath, Vlad aimed and brushed his thumb against the glyph on the end of the Lucis.

The room lit up with a brilliant white light. Otis came running back into the room, having apparently defeated Ignatius. He ducked just in time for the powerful beam of light to miss hitting him square in the side of the head. Vlad brushed the glyph again, closing the greatest weapon known to vampirekind.

D'Ablo howled. His hand had been blown completely off, leaving nothing but a charred stump behind. But "off" wasn't an exact description, as the hand was nowhere to be found. It had been blown into oblivion, into nonexistence.

D'Ablo's screams echoed in the lobby of the empty office building, blending with a myriad of curse words in every language he could think of, including one that Vlad guessed to be Elysian code. Vlad gripped the Lucis tightly, but he didn't turn it on again. Something sick and horrible filled his insides. He couldn't kill D'Ablo. He couldn't kill anyone that his father had called friend, despite the fact that he hated D'Ablo with a passion. He lowered the Lucis and met Otis's eyes. *"I can't kill him, Otis. I'm sorry."*

Otis stood, his eyes wide in disbelief. He stepped toward his nephew. *"I can. Give me the Lucis. This menace will not be stopped until we stop him, Vladimir. It ends today."*

Vlad flung the Lucis away, letting it fly from his hand. It tumbled through the air, and time stood still.

Otis pleaded with his eyes, but Vlad tightened his jaw stubbornly. *"It does end today. But not that way, Otis. I couldn't live with myself knowing I allowed my dad's friend to die."*

Otis shook his head. The Lucis clattered onto the floor. *"He won't stop. He will never stop."*

The Lucis rolled over the slatted top of an open vent. Vlad whispered, "I know."

Otis dove forward, but it was too late. The Lucis slipped

between his fingers and down the vent shaft. He hung his head, defeated.

A curved blade sang through the air, stabbing through Otis's hand. Otis screamed, and Ignatius pulled him back into the dark shadows of the hallway.

Vlad jumped forward to follow, but something large slammed into his side, knocking him through the air. He managed to glance in the direction he was flying quickly enough to shield his face with his hands. He smashed through the glass of the front door, and suddenly he could feel the sunlight on his skin as he fell outside. The smell of acrid smoke filled his nostrils, and fire lit up his sleeve. He was burning.

He opened his eyes, but couldn't stand, couldn't run from the sun's murderous heat. Something was on top of him.

D'Ablo shrieked as his hair and flesh burst into flames, but not with pain . . . with laughter. He growled into Vlad's horrified face, "Perhaps it's better this way, Vladimir Tod. Perhaps it's better that we die together."

Then Vlad realized that the flames he felt weren't coming from him. D'Ablo's burning flesh had set his clothing on fire. Vlad was perfectly fine . . . and in full sunlight.

He screeched, "D'Ablo, get to the shadows! You're dying!"

In a horrific, gravelly voice, flames framing his face as his skin charred before Vlad's very eyes, D'Ablo said, "We're both dying."

He withdrew the ritual dagger with his only hand from somewhere behind him and lifted it high in the air.

Vlad almost choked from the smoke coming off D'Ablo's burning flesh. He pushed as hard as he could with his mind, into D'Ablo's thoughts, just long enough to make him drop the blade. Once metal had clanged against pavement, Vlad grabbed the dagger and pointed at his attacker.

D'Ablo stood, still aflame, and ran toward the nearest dark alley. All the while, he screamed.

Vlad dropped the weapon and rested his head on the concrete. After a moment, he held up a hand in the sunlight. It felt warm. It felt good.

And it erased any small remaining doubt that he was the Pravus the prophecy had spoken of.

25
THE AFTERMATH

VLAD PULLED OPEN THE DOOR and stepped back into the lobby, where Henry and Otis were waiting for him. Otis lurked back near the elevator, where the shadows were at their heaviest, covered in what smelled like Ignatius's blood. Vlad threw his uncle an exhausted glance. "I thought drinking my blood would render the drinker immune to sunlight."

"You thought wrong." Otis frowned, watching the alley across the street. "As did he. I told you, Vladimir. Fairy tales and nonsense."

Henry stood near the front windows, gazing at the alleyway that D'Ablo had disappeared into with an intensity

Vlad didn't know he was capable of. Henry pursed his lips. "We should go after him, Vlad. Finish him off. Otherwise, he'll never stop trying to kill you."

Vlad looked back over his shoulder at the bright, sunny day and shook his head. "My dad would have let him live."

Otis's voice was gruff. "Are you so sure of that, Vladimir?"

Vlad paused. In truth, he wasn't, but he hoped that his assumption was right. "Even if he wouldn't, I'm going to. It's the right thing to do."

The sidewalk began to fill with people. The city had awakened, and very soon, the building would be bustling with activity. "We should find some sunblock for you, Otis, and get home. I'm sure Nelly will be furious that I've been out all night."

"Not to mention worried out of her mind." A small smile curved Otis's lips. "But I'm sure she'll understand once we explain that you had important vampire business to attend to . . . such as saving my life."

Otis grabbed Ignatius's corpse from where he had left it near the end of the hallway and slid it along the floor to the waiting elevator. He dropped it, ran a shaking hand through his hair, and sighed. "That's going to mean a lot of paperwork for someone."

Vlad chuckled. "After everything we've just been through, you're worried about somebody's paperwork?"

Otis merely blinked at him.

Vlad sighed. "I will never understand grown-ups, vampire or otherwise."

Vlad and Henry stepped inside the elevator with Otis and what was left of Ignatius. Otis opened the panel of buttons that led to the offices of the Elysian council. With a press of a button, they were on their way back to the room where D'Ablo had attempted to steal Vlad's invincibility from him.

"You know, whatever that was that D'Ablo took out of you . . ." His voice trailed off for a moment, as if something occurred to him that had not before. ". . . we should probably get it back inside you where it belongs. If there's any truth at all to D'Ablo's ramblings, perhaps ingesting it would shield you against the Grim Reaper's trespasses once again."

"Ingest it?" Vlad looked disgusted. "You mean I have to drink that crap?"

Vlad wasn't sure he wanted to find out what flavor his essence was, but he wasn't about to take his chances. Being invincible, it turned out, came in very handy. Especially with psycho vampires lurking around every corner trying to kill you.

The elevator door opened, and the trio made their way down the hall to the room with the large metal door. Otis opened it and Henry immediately cringed. Jasik lay on the floor, dead, his gray, lifeless eyes staring up at the ceiling.

At the sight of him, Vlad felt that horrible emptiness again, just as he had at the moment of Jasik's death. And he felt an unshakable pang of guilt for having controlled Jasik's mind. After all, if Vlad hadn't intervened, Jasik wouldn't have suffered D'Ablo's wrath and he might still be alive right now.

Vlad knelt and closed Jasik's eyes with his palm. He looked around the room for a sheet or blanket—something, anything to cover Jasik's dead body—but there was nothing lying around to serve that purpose. Otis squeezed his shoulder, and they exchanged looks of understanding.

"Oh no. No ... no ... no ... no ... no." Across the room, Henry muttered several curse words under his breath. "Um, guys. I'm afraid I have some bad news."

Henry held up the vial that had contained the iridescent purple liquid. The glass was cracked in several places, and the top of the vial had been broken completely off.

Vlad frowned and crossed the floor to where Henry was still crouched down, holding the broken tube. He could see the crusty spot on the floor where the liquid from the vial had puddled and dried. His invincibility. One of his Pravus powers reduced to no more than a carpet stain. Vlad's mind began to ask questions: What if the rest of his powers could be lost as easily? What if D'Ablo did come back to try again? What else might he lose? Had he made the right decision letting D'Ablo live? He silenced the thoughts before they had the chance to consume him.

After a moment of silence, Otis said, "Look on the bright side, Vladimir. Now there is no question of your mortality."

Vlad snorted. He was about to ask a question when Henry intervened with the same thing he was thinking. "How is that a good thing?"

Otis met Vlad's eyes. The concern Vlad saw there was almost overwhelming. "Because maybe now you will be more careful when facing your enemies."

"Do you think I've been careless? I've tried my best not to have to face any enemies at all." Vlad could feel his face get hot. "I really don't find this an enjoyable way to spend my Saturday nights, Otis."

"Vladimir, you misunderstood my intent." Otis's voice was soft and understanding, as if he could sense Vlad's emotions starting to get the better of him. "I simply meant that with these vampires believing that you are the Pravus—"

"Really? Because it sounded like you were saying that I tend to seek out all this life-in-danger crap." After all that he had been through in the past twelve hours, it seemed so unfair that his uncle blamed him for it all. Vlad had to fight to hold back the tears. "I just want to be left alone to live my life, but the psycho fanatics won't let that happen. And frankly, knowing that I couldn't be killed made facing them a lot easier. Now I . . . now I'm just scared."

Vlad fell to his knees. Though he had won his fight against D'Ablo, he'd never stood a chance in the battle he now fought. Now he had to face the world, and whatever lurked in the shadows, without his ability to survive it.

His emotions won out. Vlad let out a shuddering sob and wrapped his arms around himself.

Henry took a step toward Vlad to comfort his friend, but Otis held up his hand, stopping the boy in his tracks. He spoke softly to his nephew. "Vladimir, you have been through a lot in the last few years. More than any boy. More than any vampire. I wish I could say that I understand what you are feeling, but I can't. When you've lived for centuries you learn to deal with fear and loss in different ways."

Otis bent down in front of his nephew and put his hands on Vlad's shoulders. "All I can say for sure is that whatever it was that was in that vial is not you. It is not who you are and it is not what you do. There is nothing different about you now than there was before D'Ablo took out whatever that was." He pulled Vlad in closer and let him cry into his chest. "And you don't have to worry anymore. You've shown D'Ablo that you're a lot tougher than he thought. I don't think he'll be trying anything anytime soon. And if he does, I'll be here to protect you."

Vlad lifted his head and looked into his uncle's face, blinking away his tears. "Does that mean you're staying? For good?"

"For now, not for good." He smiled down at Vlad. "After what I've endured in the months since my capture, I could certainly use a vacation. However, I am still a fugitive in the eyes of Elysia, and I cannot stay in one place for too long. Speaking of which . . ." Otis's eyes scanned the room to make sure that Henry was still nearby. He spotted him rummaging through the drawer of a cabinet against the wall. "We should find a way to get out of here before council members show up."

From across the room Henry held up a small bottle of sunblock, SPF 40. "It looks like this is all they have. Will it be enough?"

Otis took the bottle, frowning a little. "It'll have to be."

Vlad regained his composure. Otis was right. There was more to him than some weird purple liquid. He was the Pravus. He knew that to be true now, could feel the . . . rightness of it down to his very cells. And no one, not even D'Ablo, could ever take that away. He crossed the room and pulled open the large metal door, but Otis stopped him with a thought. *Aren't you forgetting something? Your father's journal, perhaps? After all, it is . . . precious to you, is it not?"*

Vlad hesitated.

"I'm not sure I want it anymore, Otis." The backs of the pages now contained a horrible memory. After all, it had been a tool for his demise—something that troubled Vlad deeply. Why would his father's journal contain such a horrible ritual, especially knowing that Vlad was the only vampire born to a human mother?

"I'm sure your father had sound reasons for not destroying the ritual when he had the chance." Otis's lips formed a thin line as he nodded at Vlad. *"We just have to trust that."*

Vlad was ashamed to admit that he didn't trust that... and that he wasn't sure why, exactly. *"Why did my dad's journal contain the ritual that could destroy me?"*

"I don't know, Vladimir. Maybe he was protecting you by keeping it close and hidden—out of the hands of the likes of D'Ablo. Or maybe he wasn't even aware that it was contained on the backs of those pages."

Vlad thought for a moment. *"Do you think that D'Ablo put it there before he gave the journal to him?"*

Otis's forehead wrinkled as his eyebrows came together. *"What are you talking about? Vikas gave your father that journal."*

"No, D'Ablo did. He told me so. There's even a D on the inside cover. For D'Ablo."

"Is that what he told you to get you to give him the journal?" Otis shook his head and laughed, his voice warm and friendly in Vlad's mind. *"No, Vlad. The D stands for Dyavol, the nickname that Vikas used for your father. The same that he uses for you. Mahlyenki Dyavol. Besides, when a vampire gifts another vampire with something, we always inscribe our name in Elysian code, not in English."* Otis placed the journal into Vlad's hand on his way out the door. *"If for no other reason, to remember him by."*

Vlad squeezed the journal tightly. It had been a lie. Just another lie told to him by D'Ablo. And he had stupidly believed it.

Vlad followed his uncle to the elevator.

When the three of them stepped inside, they were greeted by the Muzak version of "Teenagers" by My Chemical Romance. Vlad and Henry exchanged looks of horror, and Vlad sighed. "Is nothing sacred?"

26
SWEET RELEASE

ELLY PICKED UP A LONG WOODEN SPOON from the counter and stirred the concoction on the stove that she kept referring to as "soup." Vlad grinned. Otis was looking rather exhausted, not from his encounter with Elysia, but from all of Nelly's pampering. "Nelly, darling, I'm not ill. You can't treat a vampire's malnourishment with chicken soup. How many times must I tell you that?"

Nelly shook her head—desperate, Vlad wagered, to have some sort of control over the situation. She'd been trying to nurse Otis every day over the last four months. Otis had healed completely in a week, but Nelly insisted on mothering him. It was enormously funny to watch. "You had three broken ribs, a cracked tibia, countless abrasions, and a hor-rific amount of blood loss, Otis."

"Yes, but through all of that, I didn't catch the flu." He caught Nelly's hand and pleaded with her with his eyes. "Please. Stop making me eat soup. What I'd really like is a nice mulled glass of O positive."

Nelly lost herself for a moment in his eyes, and Vlad be-gan to feel uncomfortable, as if he were intruding. Finally she sighed, relenting. "Okay, but I'm mulling it myself. I have to do something to help."

Vlad flexed his well-healed wrist and pulled the Slayer coin from his pocket, turning it over in his hand. It felt like a lucky charm to him now. After all, it had been there in the clearing when he was staked last year—and survived. It had been in his front pocket during his most recent struggle with D'Ablo, which he'd walked away from virtually un-scathed. Sure, it had come from a boy who was intent on killing him, but that boy had failed. In a bizarre kind of way, maybe the coin was lucky to Vlad.

"Where did you get a Slayer coin, Vladimir?"

Vlad shrugged. "It belonged to Joss. I found it."

Otis nodded, looking somewhat troubled by the coin's presence.

Vlad slipped the coin back into his pocket, then looked at his uncle. "How long will you stay?"

"Vladimir, you've asked me that every day I've been here. And every day I have told you that I await Vikas's letter advising me on what to do next. As his letter hasn't yet arrived—" His words broke off and his eyes flicked to Nelly suddenly, as if he'd heard something in her thoughts that disturbed him.

With a sigh, Nelly pulled a thick parchment envelope from her apron pocket. "I was going to wait until after dinner to give this to you. It arrived yesterday."

Otis's eyes moistened for a moment. "I wouldn't leave without saying goodbye, Nelly. You mustn't think such things about me."

Nelly dried her eyes on her apron and gave Otis's arm a squeeze as she handed him the letter. "I know. I just . . . hoped you'd change your mind and stay."

Vlad remained quiet, both in speech and in thought. The very idea of Otis leaving again was breaking his heart.

Otis opened the envelope and read Vikas's letter, his eyes not betraying even a hint of what was on the page. With a contented sigh, he folded the letter up and placed it back in the envelope. "That's that, then."

Before his uncle could say anything else, Vlad stood and left the room. It was too much for him to bear, losing Otis over and over again like this. It wasn't right. It wasn't fair.

But the moment his foot hit the bottom step, Otis called with his thoughts. *A word, if you would, Vladimir.*

Vlad hesitated, but finally returned to the kitchen. Nelly had her arms around Otis and was squeezing him tightly, tears streaming down her cheeks. Vlad filled with venom, suddenly furious that Otis was breaking her heart like this again. Clearly, she loved Otis, and all he seemed to do was hurt her. Vlad balled his fists and glared at his uncle.

Otis slid the letter across the table and brushed Nelly's tears away with gentle kisses. Vlad opened the letter and read.

Dear Otis,

I trust this letter finds you well. I apologize deeply for my delay, but your recent adventures with the president of the Stokerton council have caused quite a stir in all of Elysia—indeed a stir that will not be easily settled, I think—and I have been engaged in numerous council meetings all over the world, discussing your fate and pleading with our brethren for a moment of open-mindedness.

And so it is with enormous pleasure that I write to share with you this happy news. It has been decided by six of the nine councils that you should be entrusted to my care until your trial. The Stokerton council was less than pleased with this decision, of course, which isn't surprising in the least, considering the torment that you and your nephew have bestowed upon D'Ablo, who I am sad to report is still alive and recovering, but for his severed hand. It troubles me greatly that the Stokerton council has agreed that even though he is scarred, D'Ablo should be allowed to continue his presidency until this matter is resolved. This, as you know, is a very strange move.

D'Ablo's deformity is a disgrace. If he were any other vampire, he would be banished from Elysia and shunned. Why should our laws, our traditions bend at the will of one vampire? I can assure you that there are many in the other councils who will be watching this situation with great interest. I, for one, would like to know what he hopes to accomplish.

Your trial is set to take place in ten months' time. A trial date for young Vladimir has not yet been discussed, but I do not think it will be long before the subject is breached. In the meantime, I will be relocating on a temporary basis to Bathory, so that you may enjoy your nephew's company for a while longer. As none of us know what your fate will be post-trial, I think it would be best for you two to be close.

I look forward to tutoring Vladimir once again, and to seeing you when I arrive in the fall. Please secure lodgings for myself and my faithful drudge, Tristian.

Until we meet again . . . be well, my old friend.

In Brotherhood,

Vikas

Vlad read the letter again and again. The second and even the third time were barely enough to make it sink in. Otis was staying. And what's more, they would be joined by Vikas in the fall. Vlad wouldn't be the only vampire liv-

ing in Bathory anymore. He'd have a family beyond anything that Nelly had ever been able to give him. He'd have
people who really understood what it was to thirst for
blood and hide your fangs in public. People who could re-
late to him in a way that no one else in town, not even
Henry, could.

So what was with the hot ball of tension forming in
Vlad's stomach?

Vlad looked at Otis, who seemed to be waiting for his
glance. "You're staying?"

Otis nodded once, a look of uncertainty crossing his
eyes. "If you want me to."

As the initial shock wore off, Vlad couldn't think of anything he'd want more. His vision blurred with tears, but he
brushed them away with the back of his hand and cleared
his throat. "It's more than that, Otis. I don't just want you to
stay. I need you to stay."

He glanced at Nelly as she left the room in search of tis-
sues. "*We* need you to stay."

Otis stepped closer to Vlad, putting a strong hand on
his shoulder. His eyes brimmed with warmth and sincerity.
"All that I have done to wrong you—not accepting you initially because of your mother's human blood, leaving you
to face D'Ablo alone, abandoning you when you needed
my council most—I will make amends. That I promise you,
Vladimir."

Vlad nodded, overcome by emotion. He knew Otis would make it right, and he would finally have the comfort of his only living relative being close by. He released a shuddering breath and said, "Thank you, Otis. For everything, but especially this."

Otis embraced him tightly, then patted his back and let him go. Vlad had never felt so loved.

Otis smiled. "Don't thank me yet. There's something I've been meaning to tell you."

As Vlad raised his eyebrows, Otis set the *Encyclopedia Vampyrica* on the table and flipped it over. Then, with a small, moist cloth, Otis wiped the back cover, removing a glyph Vlad had not realized was there. Vlad flashed him a questioning glance, and Otis grimaced. "You have not been able to read any passages that contain the word *Pravus*. I confess, this is my doing. I hadn't thought you were ready. I didn't want your thoughts clouded by this fairy tale. But, after all you've been through and all you've learned, I feel you are in a position to decide for yourself what to believe in."

Otis swallowed hard and held Vlad's gaze. "Please ... accept an old fool's apology."

Vlad shook his head. "There's no reason to apologize, Otis. You were protecting me. I get it."

Otis relaxed visibly. "Why don't we celebrate my new residency over a glass of O positive? Nelly can mull some later. For now, we drink."

Vlad offered a one-shoulder shrug. "Actually . . . I'm not all that hungry."

It hadn't seemed like a remark worth Otis's reaction, but nevertheless, his uncle furrowed his brow and leaned closer, as if they were about to share a dire secret. "Is there something you wish to share with me, Vladimir?"

"What do you mean?"

Otis wet his lips, as if searching for the right words. "Before I left you those months ago, you were famished at every turn. But now . . . you seem satiated somehow. Would you care to tell me why that is?"

Images flitted through Vlad's mind, but he clamped down on them so that Otis wouldn't see. They were pictures of darkness, blood, alleyways, and a beautiful goth girl named Snow.

And even though he knew that the best thing he could do was to confess his mistake to the one man who would truly understand, he kept his mouth and mind shut, pressing his lips firmly together before saying, "Nope. Nothing. I guess I just got a handle on it."

Otis nodded slowly. And what Vlad saw in his uncle's eyes tore at his insides.

Otis knew he was lying.

But there was no way Vlad could tell him the truth, that he'd fed from the source and liked what he tasted and how the blood had made him feel. After all of Vlad's lecturing on why it was better to drink bagged blood, after his refusal to learn how to hunt, he just couldn't tell Otis that not only had he fed from a person, but he'd been wrong in his stubbornness. Because Vlad didn't feel like he'd been wrong. He still thought it was a bad idea to bite people. He still didn't plan on feeding from the source. What he intended to do was apologize to Snow, and never, ever let it happen again.

Everything would go back to the way it was. It had to.

Otis nodded, seeming to silently agree with something he was thinking. Vlad seized the moment to change the subject, and fast. "I wanted to ask you something. About Henry."

Otis folded his arms in front of him and leaned back against the counter. "Now that I've bitten him, you're wondering if Henry is my drudge."

Vlad furrowed his brow. "How'd you know?"

"Call it a guess." Otis smiled, then shrugged. "It's a fairly common concern amongst newer vampires. The answer is no. Only the first vampire to administer a bite can share that bond. To me, Henry is no different now than he was before."

Vlad sighed in relief. He'd been fretting over just how to convince his uncle that Henry deserved his freedom. Not that the thought of releasing his drudge wasn't a painful one. But he respected Henry, and if Henry wanted freedom, he certainly deserved it. Still, Vlad would miss their connection. "He wants me to release him, Otis. And I'm going to."

Otis looked briefly troubled, but spoke in a reassuring tone. "It's not the end of the world to lose a friend, Vladimir. Even a friend who is bound to you by blood."

Vlad's voice caught in his throat. His eyes brimmed with tears at the thought of losing Henry. "Then why does it hurt so much?"

Otis went quiet, and Vlad was almost certain he was thinking of Tomas. Just as Vlad was about to ask if his intuition was right, Otis spoke. "Because all endings have a certain amount of pain, just as all beginnings contain a certain amount of joy. It's just the way of things. I'm sure you and Henry will manage just fine."

As though the mention of his name had called him forth, there was a knock on the door. Vlad was not at all surprised when he opened it to find Henry there, looking happier than he'd seen him in months. It was bad enough that Vlad had to release him today. The least Henry could do was appear a bit more somber about it.

Vlad swallowed hard and averted his eyes. "Let's go up to my room so we can talk before . . . well, you know."

Henry nodded and followed him up the stairs. Once they were inside Vlad's room, he said, "So you're really going to do it? You're really going to release me as your drudge?"

Vlad nodded, and Henry said, "Why?"

"Because I can't stand seeing you bound to something you didn't agree to. Because you deserve to be free of any kind of control. Because . . . because you're my best friend. And you want me to." The tears threatened to fall once again, but Vlad somehow managed to keep them at bay. He cleared his throat, but his voice cracked anyway. "Anyway, I just wanted to go over the procedure with you before—"

"I don't want you to do it."

Vlad blinked. "What?"

"I don't want you to do it. Don't release me."

Vlad cocked his head. He looked at Henry with a mixture of intense relief and immense anger. "If this is a joke—"

"It's not. I just had to make sure that you really would release me. I mean, for a long time, I really thought I wanted that. But not anymore." Henry had grown serious, and in his eyes lurked the truth.

Vlad held his breath, too fearful that in the next second, Henry would change his mind again. "What happened to change that?"

Henry's voice grew gruff. "You did. You saved my life in Stokerton, Vlad. And it's not just that. The truth is I like having this connection with you. I like that you can call on me for help without either of us even realizing it. I like that we have each other's backs—whether it's reading the minds of random girls or fighting off ruthless vampires. I like that we're a team. And I'd be an idiot to give that up."

Vlad swore he saw the threat of tears in Henry's eyes. He sighed and allowed a small smile to dance on his lips.

He wasn't losing Henry. Everything really was going to be all right. "I don't know whether to punch you or hug you."

"There's more." Henry fumbled with his words for a minute. "I'm not going to ever ask you to mess with Melissa's mind for me again. That was a really crappy thing of me to do, and I'm sorry."

Vlad nodded in reply, and Henry ran his hand through his hair. "Anyway, I better get home and change before Freedom Fest. You walking over with Meredith?"

Vlad nodded again. His soul felt so much lighter. "Meeting her there, actually."

"Cool. I'll see you in a bit." Henry left his room, closing the door behind him.

Vlad sat on his bed and took a deep breath. As he blew it out, he lay back and felt the stress of losing Henry leave him. It was strange, like waking from a really bad dream. And Vlad was tempted never to sleep again.

27
FREEDOM FEST

VLAD WEAVED THROUGH THE PEOPLE who had gathered in front of the Ferris wheel, surveying the crowd for any sign of Meredith. The high school stadium had been transformed into a carnival this year, which was much better than previous incarnations of the Freedom Fest. Several rides had been erected on the high school football field, as well as various tents containing whatever a carnival-goer could want. Food, drinks, jugglers. Even in its mildly dorky array, it was probably the coolest thing the town of Bathory had ever done. And all of this was merely a prelude to the big street dance that would begin at midnight and end at one in the morning. It had begun as a tradition back in the 1800s, a public dance held during the witching hour and said to chase away demons. Vlad wasn't sure about that. But he was sure that the dance had a way of chasing away the curfew demons for many kids that night.

After he rounded the corner of a tent, he spotted her and smiled. Meredith caught his eye and smiled back.

They wandered the carnival for a while, checking out the rides, devouring handfuls of cotton candy, until the sun finally set and the stars came out overhead. Once it was dark, Meredith found his hand, confident at last that her father would have a hard time seeing them, and Vlad's life wouldn't be in too much danger.

Vlad tugged her over to a booth and dropped five dollars in the carnival worker's hand. After six tries, he managed to knock all the clown's teeth out and won a giant pink poodle for Meredith. She hugged him tightly, all warm and close, and Vlad froze.

Suddenly he had the urge to bend her neck back and slip his fangs into her flesh, slurping and swallowing every last drop of the sweet crimson that flowed within her veins.

In his mind, he could see himself killing her, and an excited thrill shivered through him. He pushed Meredith from him and took two steps back. It wouldn't be enough to save her if he didn't get a grip soon.

Meredith looked confused. "What's wrong, Vlad? You look like you saw a ghost."

And he had. The ghost of his true self, the monster that lurked within him. Always hungry. Never satisfied. Forever tormented by an unquenchable thirst.

And in a blink, he knew what he had to do to protect her. The answer had been there all along. Vlad had just been too stubborn, too selfish to see it. If he loved her—and he did, deeply—he didn't have an easy choice. In fact, he had no choice at all. If he really cared for her safety and well-being, he had only one option, one way to make certain that she would be safe from his dire thirst. He met her eyes and swallowed the enormous lump in his throat. It choked him on its way down to his stomach, where it formed a knot. "I'm sorry, Meredith. But we have to break up. I can't go out with you anymore."

At first, Meredith looked stunned, as if she hadn't really heard what Vlad had said to her, or hadn't understood, like he was speaking in a foreign tongue. Then her face twisted into a horrified expression. Her eyes filled with the tears of dawning realization. When she spoke, her voice was soft and trembling . . . like her lips. "Why?"

Vlad considered telling her the truth—that she would get hurt if she kept getting closer to him—but he knew it wouldn't be enough. He had to hurt her. Badly. To keep her from coming back. To keep her safe. "I don't love you. I never did. Now just . . . just get away from me."

Tears poured down Vlad's cheeks, so thickly that he could barely make out those on Meredith's. But it was the right thing to do, the only thing he could do to protect her.

She croaked out, "You're lying. Why are you lying to me? Why are you doing this?"

The ever-thirsty monster within him moved closer to Meredith, ready to feed, despite the crowd. With his last ounce of strength, he shoved her away and yelled, "Just get away from me!" before turning and hurrying away through the crowd, leaving Meredith to fall on her knees in tearful anguish.

His heart had completely evaporated, leaving him as nothing more than an empty shell. Broken, he moved past tents and rides and people until he was free of the festival at last. He barely noticed Henry on his knees in front of Melissa, who was laughing in an oddly flirtatious way. He hardly noticed the goth kids waving to him and almost couldn't remember which direction was home. All he could do was move, get away, hide his horrific self from the human girl he loved . . . before he killed her, all for the sake of hunger.

As he walked home, he kept to the shadows, hoping no

one would notice him. Three blocks from the park, despite Vlad's wishes, someone did.

A bright flash assaulted his eyes.

As his eyes adjusted once again to the darkness, a person came into view. Eddie's voice was strong and sure. "Out for a walk, Vlad? Or is it a snack?"

Vlad hesitated, then pushed the demon within him back down and kept walking.

Eddie kept the pace, and was only about two steps behind him. "What's the hurry? Gotta get back to your coffin before sunrise?"

Eddie chuckled to himself and Vlad tensed, pausing mid-step. "What do you want from me, Eddie?"

"I just wanted to show you a picture of my new friend." He held out a photograph of a girl with black hair, pale white skin: Snow. "Oh, she doesn't know it yet, but she and I are about to become the best of friends. And oh, the conversations we'll have—some, I'm sure, about you."

Without thinking things through with his rational mind, Vlad grabbed Eddie by the shirt collar and slammed him up against a nearby tree. Eddie yelped, then made an *oof* sound. Vlad gripped his collar tighter and hissed into his ear. "Listen to me, because I'm not going to say this again. If you don't stay away from me, you're going to get hurt. I'm going to hurt you, Eddie, and I will take guilt-free pleasure in your pain. You got me? Now back off!"

He let go, and Eddie slid down the trunk, trembling. Vlad turned and walked away before the hunger raging within him ended Eddie's young life.

Vlad moved through the gate and into his house, slamming the door behind him. His secret was out. He had no way of stopping Eddie. He had no way of leading a happy, normal life without becoming a danger to those he loved. And he couldn't even ask for help from Otis, all because of his stupid pride. He ran his hands through his hair and released a shuddering sigh.

As he moved toward the stairs, the sound of television drew his attention. Otis and Nelly were cuddled up together on the couch as a movie played on television. Nelly had fallen fast asleep, and Otis was on his way. Otis offered Vlad a concerned look. "You're back early."

Vlad watched Nelly snoozing quietly against Otis's chest, then turned his eyes to his uncle. "How do you do it, Otis?"

Otis pushed the power button on the remote, silencing the television. "What do you mean?"

Vlad licked his lips. "How do you get close to her without wanting to feed?"

A long silence went by. Then Otis whispered, "It's not easy, but I manage."

"And if you couldn't control your . . . urges?"

"I'd keep my distance." Otis paused, a look of concern on his face. "Is everything all right, Vladimir?"

Vlad's heart sank. He took a deep, shaking breath. "It will be."

He started up the stairs and sighed, his heart heavy, his chest tight. "I don't know how...but it will be."

28
An Overdue Apology

VLAD TRIED HARD TO STOP PACING, but he was having little luck with his efforts. A breeze blew through the alley, brushing his hair from his face and cooling his skin. The temperatures had risen to full-blown summer heat in the past week, and this evening was no different. Vlad blamed the heat wave for the beads of sweat on his forehead, but knew that he was kidding himself. It was his nerves, plain and simple.

The back door of The Crypt swung open, and, for a brief moment, music blared into the alley. Something raw. Something dark. Snow stepped out and the door closed, muting the sounds once again. Vlad caught her glance and cleared his throat, but didn't speak.

She approached, gliding dreamily toward him, her steps not cautious in the least. Vlad wondered for a moment if she remembered the night he took her blood, or if it was all just a blur. Still, he had a burning need to apologize, even if she didn't understand. "Thank you for meeting me. I need to apologize to you, Snow. I did something that I'm not proud of, and I can't go into details, but—"

"You mean when you fed on me?" Her head was tilted slightly in a curious fashion, her well-plucked brows raised.

Now it was Vlad who didn't understand. "You ... you remember that?"

Snow nodded, and her burgundy lips spread into a grin. "Remember it? I'll never forget it. It was great! I mean, at first I was confused. But ever since the fog lifted, it's all I can think about."

A brief flash of Eddie's face invaded Vlad's thoughts, and he frowned. "You didn't tell anyone, did you?"

Snow looked mildly insulted. She shook her head, her bangs draping across her eyes like a curtain for a moment. "I would never tell anyone about that night. That is just between you and me."

Vlad stayed quiet for a long time, uncertain what to say or do. After all, technically the girl standing before him was his drudge. Had she not recalled their previous encounter, it wouldn't really matter, but here she was, fully aware. He had no idea what to do with her, other than the obvious. "Don't tell anyone about me. And if a boy named Eddie Poe tries to talk to you, ignore him."

Snow nodded eagerly. "Is there anything else?"

Vlad wet his lips, hesitant. "You should know that you're my drudge now. It's ... well, pretty much a vampire's human slave. You won't be able to resist any direct orders."

She seemed to mull this over for a minute, then nodded, seemingly satisfied with her predicament. "I'm cool with that. Are you ... hungry?"

Vlad shook his head curtly. "Let's get something straight. I don't feed off humans."

Snow furrowed her brow, questioning. "But ... you are a vampire, right? And you bit me. And I know you drank. It made me dizzy."

"That was a mistake. One I don't plan on repeating." He inhaled a delectable whiff of her blood as it rushed through her veins. Her heart beat quicker, and he could also smell the adrenaline in her blood. Vlad lowered his voice to a near whisper, terrified of himself, of his growing need to feed. "No matter how good you smell."

She stepped closer and, against his will, he remained very still. Carefully, she swept her hair to one side, exposing the smooth porcelain of her neck—just as perfect, just as flawless as it had been before Vlad had bitten her. Vlad recalled Henry's wound when they were eight healing within seconds after Vlad had removed his fangs—apparently, that was the norm. It looked as though that initial feeding on Snow had never occurred, though Vlad's appetite recalled otherwise. The blue vein there pulsed, and Vlad felt his will break. He wet his lips again, suddenly famished.

Her whispered words brushed his cheek, enticing him further. "It's okay. It's just between us. Feed. You need it. I can tell."

Vlad inhaled again, and his head spun with thirst. "It . . . it has to be a secret. From everyone."

Snow was still nodding in understanding when Vlad leaned closer and bit hard into her neck. He drank deep, the rubies of her veins spilling over his tongue and filling his stomach, gifting him with the greatest pleasure he had ever known. He fed and fed, mindful of her heartbeat, but more mindful of his hunger and the taste of the forbidden.

He wouldn't tell Otis. Or Nelly. Even Henry. This was his secret, his and Snow's. And he would feed on her in surreptitious shadows.

Until he learned how to tame the beast within.

If, indeed, he ever would.

Vlad shut that thought out and pulled Snow closer, swallowing mouthfuls of her sweet crimson and blocking from his thoughts all the lies that he would be forced to tell in order to satiate his need for blood.

There would be many.

ADDENDA

A CRUMPLED PIECE OF PARCHMENT poked out of Vlad's top dresser drawer. The paper was frayed, its edges soft, as if it had been unfolded and refolded several hundred times. It had, in fact, as it had been in Vlad's possession since the summer before his freshman year. The words were scribbled in black ink, the handwriting almost unreadable. And if asked, Vlad could have recited the letter by heart.

June 15

Dearest Vladimir,
I hope that this letter finds you well. It is my understanding that as of the date of this writing, you have a little more than two months until you begin your freshman year at Bathory High. That leaves us with a very

tight schedule, as the time has come for me to teach you how to read Elysian code, the language of all vampires. I'm certain you are as excited as I am that you will begin this journey of understanding, as know-ing Elysian code will open up worlds to you, and you will be able to study the Compendium of Conscientia— *a book traditionally passed down from vampire to vampire since before time existed.*

A brief history lesson: The first written language, according to humans, occurred around 3500 B.C., but Elysian code predates even the most absurd scribblings of the oldest human caveman by several hundred years. It is both simple and complex, and has been echoed in every form of writing that has ever been written. Our vampiric ancestors chose not to share our language with humans, for much the same reason that they chose to keep their very nature secret—humans were not considered (nor are they today) worthy of the blessings of Elysia. They were (and are) considered a food source, and nothing more.* Should a human come across something written in Elysian code, it was thought, its inferior intelligence would find the elegant script a jumble, and the secrets of all of Elysia would fail to be revealed.

But enough of history. On with your lessons.

As with wooden stakes, sunlight, and Italian food, vampires have a natural aversion to both punctuation and capitalization. Each letter written in Elysian code is enclosed in Teneo indicators, shown here: ( ). As you can see, Teneo indicators are roughly similar to human parentheses, but far more eloquent. Names (otherwise known as a vampire's Mark**) are also enclosed in Teneo indicators, but the names themselves are almost always a jumbling of the vampire's initials, as the Mark is formed by the vampire's essence and not by the vampire him or herself. (Remember how your Mark formed after I fed some of my essence into you? It was a natural reaction by your own essence that formed your Mark.) Though Marks may be similar to one another, each Mark is completely unique, and no Mark has ever been repeated through the course of Elysian history.

Elysian code, translated below into English, is really quite simple in written form:

-	-|	-\	|--	|||	|-	/-	|-|	-|-	-/
A	B	C	D	E	F	G	H	I	J
|/\	|	|∧|	|\\|	///	|-\	\\\\	\\	--	\\\\\\
K	L	M	N	O	P	Q	R	S	T
	//	||	|/\\|	\\	\\/	/
	U	V	W	X	Y	Z

Therefore, if one wanted to write "Let's go out for a bite" in Elysian code, one would write:

(|) (|||) (\\\ ) (--) (/-) (///) (///) (//)
(\\\ ) (|-) (///) (|\ ) (-) (-|) (-|-) (\\\ ) (|||)

Likewise, if one wanted to write "I sucked rubies from his veins" in Elysian code, one would write:

(-|-) (--) (//) (-\ ) (|/\ ) (|||) (|- -) (|\ )
(//) (-|) (-|-) (|||) (--) (|-) (|\ ) (///) (|\/|)
(|-|) (-|-) (--) (||) (|||) (-|-) (|\ ) (--)

Speaking Elysian code is another matter altogether, as the complex sounds of the vampire language cannot be translated onto a page. One must hear Elysian code spoken often in order to learn to speak it oneself. In fact, many young vampires of one hundred years of age or less are commonly confused by the spoken vampire language, despite their daily exposure to it. It is doubtful that you will learn to speak Elysian code at all, Vladimir, as you do not experience daily interaction with other vampires. But fear not—reading the vampire language is just as important.

Please work hard to memorize Elysian code, and immediately begin your studies of the Compendium of Conscientia. It is very important that you do.

On a personal note, I'm enjoying our exchange of letters greatly. I confess I have not felt this great a connection with another vampire since your father left Elysia. Please do keep writing. And give my best to Nelly.

Yours in Eternity,

Otis (///)

---

* *Please know that I do not feel this way about humans anymore, Vladimir, as knowing Nelly has most certainly changed my point of view of what wonderful beings humans are. I just wanted to illustrate that the majority of vampires do feel superior to humans. It is greatly frowned on by all of the Elysian councils for a vampire to interact with humans in any way that acknowledges them as our equals.*

** *Marks are generally given to vampires by their creator (but for the few who are abandoned by their creators early on—or as occurred in your case, but I believe yours is a unique one). As with glyphs, the vampire must feed his intention into his bite in order for the Mark to be effective. This, of course, leaves the creator with a certain amount of control over the vampire he has Marked, but as it is such a minimal amount, very few ever utilize it. (Please do not have concerns about this, Vladimir—I respect you and will not utilize that small amount of control unless your life depends on it.) Removing one's Mark not only breaks a vampire's bond with his or her creator, but also severs the bond with all of Elysia.*

Check out the next chapter in

THE Chronicles OF
Vladimir Tod

ELEVENTH GRADE
BURNS

1

A Slayer's Resolve

THE VAMPIRE SPUN AROUND, a wild, unhinged look in his eye. He lunged forward but the slayer skillfully dodged his blow, delivering a hard roundhouse kick to the creature's throat. The vampire fell to the ground, coughing, choking on its own blood. The slayer could have killed the beast a half hour ago. But this wasn't just about ridding the world of another abomination (though that was definitely the end goal). It was about a slayer needing to release some pent up hostility and cleanse himself of all of his clouded thoughts.

Thoughts that were now perfectly clear.

These bloodsucking *things* could not be trusted. Not even when they donned the mask of a relatively normal teenager. Not even when they claimed to be your friend. Especially when they used their insidious powers to gain your trust and get you to reveal secrets that even those closest to you didn't know. Especially when their name was Vladimir Tod.

Joss was done playing games. With Vlad's face planted firmly in the forefront of his imagination, he slipped the silver-tipped wooden stake from his backpack and approached the vampire on the ground with an eager step. He whispered, "For you, Cecile," and thrust the stake forward, before the beast could draw a single breath. Blood—hot, slick, so deep red that it seemed black in the light of the moon—poured out over his hands. The nameless vampire fell still.

Joss straightened his shoulders, triumphant.

From his backpack, he withdrew a cell phone and hit number two on speed dial. When the voice at the other end answered, he said, "This is Joss. I need a cleanup on the ocean side of Russian Gulch State Park. The target is secure. Am I cleared to move on to my next objective?"

When the voice on the other end answered in the affirmative, Joss hung up the phone. There was no need to continue the conversation. Small talk didn't matter.

All that mattered was that he was going back to Bathory.

And this time, he would walk away with no regrets.